The Degrees of Barley Lick

The Degrees of Barley Lick

A Young Adult Adventure Novel

Susan Flanagan

For the Cowburns, Kurahashis, and Gibsons,
for making us Flanagans feel so welcome
during our three years in British Columbia;

And for the Ram's Head Writers' Group in Langley, BC,
especially Lisa Hatton, Michael Hiebert and Bob Jacoby.
Without you, this book probably wouldn't exist.

"My father taught me global positioning. Ever since then, it is such a part of me that I wouldn't be able to sleep if I didn't know down to the second—and I mean geographical second—where I was laying my head at night."

– Barley Lick, interview notes for the GeoFind competition

"Geocaching is a cross between treasure hunting and high-tech orienteering," said Phyllis Henderson, 2005's GeoFind champion. "Picture a tiny bucket hidden completely out of sight in an area the size of British Columbia and you have to find it, by yourself, using only latitude and longitude. You can use a GPS, but that only gets you so close to the treasure. You have to go the last eight or nine metres on your own. If you're in the middle of a dense forest, and the bucket is well camouflaged, you need clues.

"To win the GeoFind contest, you have to be the fastest to decipher and follow the clues to find the treasure. GeoFind basically involves a bunch of teenagers running around in the woods like crazed maniacs searching for objects of no value, just for the thrill of the hunt. It's the most fun I've ever had."

– Cloverdale Reporter, June 1, 2006

Contents

Prologue
Vancouver Island, 2006

Benjamin Fagan crawled along the forest floor pondering his next move. He was alone, and the undergrowth was almost impenetrable; there was no way he could stand up. The skies had just opened, and even way down here, the rain pelted through the trees like angry nails. His cotton sweatshirt was soaking wet and more muddy-brown than red. If only he had worn his rain jacket, but no, he had to be cool. Damp earth was ground into his hair and even one ear. He had been out here in this rain forest in misty drizzle for the better part of the morning, and his small daypack was beginning to weigh on his shoulders and back.

With the tangly ground cover, it was taking Benjamin more time than he expected to get around, and his stomach was beginning to scold him. He was accustomed to eating a second breakfast at about 10:00. Today he had only had one granola bar since 7:00. He hadn't expected the under-brush to be so dense and tangled that he couldn't advance in an upright or even a stooped position. Although the giant Douglas fir trees prevented light from reaching the forest floor, they didn't discourage growth. The only way Benjamin could get through the maze of vines and roots was to slither like a garter snake, one of which he had just met. He had told his father that he didn't want to come to this Outdoor Extreme Camp on Vancouver Island. None of his friends were shipped off to camp in the first week of summer vacation. But he had an extra week with his father, and as usual, his father was working 24/7. Maybe his father was preparing him for a future career in the family business.

Benjamin looked up into the canopy high above. The sky was not visible through the network of branches. Some of these trees had to be a thousand years old. He checked his special orienteering compass, which attached to his thumb by a small strap. He had two hours to go to locate the rest of the white Styrofoam cups tied to the branches of the towering trees. He was on the right track. There. In the tree, he caught a glimpse of something unnaturally white. Yes, it was a cup. It was attached to the furrowed bark of a Douglas fir with a trunk so wide that it would take him and at least eight or ten of his school friends to surround it holding hands. He stood up to check the number on the inside of the cup. Yes, #9. There it was, written in Sharpie. Things were looking up. Only five more to go. He recorded the coordinates listed on the cup before surveying the tangled mess of undergrowth ahead. Maybe he would try to get through walking. His long pants would protect his legs. His hoodie proved no match for the branches and thorns, however. And, although he kept them above his head as much as he could, his hands looked like sliced meat.

Benjamin thought of his mother, off in Portugal with her friends. Did she care what happened to him during the weeks he was with his father?

He doubted it.

Benjamin's thoughts turned back to the task at hand. He had arrived at a rugged path that led back to camp. He couldn't go back yet. He still had five cups to find if he wanted to earn his orienteering badge. He grimaced and turned away from the tents that were his only shelter from this unending rain. Usually he loved being outdoors, but in his whole nine years, he had never been so wet for so long. If he could find #10 soon, he could probably get back and dry by 2:00. As he lowered his face to check his watch, Benjamin noticed large coils of animal scat on the path ahead of him. Bits of hair and what looked like white bone stuck out of the individual coils. It didn't look like bear scat. Bear scat looked like how a kid would draw poop. Was it fresh? He prodded it with a stick. Steam drifted skyward when he disturbed the top crust.

That's fresh all right, he thought. Just as he was pondering whether to proceed, he caught a strong whiff of urine. He looked down. Near the scat, he noticed four-toed tracks, like cat's paws but the size of a coffee mug. He looked up and saw the cougar. Or was it a mountain lion? Maybe they were the same thing. It stood about thirty feet up the path, salmon-coloured nose high in the air, sniffing out the intruder.

Benjamin could make out its ribs through the beige coat. The long tail flipped from side to side, sending wet leaves in the air as it swept the ground, and a threatening rumble came out of the white muzzle, followed by a hiss, like from something possessed.

Benjamin inhaled a long deep breath through his nose and backed away slowly… Until he spied the cubs, rolling around like two toddlers in the undergrowth. The babies scrambled into the undergrowth and disappeared. The mother did not.

Benjamin screamed, "Go away." He screamed again. It had little effect. He knew little about cougars except they were the top of the food chain, the largest wild cats in North America. One of the camp counsellors said a cougar could take down a moose. Here he was face to face with one of the most savage predators on the planet. He continued backing away, screaming the whole time. The cat kept advancing, her ears flat to her head.

"*Go away, cat. I'm not going to die today. Go back to your babies.*"

The cat hissed, showing its sharp teeth. Although he knew he shouldn't, Benjamin turned and began to run. He ran as fast as his lungs would allow. He ran, gasping for breath, wishing he had remembered his inhaler back in the tent.

Was the cougar coming for him? Benjamin turned back to see and tripped over a dead log lying across the path. He landed on his chest with a thud, and lay there for a few seconds, the wind knocked out of him. He felt his bowels let down. He pushed himself up into a sitting position and tried to calm his breathing.

Disoriented, he tried to stand. His legs wobbled and he felt light-headed; he sat on the log. Please, he thought, please just let me get out of here alive.

It was at that very moment he heard a voice call his name.

1

An Intruder in June

Cloverdale, 2006

Barley Lick jumped out of his friend's car and sprinted through the raindrops past the six-foot grizzly bear carving and up the steps of the pink stucco storey-and-a-half on 62A Avenue. If he was quick, he wouldn't miss any of the hockey game. These were the first play-offs since the 2004 lockout. He laid his pizza on the porch railing, and tucked his Coke into a crooked arm so he could dig out his key to open the door. That's when he noticed the oak door was ajar. Hmmm. It wasn't like his mother to leave it open. In fact, every night since last December, she had locked the door with the deadbolt.

Cautiously, Barley pushed the door, his heart pounding out a warning—the upper and lower portions beat individually like separate organs. He heard a muffled sound and his heart rate rose.

Barley Lick dropped his drink and grabbed one of the pink golf clubs from the bag in the entranceway. Brown liquid hissed onto the floor, a syrupy river seeping into the seams of the hardwood.

He yelled like a blackbelt in karate, took two running strides, and raised the five-iron poised to strike.

A huge man, a stranger, had someone pinned on the couch. And that someone was his mother.

Was she gagged? In peril? Barley would protect her against this ... this ...this sexual predator. *No one could hurt her. No one. She was all Barley had. After what happened to his father.*

That was when Barley took note of two sets of middle-aged eyes turning towards him. Not quite in unison. One a split second ahead of the other, but in both sets, he saw the same recognition and horror taking hold.

This wasn't an intruder attacking his mother. It was some nerd in a tartan vest.

"What the hell," Barley said, lowering the club.

With the speed of a mousetrap, Mary Jane Lick snapped to a sitting position and began smoothing her hair with her fingers.

Could this really be his mother? His forty-five-year-old mother? And who was the massive mound of male hormones?

The vest guy jumped up, tucked in his shirt tail, and turned to face Barley, revealing ruddy cheeks, a salt-and-pepper mustache, and a receding hairline. He was a mountain of a man. At least 6'4" and 250 pounds.

Barley's mother cleared her throat. "I, uh, I thought you were working." She looked like a sheepish teenager.

"Mr. Franklyn let us go early." Barley averted his eyes.

His mother's face was flushed. She began again. "Barley, this is my friend, Fred. Remember I was telling you about him?"

"No." Barley let the single word hang there between them.

The mountain moved into Barley's field of vision, smiling, showing pointy incisors. He extended his right hand.

Barley laid down the golf club but could not bring himself to offer his hand in return. It was just too gross.

The mountain lowered his arm.

"Barley Lick, show some respect. Shake hands with Fred."

"Pfft. Me, show respect? Dad's only been gone seven months and you're getting on like..." Barley didn't finish the sentence, even in the silence of his own mind. "This guy better get out of our house before..." Before what? Barley had never thought of himself as a violent person.

"I'm sorry, Fred," said Barley's mother.

"It's OK, M.J. I'll see you tomorrow after work."

M.J.? He's calling her M.J.?

The mountain straightened his vest—my God, it really was tartan—and started towards the door.

He padded straight through the puddle of Coke, slipped on his loafers, and with one quick glance back at Barley's mother, was gone.

Barley waited until he heard the door click before he spoke. "'M.J.'? Mom, no one ever calls you M.J. besides Dad." He looked out the window to see an older-model, silver Mercedes pull away from the curb.

Mary Jane Lick sunk down into the couch like a deflated balloon. "I know, Barley, but your father's...." She didn't finish.

"He's what, Mom?" Barley knew his mother had trouble saying the word.

She turned to him with a look so pained etched in her cheeks that Barley knew he should stop shouting and go to her. But he couldn't. He felt like someone else had inhabited his body. That it wasn't him speaking. "He's what, Mom? Oh, that's right, he's dead. Dad is *dead* and you brought some loser home with you. What were you thinking?"

Barley knew what *he* was thinking—that his father was spinning in his grave. That it was way too soon for his mother to have a boyfriend. That he had to get himself out of that room. Otherwise, the deluge of tears he was fighting back was going to break free.

"I'm going to bed." Barley didn't even clean up the pizza and drink. His mother could do it. He stamped up the stairs, and slammed the door to his room so hard the windows shook.

2

The Next Day, Monday

During the night the incessant rain that had plagued the Lower Mainland for months finally came to an end. Barley had a terrible night's sleep. He spent hours lying still under the covers listening for the hammering on their tin roof. It had been predominant for so long that now he couldn't seem to sleep without it. He had finally sunk into a deep slumber after he watched the digital clock numbers click over to 3 a.m.

"Barley?" His mother's voice was strained. She pushed open his bedroom door with a creak. "You awake?"

Barley was not quite awake. He was still in the clutches of a dream in which he and Phyllis Henderson, his former-girlfriend now-nemesis, were blazing a trail through dense old-growth forest searching for something. It wasn't evident what it was until they reached a ravine, and there on the other side, Barley could see his father. His leg was stuck in a tangle of trees and he couldn't get free. A massive redwood had been uprooted and was going to fall and crush his father. A raging river coursed through the ravine preventing Barley from reaching him. Phyllis ran back and made a leap clearing the eight-foot span. From the other side, she held out her hand to help Barley across. He refused to take it, tried to jump the chasm without help. He was just falling to his death....

"Barley," his mother said again, louder this time. "I think it's time to get up."

Barley squinched open his eyes, blinded by the sun beams that pierced the sheer curtains warming his pale, sun-deprived face.

Yesterday's disgusting scene replaced the dream. Barley tried unsuccessfully to erase it from his mind. The guy's pudgy cheeks, his tartan vest, the outstretched hand. Ugh.

His mother sat on the bed and took a deep breath. "Barley, I know you're upset, but you have to talk to me."

Barley turned his face to the wall.

"Can you please try and see things from my point of view."

Barley kept his lips pursed.

His mother tried again. "Barley, I can't help that Dad had that heart attack." Pain came through her words.

Barley slowly turned his face toward his mother. "I know, but you don't have to go bringing home every guy you pick up."

"Barley, Fred is the first man I've brought home, and he is not some guy I picked up." She enunciated every syllable in the final five words.

"So where did you meet him?"

"At the Grief Support Group. He lost his wife too."

Barley scanned his memory banks for any mention of this and came up blank. "You didn't tell me about any Grief Support Group."

"I started going to one at the Y."

"Is that how you comfort each other at those things?" I will not cry, Barley told himself. I refuse to cry. He kept his eyes trained on the wall, so his mother wouldn't see the tears wetting his eyelashes. He blinked rapidly.

"Barley, honey, just because I care for Fred doe mean I loved your father any less. Your father would want me to be happy. He'd want me to date again."

"How do you know?" Barley sneered. "It's not like he died a long, lingering death and you had time to discuss it." Instantly, he regretted the words. The moment they left his lips, he knew he'd hurt her.

"No, but I did live with the man for twenty years. I think I can say I knew him." She'd been in the car with his father when he had the attack. They had just exited the Massey Tunnel on their way home from Vancouver. According to her, one minute he was telling her about some wolf that had been hanging around his work camp, next thing he was slumped over the wheel. No warning. No history of heart disease. No apparent stress. Just bam... gone. Luckily, they were at a red light, so the Corvette didn't wrap around a pole or anything. Barley turned his head away from the wall and looked his mother square in the face.

"I knew him too." Barley felt his lips start to tremble. If only he'd had a chance to say goodbye; to say he loved him; to thank his father for all he had done for him—giving him confidence, pushing him to appreciate the outdoors, teaching him how to use a compass and GPS. Barley would never have accomplished anything without his father's encouragement. His mother took him in her arms and held him there. He felt like he was five years old again. Sixteen was too old to be hugged by his mother, but it felt good, so he let her stay wrapped around him.

"I know you did, honey. And he knew how much you loved him. He loved you even more. Never forget that." She pulled away and drew a deep breath. "Good luck today. I'll be thinking of you." She kissed the top of his head and stood up. "If you run into that nice girl Phyllis, tell her I said hello."

Phyllis. Phyllis Henderson. His arch-enemy. The Phyllis in his dream. The Phyllis he hadn't said a word to in more than eight months. Barley had seen her plenty of times; she was at the same school, Cloverdale High, a year ahead. And she spoke to him every time they ran into each other in the corridors; he just didn't speak back. He had no idea why she persisted. In fact, he had no idea why she bothered with him at all. Just hearing her name made Barley's stomach churn like the time he had eaten too many donuts at the Cloverdale Rodeo.

He forced himself to think of other things. His mind went to Big Bite. He had been working there since February with his friend, Colin. When school let out last week, Mr. Franklyn had asked each of them to work three days a week starting at noon. Barley said fine, except for the first week. He was one of fifteen people chosen to compete in GeoFind, the biggest geocaching competition that Vancouver and the Lower Mainland of British Columbia had ever hosted. After years in Washington state, it had finally come to Canada. The contest would determine the best geocacher in Washington and BC, and Barley had a chance of winning. That is, if he stayed on his game and didn't let things like his hormonal mother or Phyllis Henderson wreck his concentration. Barley couldn't risk falling behind, not even for one day. Otherwise, Phyllis would swoop in like a vulture, leaving nothing but shreds of him behind. She was the only other competitor who had a chance against Barley. Even though she had just turned seventeen and Barley was six months younger, people said they were two of the best geocachers Canada had produced. But GeoFind could only make one of them famous.

It wasn't the fame Barley wanted. He wanted to win GeoFind for his father. He wondered if he could. Yes, he thought. Dammit, he could, and he would. But would his father know? Did he know how much Barley wished he was still here?

Seagulls sounded from under Barley's pillow. It was Colin, calling to say he was on his way. Barley hopped out of bed and bolted for the shower.

Colin Carter was Barley's best friend and driver. Best friend since second grade, when they met at a Christmas party at their fathers' work. And driver, because Barley's mother had yet to renew the registration on his father's car and set up Barley on the insurance.

Barley had to hide his nerves. He tugged on his jeans, pulled his new geocaching shirt over his wet head, grabbed a cinnamon raisin bagel and a water bottle, and raced out the door to Colin's waiting car.

★

Colin pulled his grey PT Cruiser onto 62A Avenue and Barley stretched over a puddle to reach the door handle and climb in.

"Hey, nice shirt." Colin read the words aloud. "'You are the Search Engine.' That's pretty cool."

"Thanks, I got it at Latitude," said Barley, arranging his stuff and shutting the door. "You know that geocaching store in Langley?"

"Yeah, what else do they have?"

"Geocaching license plates and some sick Travel Bugs."

"I'll have to go check it out." Colin turned around in the driveway. "So where are we going, your highness?"

"Colossus."

"The movie theatre?"

"Yeah, that's where GeoFind headquarters is. We have to go there every day to get our clues. Colin, do you think I have a chance of beating Phyllis?"

"Sure. As long as you start in the lead and stay in the lead."

Barley spoke around a chunk of bagel. "Easier said than done with Syphilis."

"You shouldn't call her that, Barley. I don't even know why you're still mad at her. She said she never was dating Tyler."

"She brought him to the dance, didn't she? Anyway, I don't care. Can we talk about something else?"

"You brought her up." Colin looked offended.

Barley drummed his leg with his fingers. "I haven't told you about yesterday's peep show."

"What do you mean?"

"You know when you dropped me off? I walked in on this guy going at it with my mother." The instant the words crossed his lips, Barley felt better. Things always felt better when he was with Colin.

"No way." Colin turned to look at him. "That would be emotionally scarring. What did the dude look like?"

"He was huge—like some random mutant from WrestleMania. But without the muscle mass."

"He sounds gross. What does your mother see in him?"

"Exactly my point." Barley sighed and looked down at the Global Positioning System he was twirling in his fingers. It was his father's GPS, a black Magellan. The company, named after the first explorer to circumnavigate the globe, built the world's first handheld GPS in 1989. The Magellan eXplorist XL was water resistant with a backlit display that made it easy to read in either dim light or sunlight. How he wished his father could be here with him. But at least he had Colin. Hanging out with Colin made life seem almost good. Well, as good as it could get with a dead father and a mother acting like a sex-crazed teenager. He took another bite of the bagel.

"I was so mad; I didn't even stay downstairs to watch the game."

"What did you do?"

"I went to my room and punched a hole in the wall. Look at my fingers." Barley held up three blackened knuckles on his right hand.

Colin's eyebrows disappeared into his bang. "Where's the hole?"

"Right above the Luongo poster."

"That's not good at all. Your mother is gonna go ballistic when she sees that."

"Naw, I moved the poster up a few inches."

Colin grunted to show his approval, braking to allow two young girls to skip across the street.

"So, what am I supposed to do, man? What would you say if you walked in on your mother making out with some dipstick?" Barley swallowed.

Colin put the car in gear and laughed.

"What's funny?"

"I just thought of what Dad would do if he walked in on Mom getting it on with someone else."

Barley couldn't help but smile at the thought. Colin's father was 6'6" and built like an oversized fridge. His mother was not even half his body weight and built like a bird.

Colin's and Barley's fathers used to work together until the undiagnosed heart defect dropped Barley's father at forty-eight.

It seemed like a lifetime ago that Colin and Barley and their fathers would watch hockey together. Sitting on the couch, eating Miss Vickie's Salt and Vinegar chips. Cursing Don Cherry. Trying to figure out if the Sedin twins could actually read each other's minds. This year Vancouver hadn't even made the play-offs, and this was the first time in the history of the NHL that the final round was between two teams that hadn't been in the play-offs last time. The last game Barley saw, Edmonton had beat Carolina 4-3 in overtime. It was a nail biter of a series.

"So, who won the game?" asked Barley.

"Edmonton. Four-nothin'."

"Wow, that's two in a row. They might take it."

Colin shook his head. "Not sure; it could go either way. Remember, Carolina had that shut-out in the second game."

"True enough. I'd like to see Edmonton win though. Be the first time in sixteen years," said Barley.

Colin drummed his fingers on the steering wheel. "Be good for a Canadian team to win. And even though Pronger has asked for a trade, that penalty shot goal he scored in the first game was sick."

"Yeah, he's the first NHLer to score a penalty-shot goal in the Stanley Cup finals."

"Whichever way it goes, it'll be all over tomorrow night."

"I can't wait. I didn't think it'd go to Game 7. You want to come to my house to watch?" Barley put down the window and extended his hand outside to feel the breeze.

"I can't. Mr. Franklyn gave me extra shifts to cover for you while you're competing and tomorrow night is one of them."

"Oh no. Sorry 'bout that."

"It's OK. We have that TV up in the corner. He said I can turn it to the game."

Barley wasn't sure what to say. It was because of him that his best friend was going to miss the first Stanley Cup final game in two years.

Colin pulled the PT Cruiser off 200 Street in Langley just past the onramp to the TransCanada, and parked in the space nearest the movie theatre's front door. Colossus looked like a giant alien spaceship; disc-shaped with coloured lights running all around the outside. "Is this really where the contest is being hosted?"

"Yeah, this will be my first time inside. We always go to the Clova. Way cheaper." Colin removed the key and undid his seatbelt.

"I've only been once. Mom took me to see *Harry Potter*." Barley gazed up at the building. A sixty-foot sign advertised *GeoFind, The Movie. Coming August 2006*.

"I heard they're using actors and not you guys for the geocaching movie," said Colin, opening his door. "That sucks."

"I know, but Mom says that they need big names to draw big crowds."

"Is she working on it?"

"Just a few logistics. But she's super excited that it's made-in-BC, and they've got Ryan Reynolds as the lead."

"That's wicked."

"I know. And I'm psyched because it opens on my birthday. You gotta come with me."

"All right. Who's making it anyway?"

"You're about to meet him."

"Really?"

"Yeah, it's Marvin Czanecki, you know... Mr. C., he owns the theatre."

"Mr. C., the guy in the commercials with the crazy suits, is making the GeoFind movie?"

"Yup, bankrolling the whole thing."

"Yeah, they say the reason he's sponsoring GeoFind is to get publicity for the movie." Barley took out his Blackberry Pearl, his gift for doing so well in school last year. "Shoot, it's almost 8:30. We gotta beat the feet."

Colin clicked the locks on the PT Cruiser and ran behind Barley into the movie theatre.

But it wasn't Mr. C. they saw when they got inside; it was Phyllis Henderson.

3

Phyllis

Phyllis Henderson was super fit. She walked faster than most people run, and she ran faster than she talked, which was saying something, because she talked fast—like an auctioneer on Red Bull. At seventeen, she had a couple of marathons under her belt. She once told Barley she was disappointed in her last time because she had finished in 3:45. She wanted to break 3:30.

Phyllis said the reason she was always in a hurry stemmed from the fact that, growing up in Turkey Gulch, she had to travel everywhere on foot. "Shank's Mare," she called it. "I wouldn't have it any other way," she added. "It's so beautiful up there."

All Barley knew was it made her a force to be reckoned with during any speed competition. After geocaching with her the previous summer and fall, Barley knew that if Phyllis and he were given the same coordinates at the same time and place, Phyllis would get to the cache first. She could outrun him, and all the other guys, hands down. She was built like a gangly spider. With big hooters, mind you. In Barley's mind, she was a perfect female specimen. Physically anyway.

"Look what the cat dragged in." Barley whispered to Colin over the electronic cacophony of Axel F's "Crazy Frog." *Bing, Bing…*

Phyllis walked towards Barley and Colin, her breasts perky under her tank top. "Ah, my favourite geocacher, Barley Lick." She smiled and the smell of her strawberry shampoo tickled Barley's nostrils.

Barley felt a flush rise to his cheeks and a trickle of sweat run over his left ear and drip onto his shirt. He kept his gaze over her right shoulder.

"Hi, Colin." She seemed to add this as an afterthought, nodding her head in Colin's direction but keeping her eagle eyes trained on Barley.

"Hi, Phyllis," said Colin. "Pretty wild place." He gestured to the massive planets hanging from the ceiling and the ticket booth that looked like the fuselage of a spaceship.

"It is. I came to see *Mission Impossible* a few weeks ago." Phyllis turned to face Colin. "I didn't know you were one of the fifteen competing."

"I'm not; I'm just driving Barley around."

"That's nice of you. You know you're not allowed to help him though."

"He doesn't need any help. Plus, he said he'll give me fifty bucks and take two of my Big Bite shifts when he wins… if he wins, I meant to say."

"Proof's in the pudding." Phyllis twirled her orange GPS in her hand.

Barley shook his head, trying to give off the impression that he had no time for Phyllis or her frivolities. But it was hard to divert his eyes. She was all legs in cut-off jean shorts and a pair of ASICS. No socks. She had so much definition in her calves that Barley wondered if she took steroids.

Phyllis must have felt his gaze on her because she turned back to him and looked directly in his eyes. He stopped breathing.

"Not sure if we'll run into each other out there today, Barley. I think we all start with different coordinates. Anyway, if I don't see you, good luck." She smiled good naturedly, turned, and walked over to talk to a guy from Washington.

Barley rolled his eyes and caught sight of four Plexiglas aliens looking down on them. They hovered high above in the four corners of the fifty-foot atrium. He shivered. Suddenly instead of aliens, Barley imagined the towering marble statues of Matthew, Mark, Luke, and John in the big cathedral where his father's funeral had been. Funny how memories of his father could sneak up on him and punch him in the throat when he least expected. He had perfected a coping mechanism just for times like these. Instead of thinking about how much he missed his father, he thought about how much he hated Phyllis Henderson. It always worked. I will beat Phyllis in GeoFind, he thought. I will crush her into the dirt and win this contest for Dad.

"Phyllis looks good," Colin said after she was out of earshot. "I don't think she's wearing a bra under that tank top."

"Give me a break. Just because she looks good doesn't disguise the fact that she's the spawn of Lucifer."

"You're nuts, Barley. You've got to get over yourself and give people a chance. Phyllis was being friendly."

"How? By saying how nice you were to drive me around?"

"I don't even know why she gives you the time of day." Colin gave Barley the evil eye.

"Because I'm the only one who's as good as she is at geocaching. She just wants to keep the enemy close."

Colin began to counter, but their argument was cut short by a thunderclap that drowned out "Crazy Frog." A sour odour filled the room, and all heads turned to the back of the atrium; it had disappeared into thick smoke, out of which emerged Mr. C. striding down a flight of stairs like Moses, or maybe the BeeGees.

Wearing a shimmery pale blue suit and square blue-framed glasses, the short man raised his hand in a regal salute. His goatee shimmered with gold flecks.

"Whoa," said Colin. "That's over the top."

"Welcome, everyone. I am thrilled to finally bring GeoFind to Canada." A round of applause and a few who-whoos carried through the crowd. "I especially welcome participants from the United States." More cheers and a whistle from Colin.

"Fifteen of you have been deemed by your peers to be the best geocachers in British Columbia and Washington. Congratulations." More applause. "I hope in the years to come, we can expand GeoFind beyond these borders. For now, let us get right to it. As I speak, my assistant…" Mr. C. indicated to a smartly dressed middle-aged Japanese woman with wide eyes and olive skin. "Keiko is distributing your clues. Please do not open the envelope until I say. You are welcome to arrive at the cache sites however you see fit. That means you can have someone else chauffeur you, as long as they do not assist you in the hunt. But," Mr. C. paused here and looked at every face, "you must check in after each find."

Keiko arrived and passed an envelope to Barley. She held one out to Colin, but he shook his head and held up his hand, palm vertical, to indicate he was just along for the ride.

"Fifteen Geocoins have been placed in each cache. When you find a cache, you are invited to take and keep one Geocoin. One and one only. On that coin, there is a number. It is that number you must record and bring back with you to Headquarters…" He swept his arms open to show that this room was Headquarters. "My assistants will note your time and numbers until 4 p.m. sharp. If you arrive at 4:01, that cache will not be counted."

Barley stole a glance at Phyllis, but she had her back to him looking up towards Mr. Czanecki, who again swept his right arm in a wide arc around the room. The assistants, dressed like aliens with rubberized cone heads, appeared at their stations. Nervous laughter rolled through the competitors. Colin took out his phone and snapped a picture.

"Once you have checked back, and your Geocoin number has been recorded, my assistants will provide you with further coordinates. After the second cache of the day, you may go home and rest up. Each morning at 8:30 you will receive a fresh set of coordinates. At the end of the six days, whoever has found all twelve Geocoins in the least amount of time will be the winner and receive a new Garmin eTrex, five Travel Bugs, and free admission, transportation, and accommodation for the 2007 GeoFind competition in Seattle."

"One final point, and this is most important: you can remove only one Geocoin, and when you replace the cache, it must be in the same place you found it. Any questions?"

Larry raised his hand. "What happens if someone cheats and takes more than one coin?"

"Excellent question, Mr. Lobez."

Larry beamed and looked around at everyone else to make sure they shared his self-admiration. Barley frowned. He couldn't help but think that last October Larry had screwed Barley's life up more than he could have done on his own.

Mr. Czanecki continued. "Each of the caches has a hidden camera trained on it. Do not waste time trying to find the cameras. They are well camouflaged. But know you are being watched. And if it comes to my attention that you are not following the rules, you will be disqualified immediately."

There was a murmuring in the crowd, and Marcie Redding raised her hand. Barley had first met Marcie at a geocaching blitz last fall. She was from Bellingham in Washington and was, by far, the quickest at finding a cache once the GPS got you as far as it was going to take you. She was like some kind of Wunderkind. He didn't know her well, but she had driven up to Cloverdale for his Hallowe'en party in October.

Marcie sucked in one cheek. "Is it true we won't know how we're doing until the end?"

Mr. Czanecki smiled. "Indeed, Miss Redding, although all of you will attempt to find all the same caches, you will do so on different days and at different times. These clues will take you far and wide over the Lower Mainland. Some are close and some may be quite far. So, until all of you have attempted all the clues and the contest is complete, we will not be able to determine who has found the most caches in the shortest amount of time."

"What happens if we cross paths with another competitor at the same cache site?"

"Just carry on your way and do not provide any clues. My assistants have arranged it so there shouldn't be much overlap." He scanned the room. "Any other questions?"

"Yes." Chase, a quiet boy from Burnaby, raised his hand. He was about six inches shorter than the next smallest person in the room and looked around like he thought someone might tackle him. "What about if someone not connected to GeoFind sees us looking for a cache and goes back and takes the bucket?"

All eyes were trained on Mr. Czanecki. This was a constant concern for geocachers the world over.

"Not to worry, Chase. My team will be monitoring the caches and making sure there is no interference." He gave a perfunctory nod. "Any other questions?"

When no one said anything, Mr. C. put his right index and middle fingers to his forehead and saluted. "GeoFinders, open your clues. Let the hunt begin."

Barley tore open the envelope and read the clue aloud in a low voice, but loud enough for Colin to hear. "Kinder cache. Salt beef, children?"

"What the heck does that mean?"

Barley lifted a finger, looked at the coordinates and raised his eyes to the left. He took a deep breath and turned to his inner GPS.

Colin looked over his friend's shoulder at the paper. "Where do you think it is, Barley?"

Barley took a second to come back from the magic geography centre in his brain. "In or near Hi-Knoll Park."

"Are you sure?" They reached the door and Colin held it for Barley.

Barley put on a voice like a snooty professor. "Colin, where coordinates are concerned, am I ever wrong?"

Colin laughed. "No, you're a freakin' human filing cabinet."

Barley scratched his nose and blushed. "I can only do it if I've seen similar coordinates in the past."

Colin shook his head, serious now. "You have a photographic memory."

"Not for chemistry. Ask Mr. Burns."

"Still, it's freaky."

"There's what's freaky," said Barley, pointing to Phyllis with her long braid bobbing in the wind as she raced by them on her way to her car. "Come on, we can't let her take the lead."

Colin popped the locks on the PT Cruiser. They jumped in and buckled up.

"I think you have home advantage," said Colin.

"What do you mean?"

"Phyllis only came here in high school. You know the Lower Mainland better than she does. Just like she'd know the back woods of Turkey Gulch better than you."

"Maybe so, but that girl could direct a plane to any airport in the world using a bargain basement GPS."

Colin put the car in drive, and they ripped out of the parking lot with only Larry Lobez between them and Phyllis. Larry turned and wiggled his fingers at them as he exited.

"I wonder where their caches are?" Colin said, as they watched Phyllis's yellow Mini Cooper turn south.

"Pedal to the metal, Colin." Barley held onto his door.

"Go easy on me, Barley, man. I can't risk getting another speeding ticket."

"How many you got now?"

"Only two, but if I get any more, I'm dead meat."

"Gotta do what we gotta do," said Barley. "Can't let Phyllis get ahead."

"Guess not. I still wish you two would get over things, have some steamy sex, and..."

"Listen, dingus." Barley's voice was louder now, his face unsmiling. "Get one thing straight. I will never speak to Phyllis again—ever. Got it?" Barley's face was so close to Colin's that his breath was steaming up Colin's thick glasses.

"You don't have to speak to make a mix tape," said Colin.

Barley punched him in the arm.

"Ow, that hurt. If you do that again, I'll drive off the road and then you really won't win."

"Sorry, man. Mom's gonna deal with the insurance and stuff today."

"I can't believe you're going to get to drive a Corvette and I'm stuck with a Geezer Mobile," said Colin. Mr. Carter had asked Colin what kind of sporty car he'd like when he got his license. Colin said something like a Dodge Charger or maybe even a Mercedes. He thought the heated leather seats might be a draw for picking up girls. When Mr. Carter came home with a second-hand PT Cruiser, Colin was gobsmacked; it looked like something out of the

Cars movie. "I had to buy it," said his father. "It looks just like the car your grandfather drove." Colin didn't dare protest. He knew not to mess with his dad.

"I always wondered what the PT stands for?" said Barley.

"Plymouth Truck."

"But it's not a truck."

"That's exactly what I said. Mom looked it up. She said that Chrysler had to fulfill some requirement to bring down the average fuel consumption of their truck fleet. In order to do it, they called these things trucks."

"No way."

"Yes way, and as soon as you get that car on the road, you're gonna drop me and this truck just like you dropped Phyllis."

"Give me a break. She proved herself unworthy of my company. You, however, would never let me down."

As Colin turned off 192 Street onto Colebrook Road in Langley, Barley once again opened the window of the PT Cruiser again and let the warm June air blow through his hair.

4
GeoFind Stage 1

Hi-Knoll: N 49° 05.497, W 122° 40.851

Fleetwood Park: N 49° 08.465, W 122° 46.897

Barley bounced out of the car into Hi-Knoll Park and started running up a wooded path with Colin in hot pursuit. The woods smelled damp from the months of rain; spring had turned to summer overnight and the day wasted no time heating up.

Colin splashed through a puddle. "You using your dad's GPS?"

"Yeah." Barley launched his body over a tree that had fallen across the trail. Bright green moss covered the branches. "It's a Magellan eXplorist XL."

"How does it compare to your Garmin?" asked Colin.

"Way bigger screen. Colour, too, and Dad had all the maps of BC already downloaded."

"But it still needs a clear view of the sky?" asked Colin, over the raucous cries of crows in the trees.

"Of course." Barley turned his head and lifted his eyebrows. "Every GPS needs to hook up with at least four or five satellites before it can navigate."

"So is the bigger screen the only reason you're using it? It seems like you'd be more familiar with your own."

"I dunno," Barley lied, as he used the tiny joystick

to plug the coordinates into the device. He knew why he used his father's GPS instead of his own. He used it because it made him feel like his father wasn't gone. It made him feel like his father was just out in the field working. And when Barley got home from a day of geo-caching, his father would be there to hear the details. To recommend the best way of finding a cache. To laugh at Barley's stories. *Shit.*

Barley looked at the machine in his hand. "We have to go about a hundred metres that way." He pointed towards a lagoon where ring-necked ducks bobbed, heads down in the water, and a double-crested cormorant sat on a flat rock. When they reached the far side of the water, the tiny black needle began to spin. Barley's heart skipped a beat, like it always did when he knew he was homing in on Ground Zero. He stopped abruptly and Colin banged into him from behind. "We're close."

No matter how much a person paid for one, all GPSs did the same thing once they got within eight metres of the chosen coordinates. The little needle would start spinning and then you were on your own. The machine couldn't help you anymore.

"Already?" said Colin, panting. "That was quick."

Barley pulled the paper out of the envelope and reread the clue. "Kinder cache. Salt beef, children?"

"Does it say anything else?"

"Nope. Now shut up and start looking."

"I'm not allowed to help, Barley."

"Come on, who's gonna know?"

Colin shrugged. "You heard Mr. C.—the trees have eyes."

"All right, all right. You warn me if you see any Muggles."

Barley got down on all fours in the damp soil and advanced into the undergrowth like a large rodent. His rear end disappeared under young ferns. "There's a heck of a lot of ants in here."

"Forget about ants, you wuss. You see a bucket?"

"Nothing yet." Barley continued his slow advance. "Ouch. One of them just bit me."

"Shh," said Colin. "Muggles."

Barley lay still, trying to blow the ants off his arms, while Colin pretended to get a water bottle out of his backpack. Barley kept his face down until he felt the people pass.

"Coast clear?"

"Yep, they're gone."

Barley crawled in deeper flushing a pileated woodpecker from an old dead tree trunk. Delicate white lilies grew at its base. "It's really mucky down here," he called out.

"First ants, now muck. Be a man, Barley."

Barley swore under his breath and kept rooting around until he spied a flash of white plastic. Satisfaction surged through him. Finding a cache was the greatest rush ever, better than winning a prize or scoring a goal, well maybe not a game-winning goal but it was right up there with that. "Got it." He pulled out a five-gallon plastic bucket from where it was shoved under the bark of a fallen tree.

"Wicked," said Colin. "If you can find them all this fast, you're off to the races."

Barley shimmied out backwards the same way he went in, in an effort not to disturb the ferns so it wouldn't be evident to the next searcher. The white bucket appeared after him, and he sat back on his butt, arms and clothing mud caked, and held it out to Colin who raised an eyebrow. "Who would eat two gallons of salt beef?"

Barley shrugged and pulled off the red lid.

"Anything in it besides Geocoins?"

"Yeah, it's full of Kinder Surprise toys." Barley tilted the bucket toward Colin, showing him the collectable mini toys that usually came encased inside chocolate-covered orange plastic eggs.

Colin looked in. "Ah, so it was 'kinder' like 'tinder'. I assumed it was 'kinder' like 'finder'. Do you think we can take one?"

"Don't see why not as long as we put the bucket back where it was. There must be a couple of hundred. Fill your boots."

"You sound like your father. Remember he always used to say that?"

Barley nodded silently, took off his muddy jacket, laid it on the ground, and dumped out the entire contents of the bucket. "Keep watch, would you."

Colin looked up and down the path. "All clear," he said and crouched down to pick up a tiny troll resting with his back against a mushroom. "I like the one-piecers best. Some of the multi-piece ones drive me crazy."

"The toys aren't going to help me," said Barley. "What I need is a Geocoin." He dug through hundreds of plastic orange rabbits, mini cars, and aliens until he touched a small Ziploc bag containing fifteen Geocoins. The silver-coloured discs were essentially worthless, but geocachers treated them like gold. Barley opened the bag up and took one out. It was about the size of a toonie and engraved with an eagle.

"Let's see," said Colin.

Barley handed him the coin. Colin moved his palm up and down to feel the weight of it. "Sweet. Looks like they were made especially for the contest."

Barley took out a small notebook. "Read out the number, would you?"

"Why? Don't you get to keep it?"

"Yeah, but I could have a hole in my pocket."

"Are you serious?" Colin laughed.

"What? I don't want to take any chances." Barley had his pencil in hand, poised to record the number.

Colin read out nine digits and Barley read them back to him before pocketing the book. "Oh yeah." Barley made a fist and pulled it back to his side, elbow crooked. "One down. Eleven to go."

Before returning the bag of coins and toys to the bucket, Barley pulled a small white plastic goat from his jacket pocket and dumped it in. These goats had been his signature item since he started geocaching in 2004. They were super cheap at the dollar store. His father had always told him he was like a billy goat when they were hiking.

"You supposed to put something in there?"

"Dunno. Mr. C. didn't say we couldn't." Barley picked up his coat by the corners and dumped everything back in the bucket before closing the lid. He waited until a couple of people passed before re-hiding the bucket in the undergrowth by his feet. Once they were out of sight, he crawled into the ferns and placed the bucket exactly where it had been under the bark of the fallen tree, near the white lilies.

A group of middle schoolers gave Barley the hairy eyeball when he, once again, materialized out of the ferns, butt first. They pointed and giggled. Barley ignored them, as if it were normal for teenagers to be crawling around the forest floor. Once upright, he high-fived Colin and the pair ran as fast as they could back to the small parking lot on Colebrook Road.

"Good job," said Colin. "Not even 10:00 and you've got one done."

Barley smiled, a genuine smile. Finding a cache was one of the only things that made him truly happy. He felt the hunger for more. One cache was never enough. He had a fire burning inside him. He was a cache-finding machine.

Back at Colossus, Colin stayed in the lot by the door with the car running while Barley ran in to log the Geocoin with one of the alien assistants. Inside the movie theatre, Barley saw Marcie Redding and the quiet boy, Chase, each at a different cubicle to record the number on their Geocoin. Marcie turned to look at who had come in, and her eyes widened at the sight of Barley's muddy jacket. Barley ignored her, and Chase; they didn't concern him. Phyllis was the one to worry about, but there was no sign of her. Either she had already been, or she hadn't found her first cache yet. Barley hoped it was the latter. In fact, he hoped Phyllis got a flat tire.

The conehead assistant Barley approached sported five-inch-tall green pointed ears and spread the fingers of his left hand into a Vulcan V. He refused to record Barley's numbers until Barley gave him the same hand signal. Barley obliged, but he felt there was no time for Star Trek games. Every second counted. He had to win. He read out the number and made sure the assistant wrote it correctly. "May the Force be with you," the conehead said. Barley shook his head. The guy had his sci fi shows mixed up. Back in the car he ripped open the envelope.

"Hey, here comes Larry Lobez," said Colin. The skinny platinum-haired boy zipped past, glancing nervously at them on his way into the movie theatre.

"Don't worry about him. Phyllis is the only one we have to keep an eye on." Barley read the coordinates, "N 49° 08.465, W 122° 46.897," and closed his eyes, breathing deeply.

Colin knew not to interrupt.

Barley opened his eyes after ten seconds. "I think it's in Fleetwood Park."

"Got it." Colin pulled out into the northbound traffic.

Fleetwood Park was another urban green space in Surrey. The trees there were not nearly as old as at Hi-Knoll, but it had amazing gardens and a lot of families used the space. Barley and Colin used to compete in track and field there in elementary school. Barley never won any races, but Colin was a rabbit.

Colin passed a driving school car. "What does the clue say?" he asked, as he whipped around the novice driver.

"It says: Square dance medicine. Branch out like twins joined at the hip."

Colin overtook a Volkswagen Beetle covered in trinkets. "Doesn't sound like it'll be too hard to find."

"Naw, easy peasy," said Barley, plugging the coordinates into his father's GPS.

Half an hour after arriving in the park, they were still searching. Barley looked at his watch and wiped his brow. "Damn, it's hotter than all get out. I'm sweating like a pig." Sweat rolled down his back leaving dark patches on his new t-shirt. Nothing frustrated him more than not being able to find a cache. "I can't believe this. Every tree I look at has two branches splitting off in separate directions." He looked through the trees to where two bearded Sikh men played chess at a picnic table.

"Be patient, we'll find it." Colin was good at calming Barley down, but after ten more minutes, Barley sat on a log deflated. A greyish Great Blue Heron with a long orange bill and black head plumes edged nearer as if to commiserate. He stood stock still for over a minute; one long leg bent at an angle like a flamingo. The heron looked at Barley as if to convey some important message, then quick as a flash, grabbed something from a small pool of water, stretched its neck into a tight s-shape, and with several slow flaps of the wings, rose into the sky, its slender legs extending beyond its tail.

"Holy cow, Batman," said Barley, blowing out. He hadn't realized he was holding his breath.

"Wow, that was pretty rad," said Colin. "Look, is that something there?" Colin pointed at something four feet off the ground sitting in the fork of the tree. "Oops, I'm not supposed to help..."

Barley jumped up as quick as a mink, hot blood coursing through his veins. It was if he had a jolt of caffeine. "Yee haw," he said, pulling out a small plastic pill bottle.

"We're back in the game."

"Let's see," said Colin.

Barley pulled the top off. "It's full of lapel pins," he said. He spread the contents out on his coat, just as he had done with the Kinder Surprise toys.

Colin picked up a pin, a cowboy hat with legs. "They're all related to the rodeo."

Barley chose a Geocoin and recorded the number before pocketing it. He gathered up everything else to put back in the pill bottle. No room for a goat in this one. Barley wasn't fond of microcaches. Not only was there was no space to leave something behind, but they were usually much harder to find than traditional caches. Barley loved the thrill of the hunt, but he didn't like to waste time searching for cigar tubes and the like. He had better things to do. Like beat Phyllis.

They ran back to the main path and arrived at a water park where dozens of children happily screamed under spouts of water projected up out of the asphalt. Barley ran through the spray. Colin followed his friend, laughing, until they reached the PT Cruiser, dripping and out of breath. "It's gotta be 30 degrees Celsius," he said. "Must be cooking at Big Bite. We have to convince Mr. Franklyn to get a fan."

"You do it, you've known him longer."

Colin had started at Big Bite before Barley. He had put in a good word with Mr. Franklyn, and Barley got called in for an interview. That was back in February. Mr. Franklyn seemed to know Barley's father had died and times were tough. The Big Bite job was a really good distraction, and the income was a help.

"I already asked him. He said he'd have one before my next shift. He's a good guy, Mr. Franklyn. Now, come on, unless you want Phyllis Henderson to beat you."

Back at Colossus, Barley tore in the door, Geocoin in hand, almost wiping out Mr. C.

"Whoa there, son."

"Sorry, Mr. Czanecki." Barley was breathing hard. Mr. C. smiled. "You need me alive in order to get the prizes, you know."

Barley smiled back. He wanted to tell him he didn't care about the prizes.

He just cared about the title.

5

The Dog

Probably the last thing Barley Lick expected to find in his living room when Colin dropped him home after the first stage of GeoFind was a Great Dane. But there it was, a massive mound of beige fur parked in his father's favourite recliner. Although the dog's rear end was where it should have been in the recliner, his front paws stretched all the way to the floor in front. Barley dropped his phone and GPS on the table and approached cautiously.

"Who are you?" he said, rubbing the giant furry head.

The beast gave no answer but unfolded himself from the confines of the armchair, peering at Barley, one ear at attention, the other flopped over.

Barley's mother stopped whatever she was doing at the counter in the kitchen. "Don't you think he looks a bit like Robert DeNiro?"

Barley examined the Great Dane's elongated face. "You mean that old guy in *Meet the Parents*?"

"Yes, they could be twins."

"I don't really see the resemblance."

"Come on, Barley. He's got the same smirk. And look at the mole on his right cheek."

Robert DeNiro has a mole? Barley shook his head. His mother was weird. "Mom, what's this dog doing in our house?"

"You always said you wanted a Great Dane."

"Mom, that was when I was in kindergarten."

The giant dog looked at Barley like he was offended.

Duke belonged to one of the children who lived up the hill from the Licks. Barley had been so envious he begged his parents to let him get a Duke of his own. The best they did was buy him a Scooby Doo costume that Hallowe'en.

"I thought..." Barley's mother looked crestfallen. She sighed and tried again. "Whenever we'd go to the playground, you would ignore the other children and spend all your time petting Duke." She grimaced as she hoisted a wad of green dog food out of a tin and glopped it in a dog dish.

"Sorry, Mom. It's just that... I was a kid."

"I know, honey." She wiped her eyes before she plunked the stainless-steel dish on a plastic step stool. The bowl had a rubberized bottom so it wouldn't slip off easily. The dog sauntered over to lap up the stinky green goop. The bowl was empty in less than ten seconds.

"Wow," said Barley. "He's like a vacuum."

"Does that mean you like him?"

Barley realized what his mother was doing; this was her way of apologizing for bringing that meathead home yesterday.

The dog bumped his head into Barley's leg. A string of green drool, the exact colour of the food, attached itself to Barley's jeans just above the left knee. Barley began patting the gargantuan head. The dog was so tall Barley didn't even have to bend down to reach him. Just touching the dog seemed to make the anger directed towards his mother and the world drain away.

"Where did you get him?" Barley grabbed a dish towel and wiped the dog's muzzle.

"Don't use that." She took the dish towel from Barley and replaced it with a rag she pulled from her back pocket. "I went to a dog show at the Cloverdale Coliseum. There's this lady who shows Great Danes. I asked her how to go about buying one. She said she had one she was willing to part with, I could come by her place to look at him."

"When was this?"

"This afternoon."

"I thought you were going to get the car registered and take care of insurance today?"

"Dang. I forgot."

"Mo-om, you promised." Barley took his eyes from the dog and glared at his mother. His mother was a bit of a sieve when it came to storing information.

"Sorry, Barley, I'll write it on my palm pilot." She took a pen from the counter and made a note on her hand.

Barley knew she was doing her best and decided not to make a scene. "What's his name?" He motioned towards the beast who was staring straight into Barley's eyes like he knew something Barley didn't.

"The lady called him Bailey, but she said you can change it to something else as long as it's two syllables and sounds sort of the same."

"Hmmm," said Barley, rolling around possibilities in his mind. "Why did she get rid of him?"

"Gimpy ear." His mother touched the right ear, which flopped over; its left counterpart stood at command. "She said that when he was little, she had a tracking chip installed just under the skin on his right shoulder. They do that a lot now apparently. But it drives him batty. That's how the ear got flattened." As if on cue, the dog put his back paw up to his right shoulder and did his best to scratch. It was as futile as Barley trying to lick his own elbow.

"You can't show a Great Dane if his ears don't point up?"

"Guess not."

"Why didn't they just take the tracking system out?"

"The doctor said he'd still be scratching, and he doubted the ear would ever stand straight this late in the game."

"How old is he?"

"Fred says the lady told him he's only two and a half but..."

Barley took his hand off the hound's head. "Fred—the guy from the couch? *He* helped you pick out the dog?"

"Yes, as a matter of fact, he did. I tried to tell you about him, Barley. Fred is a wonderful person..."

Barley tried to blot out his mother's voice. Talking about the molester in the tartan vest felt like a kick in the guts. *How could his mother even contemplate going out with someone when his father had been dead less than a year? Wasn't there some rule about stuff like that?* Barley could still picture the man extending his hand. He shivered involuntarily.

"I know you're probably wondering what he does, where he lives, all that." His mother's voice droned on as if she were inside a fish tank, and Barley was outside looking in.

"Actually, I don't care what he does or where he lives. I hope I never see him again."

"Barley, what's gotten into you? You used to be so well mannered."

Barley shrugged. "You thought you'd bring me a dog to make up for that disgusting scene I witnessed last night?"

"Barley, I told you, I thought you were working till later."

"I wish I had been." Barley stood, cracking his shoulder blades.

His mother sighed. "I thought we went over this this morning. It's been hard since your father left us, but we have to keep moving forward. Both of us." She came over and wrapped her arms around her son until they both felt the anger eek out of him. The dog seemed to think he was missing out on the action and pushed in between them.

His mother laughed and released Barley from the hug.

"Barley, you know I love you more than anything in the world. Your father did too. I'll give you time to think about me dating again. When you're ready to talk, let me know."

She took his face in her hands and kissed him on the forehead. Barley swallowed and felt air passing over his dry throat.

"In the meantime, I'll let you two get to know one another."

The dog looked at Barley and cocked his head.

"I have to make some calls before the morning." She went up the stairs to go to her office, the office she used to share with Barley's father. She paused on the landing. A wedding picture hung behind her on the wall. "I almost forgot to ask about the competition. How was it?"

"Good."

"How did you do?"

"Dunno. We won't find out until the last day."

"Was that lovely girl, Phyllis, there?"

"Yep." Barley spit the words. Could his mother just stop asking about Phyllis already?

"I always liked her. You should tell her to drop over."

"I'll be sure to do that." Barley fake smiled.

His mother turned and continued up the stairs.

Barley knelt down in front of the dog who was now lying belly-up on the floor in a most ungentlemanly pose.

"Hey, buddy." The dog lifted his head, and his big black nose came within a millimetre of Barley's but didn't make contact. "You smell like tuna."

The dog tilted his head.

Barley stood up and patted his chest. The animal rose like a time-lapse skyscraper and Barley took the dog's paws in his hands and they stood there like dancing partners. "Holy," said Barley. "Wait till Colin sees you."

Barley rested the dog's paws on his shoulders until he

towered high above Barley and doggy drool pooled on his head. "Woah, this is insane."

Barley brought the dog back down to stand on all fours. "What are we gonna call you, big guy? Bailey, Barley. Well, you can't have my name." Barley rubbed underneath the Great Dane's curved chest. "Smiley. Naw. Curly. That's no good. I know... Stanley. I'm going to call you Stanley, like the cup."

6

GeoFind Stage 2

Hope's Othello Tunnels: N 49° 22.207, W 121° 21.891

Barley woke the next morning to a smell of fish and a damp leathery nose gently poking him in the cheek. He opened his eyes. It hadn't been a dream after all. The Great Dane brought his face within a centimetre of Barley's, retreated, and appeared to smile.

Holy Batman. The beast was even bigger than Barley remembered. He gave the soulful face a vigorous rub and sat up just in time to see his cell phone vibrate across the night table. He caught the Blackberry before it plummeted off the edge and clicked to accept the call.

"Hey, Barley, how's it hangin'?"

"All right. You?"

"Not so good. I got called in to take the day shift at Big Bite, so I can't drive you to GeoFind today."

"Oh, no. I'm doomed." The dog rested his head in Barley's lap.

"Sorry, gotta get there early too. Gotta help Mr. Franklyn install the new oven he got when he went to buy the fan." Colin really did sound like he was sorry.

Barley swallowed. He needed something to drink. "That's OK, man. I'll figure something out."

Barley closed his phone. The dog looked right into his eyes as if he knew what Barley was feeling. His dark ears perked straight up, both of them, and his brow furrowed, a deep dark line forming between his round eyes. Barley burrowed his face in the dog's neck.

What was he going to do now? His mother still hadn't registered the Corvette. She was supposed to do it yesterday. And get the insurance straightened away. She had been promising since he got his license in February, six months after his sixteenth birthday. He closed his eyes to think things through and avoid the dog's sympathetic gaze. What if he used the car just this once without all the paperwork done? What could happen? No one would find out.

Barley was an excellent driver. Both his parents had told him so. Plus, he'd be extra careful. He'd never be in an accident. All he had to do was wait until nosy old Mr. Jewer next door left to drive to the dog park, and then Barley could sneak out in the 'Vette, pick up the clues at Colossus, bag the caches, and be back long before his mother got home from work. Piece o' cake. If Mr. Jewer noticed him coming home, then so be it. Barley would deal with his mother later.

Stanley gave Barley a look like he could read his mind and let out a snort of disapproval. Barley ignored him and planted himself in front of the window and checked his watch. For as long as Barley could remember, every morning at 8:20, Mr. Jewer left his stucco house and rolled down the street. It was like clockwork.

The seconds slipped away, the garage door opened, and there he was. Barley watched Mr. Jewer's Pontiac pull out of the garage, his current fluffy dog, Angel, sitting on his lap. Right on time.

Barley ran to the door leading from the porch off the kitchen to the garage. He'd have just enough time to make it to Colossus to get this morning's GeoFind clue. Stanley tried to squeeze into the garage with him, but Barley made sure to open the door just a crack, the space too narrow for the Great Dane's motorcycle-sized body to fit. Barley pushed the massive head back into the porch and ignored the whimpering as he grabbed his father's keys off the hook hidden behind the coveralls. Then there was scratching at the door, loud scratching. Shoot. His mother would freak if the moldings around the steel door were ripped up. New moldings had been part of her renovations after his father died. She loved moldings.

When a large beige head appeared in the high glass window looking into the garage, Barley opened the door to offer comfort and, he hoped, stop the damage to the metal door. "Hey, buddy. I'll be back..." Barley used what he imagined was a conciliatory tone.

Stanley pushed past—he was surprisingly strong—and sat waiting by the Corvette's long snout. He let out a solitary woof as if to say, let's get on with it. Barley tried to drag him back inside, but it was like moving a ton of lead. He was going to have to take the dog with him. This was insane. "Listen, mister, if you come with me, you'd better behave."

Barley opened the passenger door and Stanley stepped in like entering a classic sports car was something he had been doing his whole life. He arranged himself in the bucket seat the way he had in the recliner, front feet on the floor, butt and back feet on the seat. He sat taller than any human with the exception of maybe an NBA player. The tip of his one upright ear touched the ceiling.

On the way to the driver's door, Barley noticed a big plastic bin of Milk-Bones on the shelf they used for tinned goods, and shoved some in his pocket. He installed himself in the driver's seat and took his wallet out of his back pocket. Stanley dropped his head and nudged Barley's pocket with his black nose. "Sorry, big guy, these are for later." He pushed Stanley's head away and threw his wallet in the glove box. He turned the key in the ignition and Outkast blasted out "Hey Ya," causing the dog's gimpy ear to perk up.

He eased the Green Machine out into the driveway and hit the garage door remote. His father's sports car rolled down to the street like she was floating. Barley let out the clutch and put her in second. The transition was seamless. She was a beautiful machine to drive—a 1985 C4, with a V-8 engine, fuel injected. She could reach sixty miles an hour in six seconds flat. His father had taste. Barley remembered the day his father bought the car, the shock he and his mother experienced when they saw it. He still did a double take every time he opened the garage door.

Barley wished his father could see the massive dog in the passenger seat. Stanley looked like he should be wearing goggles. Barley turned north on 200th. As the Green Machine reached fourth gear, Barley could hear his mother's voice as he drove: 'Barley, go easy.' 'Barley, you're too close to that truck.' She said he was a great driver; yet she almost put her foot through the passenger floor whenever he was at the wheel. They hadn't been out driving since the insurance expired. In fact, this was Barley's first time driving with no one riding shotgun. Well, no human at least.

Barley pulled into the lot at Colossus with only minutes to spare. "You stay here," he told Stanley, and jogged to the door. Barley stood with the other fourteen competitors waiting for Mr. C.'s assistant—*what was her name? oh yeah, Keiko*—to give out the clues.

He did a tally. Only about four of the competitors were from the States. He knew most of them from the Geocaching Club down in White Rock. They were good guys, but they didn't seem to possess the innate ability to find the location of coordinates that he and Phyllis did.

Marcie Redding was amazing at finding clues, but Barley and Phyllis were hands down the best at global positioning. Barley felt like he could be dropped anywhere on earth, and he'd instinctively know where he was.

Without a GPS.

He was pretty sure Phyllis had that same sixth sense. He hoped it would fail her this week. She was standing on the other side of Chase. He glanced over at her. She was wearing her usual cut-off jean shorts and a t-shirt with a toaster on it.

She nodded and smiled; her braces were gone. He had somehow missed that yesterday. She looked like a movie star with her perfect physique and high cheekbones. Barley turned away. But not fast enough.

"No Colin today?" She moved behind Chase, until she was standing so close to Barley, he could smell not only her shampoo, but her breath; it was minty.

"He had to work." Barley kept his eyes straight ahead.

"Oh right, Big Bite Pizza. I heard he got you a job too."

Barley didn't answer. Just grunted. Can't make friends with the enemy, he told himself. Sometimes he couldn't believe they had actually dated. First, he wondered what she saw in him? Why she chose him? She could have had anyone down at the club. She was the hottest and smartest girl there. He'd asked her once what she saw in him. The answer came as a surprise.

"I like your teeth," she answered.

"My teeth?"

"Yeah, they're big, like horse teeth."

Barley had closed his mouth tight then. She'd laughed and kissed him, forcing open his lips with her tongue. He felt his pulse quicken. He replayed that kiss over in his mind many times. One of her tiny orthodontic elastics had popped off as they pulled apart.

Mr. C. clapped his hands bringing Barley back to the

theatre and the aliens. Back to GeoFind and his arch-enemy standing before him.

"Greetings, GeoFinders. You should all be proud of your performances yesterday. Every one of you completed the first two challenges with plenty of time to spare." Mr. Czanecki was wearing a purple suit with white polka dots and round glasses with thick sparkly frames. He looked like Elton John. "Today will be the same format as yesterday. Keiko will present you with an envelope containing your first coordinates and clue. Once you find the first cache, like yesterday, come back to register your Geocoin number and get your second clue. Everyone must complete their caches and be back here to record the Geocoin numbers before 4 p.m. Any questions?"

Larry Lobez raised his hand again.

"Mr. Lobez, always a pleasure."

"My father heard there might be some problem with the satellite signals. What do we do if there is?"

"What's Larry talking about?" asked Phyllis. Barley didn't respond, but heard similar mumblings run through the crowd. He watched as Mr. Czanecki's smile disappeared.

"No, no, Mr. Lobez. Everything is in order. Relax and enjoy the hunt." Mr. C. turned to his assistant. "Keiko, the clues, please."

As soon as Barley got his envelope, he tore it open and plugged the coordinates into the GPS. When he got outside, the machine told him what he already knew. Today's cache was in Hope, the small logging town jammed between the Coquihalla and Fraser Rivers about two hours northeast of Vancouver, that meant only about an hour fifteen from Colossus, which was pretty much on the border of Surrey and Langley.

He hopped in the Corvette, and Stanley's nose came over to meet his. He had forgotten about him when he was in the theatre. The cool leathery nasal pad left a bit of moisture on Barley's skin.

"Hey, buddy," he said, suddenly happy to have the company for the drive. "You miss me?"

Via the TransCanada, the Green Machine got them to Hope in a little more than an hour. One December, Barley's father had brought him here for a hockey tournament. They had strolled around the town to see dozens of amazing chainsaw carvings. It was cold. They had gone to a coffee shop for hot chocolate. There they met a chainsaw carver named Pete; he had sausage fingers and a huge gut. He invited them to his workshop. As soon as his father laid eyes on the six-foot grizzly bear carving, he had to have it. Pete the carver helped load it into the old truck they had at the time, and they brought it back to Cloverdale and hid it in a neighbour's garage. On Christmas Eve, when it got dark, they rolled it on a dolly to their front lawn where Barley's father had poured a cement pad while Barley's mother was out. They secured the bear, whom Barley had christened Hope, onto the steel rods his father had set in the concrete. When his father led her to the front window Christmas morning, Barley's mother covered her mouth and nose with her hands and laughed, "Where did you get him?"

Barley's father looked conspiratorially at Barley and answered: "What happens at hockey tournaments stays at hockey tournaments. Right, Barley."

Barley shook the memory from his mind as he drove the Corvette under the welcome sign. *Chainsaw Carving Capital of the World*, it said. Wooden lynx and wolves climbed the massive trunks that framed the sign. He wondered if Pete the carver was still around. No time to find out.

He had to focus; forget chainsaw carvings. Locating the cache was all that mattered now. Find the Geocoin and get back to Colossus faster than Phyllis.

Barley reread the piece of paper in his hand. "Rambo Cache. Where the sun don't shine, pirate treasure can be mine."

The Rambo reference made sense. Hope was where they had filmed the jungle scenes for *First Blood* with Sylvester Stallone. Barley's father rented the movie when they got home from the tournament. His mother had a fit. "That's too mature for Barley," she said.

"Relax, M.J.," his father said. "I'll fast forward through any nasty parts."

His father's Magellan told Barley to drive north of Hope. He watched the road but kept glancing at the GPS screen on his lap. When it told him they were close, he pulled in at a sign that said *Coquihalla Canyon Provincial Park*.

Barley parked and looked over at the dog. He had never geocached with a massive furball before. Stanley peered back at him. Let's get this show on the road, the dog's look said. Barley opened the passenger door, and Stanley stepped out like a glamorous date. He then ran and peed on a large rock. Shoot, Barley had no leash for the behemoth he'd acquired. He wondered if his mother had thought of buying one. He found a bungee cable in the trunk and tied it around Stanley's thick chain collar. Stanley scratched at the bungee like he scratched at his ear, which involved complicated contortions. He gave up within seconds and walked along beside Barley like the show dog he had been. Barley was impressed. *This is just what I need*, he thought. *Silent, uncomplicated companionship.* It almost felt like his father's spirit was in the dog, walking with him, making sure he wasn't alone.

Barley consulted the GPS again; it directed them past a sign announcing the Othello Tunnels. He had no idea what the Othello Tunnels were, but if they were really tunnels and the cache was inside one, then the GPS was not going to help him; he'd have to rely solely on the clues.

They walked down Tunnel Road until they came to a trail bordering the Coquihalla River; the river was running strong from all the rain, carrying branches along with it. It was hot for June. The season's first blood-thirsty mosquitoes began dive bombing Barley's face, their incessant drone enough to drive a person loony. Stanley was bothered too. He kept bringing up his leg and rubbing his head with his foot. Barley wondered if he could get fly dope for dogs.

The steep granite cliffs of the Cascade Mountains towered above them, with trees growing straight out of the sides of the canyon. They followed the path for several minutes until they came to a long wooden bridge with side rails and a jagged rock tunnel came into view. A middle-aged man emerged riding an old blue ten-speed bike. Torn jeans and face covered in stubble—the guy didn't look like a cyclist. A mangled cigarette hung from his bottom lip, its smoke streaming from his nose like a dragon. He gave them a weird look and mumbled something. Was that an earpiece in the guy's ear?

Barley checked the GPS. They still had several hundred metres to go before Ground Zero, but the good thing was, the cache appeared to be hidden straight ahead and not across the river or up the cliffs. Of course, the cache was most likely inside a tunnel. Barley could see that there were more than one, and although the first appeared to be fairly short, Barley took a headlamp from his pocket and pulled it over his head. He arranged the elastic head band so the light was aiming forward and down slightly, then switched it on before giving a tug on the bungee.

Stanley hesitated before entering, as if he were unsure how to proceed. It occurred to Barley that it was entirely possible Stanley had never been in a tunnel before. Barley spoke to him in a low coddling tone. "Come on, buddy. I'll be with you."

"Woof!" Stanley followed Barley into the damp shadow. Within minutes, they were back outside. The next tunnel was even shorter, but Stanley came to a standstill outside the entrance and dug in his heels.

"Come on, big guy. The first one wasn't too scary, was it?" Barley asked, pulling the bungee. Stanley resisted, forcing the elastic material to extend. He didn't make a sound, just put on his doggy brakes and refused to budge. Barley gave him a Milk-Bone and rubbed his head. That did the trick, and together they bulldozed through the dank, grey tunnel air. In no time they were outside again, squinting against the blinding sunshine.

Barley checked the GPS. They were getting closer, but the tiny needle didn't start to spin on the screen until they had gone through a third tunnel and stood outside the entrance to a fourth that was reinforced with wooden supports and wire mesh to prevent rocks from falling. Barley pulled Stanley, who once again verbalized his displeasure, towards the entrance. A family was playing an echo game inside and Barley decided to wait just at the entrance until they finished. Time was of the essence, but it was also important not to alert Muggles to the existence of the cache.

Barley reread the clue to Stanley. "'Where the sun don't shine, pirate treasure can be mine.' Hmm." He sized up the wooden beams. It was possible that the cache was hidden on top of a beam, but that was too high for Barley to reach. Stanley tried to head back towards the sunshine, but Barley stood firm. The family tired of the game and were on their way out when the younger child spotted the king-sized dog.

"Look, Mom, it's Scooby Doo." She ran and nuzzled Stanley's neck. He showed his pleasure by drooling thick Milk-Bone juice on her head. The rest of the family approached cautiously. The mother said hello, was it OK if her daughter cuddled the dog?

"Sure." Barley hoped this would hurry them on their way. Sheesh. He had work to do. Finally, after each had a turn patting the enormous head, they headed back towards the parking lot.

This tunnel smelled mustier than the others, like Barley's aunt's basement that time she had a flood. He looked upwards beyond the wooden supports: the roof had been covered with arched concrete and vertical concrete columns framed huge walls of rough granite.

Barley slowly advanced into the tunnel, pulling Stanley as he went. Four wooden supports in, the lamp's beam caught the outline of something up in the rafters. Barley drew closer and saw what looked like a metal box. Stretching his right hand as high as he could, he still wasn't able to reach the top of the eight-foot support. He dropped the bungee and went back outside to find something to stand on. Stanley trotted happily alongside, seeming to think their time in the tunnel was done.

Over an orange plastic emergency fence, Barley spied a piece of granite about the size of a jumbo box of cereal. Barley figured that would do it; he only needed an extra six inches or so of height to reach the cache. He laid his GPS on the ground next to Stanley and climbed the fence. Stanley looked stricken, and low thunderous sounds emerged from deep down in his diaphragm. Barley could hardly lift the rock but he managed to move it up to a higher flat boulder closer to the fence. God, it was heavy. Sweat popped on his forehead and under his arms, and started rolling down his spine. He looked at Stanley, who may or may not have shrugged his shoulders. Barley had an idea; he climbed back over the fence, untied the bungee from Stanley's neck and returned to the rock. With a quick glance to make sure Stanley wasn't going to run off, Barley fastened the bungee around the rock and began dragging it towards the plastic emergency fence.

When he got it as far as the fence, he scrambled back over and lifted the bottom of the orange plastic. Grunting, Barley dragged the rock under, and with the help of the bungee, began to pull the rock towards the tunnel. The rock wasn't shifting more than an inch at a time. At this rate, he'd be there all day. He hoped no one else showed up for a while. It might jeopardize the competition if a Muggle messed with the cache.

Slowly, Barley dragged the hunk of granite as far as the fourth support beam. Once in position, he stood on the rock, but his headlamp was too close to be of any use. Barley felt around until his fingers touched cool metal. He yanked; the rectangular tin came more easily than he'd expected, and the momentum caused him to fall backwards into a puddle of murky water. Stanley yelped from where he had remained on guard outside the entrance. Barley's cargo pants were drenched on the back.

"Yuck." He put a hand to his backside. They were stuck on to his skin. Although it was exceptionally hot out, inside the tunnel the air was cool, and he shivered.

He carried the old-fashioned tin box to the entrance and placed it delicately on the dirt next to Stanley. The cover was embossed with Victorian ladies drinking tea. Barley knew they were Victorian because he had done an entire unit on Queen Victoria's reign in Grade 10. The tin must have held biscuits when it was new. He opened the lid to reveal a veritable pirate booty of imitation jewelry, and underneath, a bag of shiny Geocoins. Barley took one, recorded the number in his book, and dropped the bag back in the tin, along with a small white and brown goat.

"Ha, cache in the bag at...," he glanced at his watch, "11:32." Barley grabbed Stanley by the front paws and tried to engage him in a jig. Stanley was less than enthusiastic. It showed in his dancing.

Barley didn't know why they just couldn't call in the numbers after each cache instead of checking in at Colossus. It would save a lot of time. He hurried back in the tunnel and jammed the tin back up in the rafters before anyone showed up. Even though it took time, he dragged the rock back outside and undid the bungee cord. He shoved it the rest of the way with his foot, under the fence and into the river where it disappeared with a splash. "Let those other losers find their own step ladder," he told the dog.

He reattached the bungee to Stanley's neck. Stanley seemed more than happy to leave the musty air and fell into a happy canter next to Barley.

They were just about to enter the second tunnel when Barley's phone rang. Stanley perked up at the sound of seagulls. Barley crouched down so he could kneel on the bungee, tucked his GPS under one arm, and dug his Blackberry out of its sheath on his belt. Not many people had his number. Oh God, Barley hoped it wasn't Mr. Franklyn telling him he couldn't take the week off after all. Colin had his back, though. Colin always had his back.

Barley didn't recognize the number. His panic subsided. It must be his mother calling from a work site. He saw she had called earlier from her cell. He hoped she hadn't noticed that he had taken the Corvette. She'd pop a gasket.

"Yello." Barley gave Stanley a rub on his underside.

"I'm looking for Barley Lick." It was a voice Barley didn't recognize.

"Yes."

"Barley Lick?" The voice was deep, baritone.

"This is me." Barley figured it must be a journalist. The *Cloverdale Reporter* had already done a story on GeoFind, with big pictures of Barley and Phyllis across the top of the page. Barley's mother had stuck it on the fridge.

"Where are you? It sounds like there's a river in the background."

"I'm at the Othello Tunnels near Hope."

"What the heck are you doing there?"

Barley moved the phone a couple of inches away from his ear so as not to be deafened by the booming voice. "I'm geocaching." Barley tried to keep his voice calm. He looked at Stanley, who was drinking from a stagnant puddle. Barley tugged him away. This was not the time to engage in idiotic conversations with strangers.

"Yes, yes, geocaching. That's why I called. I need some assistance in your area of expertise. I'm hoping you can help me." The man sounded like he was chewing gum.

OK, so this wasn't a reporter. "Help you do what?"

"Help me locate a set of coordinates."

"Sorry, I'm busy right now."

"I know about the contest. But what I'm working on is significantly more important."

Barley had to get rid of this arsehole. "Sorry, Mr.?"

"Newton. Fred Newton. I met you the other night."

Oh my God, it's the mutant molester. Ugh. Barley stuck out his tongue and clicked off his phone. His mother was going to kill him. But he didn't care. The thought of having anything to do with that man turned his stomach. How dare he say that whatever he was doing was more important than GeoFind. This contest meant everything to Barley, and he was going to win it for his father.

7

Nelson Lick

Nelson Lick had started his career working for the government of British Columbia in Crown Lands. After about ten years, he took a job at the Geological Survey of Canada, mapping remote sites in the BC interior and writing up reports on base metals like zinc and copper. He loved anything to do with maps and the outdoors.

Nelson Lick worked deep in the woods, helicopter deep, but whenever he was in the field close enough for his phone to ping off a cell tower, he would call his wife, M.J., at 6 p.m. to check in. M.J. always made sure she was home from work and relaxed, so she could devote all her attention to him and they could tell each other about their day. He savoured those calls; he'd sit on a rotten log, listen to M.J.'s voice, and sip lukewarm coffee from a thermos. Later he'd pretend that instead of eating smoked oysters out of a tin, he was sitting in their kitchen, eating home-cooked chicken. Then he'd crawl in his tent and ponder life's big secrets.

Nelson Lick spent so much time in the woods it was no surprise that's where he was the day his only child was born. At 6 p.m. on August 24, 1989, he called M.J. and wondered why she didn't pick up.

At 7:30, he got his answer.

"It's a boy," came her excited voice through the tiny receiver. "Darn near had him in the loo." Mary Jane Lick went on to inform her husband that she had decided to call the baby Barley after the grain that her father had grown on their farm in Saskatchewan.

"Come on, honey," Nelson said. "We can't call him Barley. People will think we're off our rockers."

"You knew if it was a boy that I wanted to name him after my father."

"Yes." Nelson wondered where this was going.

"Well, would you prefer we call him Vladimir?"

"No, but let's be reasonable…"

"I am being reasonable. The next time you give birth to a ten-pound watermelon, I'll let you call it whatever you like."

Nelson realized it was a losing battle, but he did manage a consolation. "OK, my darling wife, if our baby boy is going to have Barley as a first name, he can have Markus as a middle name." Nelson Lick was the ultimate Markus Näslund fan. He said Näslund was the glue that held the Canucks together.

Mary Jane Lick knew immediately this was to pay homage to her husband's favourite hockey player. "You drive a hard bargain," she said, the baby cooing in the background.

By the time Nelson Lick got back to civilization the next day, he had accepted his son's fate, marched into the maternity ward, and presented his wife with roses and a bottle of Glendronach single-malt Scotch whisky. He was just struggling to manoeuvre the infant's arms into a tiny monogrammed onesie when the doctor came by to do his rounds.

"Barley Markus Lick," he read. "What does that mean?"

"That's our son's name," said M.J. defiantly.

"Oh," he answered. "Why torture the child?"

But Barley it was. And people got used to the name. Well, most people anyway. Some, including Barley himself, questioned the blip that had occurred in his mother's brain the day of his birth.

★

In fact, it had taken Barley sixteen years to accept his name. It was his father's death that made him finally come around. His father had always said his name with such affection. 'Barley, come help me in the yard.' 'Barley, load up the car.' 'Barley, we're going on a road trip.' Barley found he missed that once his father was gone.

Barley missed everything about his father. Half the time his father was out in the woods mapping, but when he was home, he was really there. He wasn't hidden behind his newspaper or working on the computer; he was there playing street hockey with Barley. Or building a fort with him. Or out in the shed tinkering with his motorbike, teaching Barley how to change the oil. No matter what his father was doing when he wasn't working, Barley was always welcome and encouraged to participate. Nelson Lick taught his son to love whatever he did, and as a result, Barley came to love and excel at those pastimes he shared with his father.

Barley remembered the first time his father took him to an NHL game. It was 1999 and Näslund scored three goals. From that night on, Näslund was Barley's hero too. Barley had been playing house league hockey for years, but it was only after seeing the Canucks play that he really put his back into it. His father wasn't coach, but he came on the ice for practices and was on the bench whenever they played. He was the one who'd open the gate and tap a player on the helmet after every shift. Barley still played high school hockey. He had been MVP in Grade 10. He was a defenceman who could score. He racked up forty-seven points that season. Nineteen goals and nine assists. More than any other defenceman in the league. He hadn't done so well this year.

His father had been Barley's biggest fan, although Barley had plenty of fans his own age in the stands. And when geocaching more or less took over from hockey as the main pastime in the Lick household, Barley's father did double duty. He was always teaching Barley some new GPS function or dragging him to an obscure park to find a cache, but he found time to keep up with hockey. In fact, Barley couldn't think of a time that his father missed a hockey game or practice when he was in town.

Barley still woke up every morning thinking his father was going to be there waiting for him either to go to the rink or to head out to hunt for new caches. Then the awful truth would envelope him. When he realized his father wasn't there, was never going to be there again, the depression would settle like a fog weighing down on his body and mind. Barley had to talk to himself to get out of bed and push through the sadness. He knew it made him sullen and lash out at his mother for no reason sometimes, but he couldn't help it. The loss was too immense, the fog too thick. The only times he was able to drive the depression to the background was while he was on the ice or geocaching, so he tried to spend as much time as possible engaged in those two things. Hockey had ended earlier in the spring, so geocaching was how he occupied himself everyday he wasn't working or at school.

Although he didn't know it, Nelson Lick had prepped his son to be a champion geocacher long before geocaching existed. Before kindergarten even. At home in the den, a two-foot-wide globe provided countless hours of entertainment for a young Barley. First, he just liked memorizing the colours and shapes of the countries; by the time he was seven, Barley was learning the basics of global positioning from his father.

"See how the earth is divided up into sections by imaginary lines," his father explained, spinning the globe. "Each one of those lines has a number from the equator." He pointed at the belt that went all the way around the globe's centre. "From the equator to the north pole and from the equator to the south pole."

Barley could still see the globe and the numbers in his mind. He could see his father wearing his favourite Canucks t-shirt with the big hole under one arm.

"It's the same thing from the prime meridian for east and west. So, the captain of a ship, for example, can point at a spot on his charts and go there. All he needs to know are the coordinates."

By the age of nine, Barley knew all the world's time zones without consulting a map. He had started with the North American ones, so that if the Canucks had to play in the East, he'd know what time the game would be on in Vancouver.

Barley spent a lot of time studying the globe and the family's worn atlas while his father was in the field. By age ten, given the coordinates, Barley could pinpoint any place on earth. His father was on a two-week field study when this advance took place. Barley couldn't wait to impress him when he got home.

His father wasn't in the door two minutes when Barley said: "Dad, I bet if you tell me any place on earth, I can tell you the coordinates within sixty seconds."

His father laid his duffel bag on the floor outside the office door. "OK, smarty pants, tell me the coordinates of where we live in BC."

Barley opened the big hard-cover *Collins Atlas of the World* and flipped to North America. He picked out Vancouver Island and Vancouver no trouble, but it took a second to find Cloverdale. It wasn't labeled. Nor was Surrey. The scale wasn't that big. Barley did see the number 49 written just below Vancouver so he knew Cloverdale would be the same: 49 degrees north. "And since Vancouver is 123 west, Cloverdale should be at least one degree farther east." He paused. "Maybe 122 degrees west?"

"Good job," his father said, patting him on the head. "You have a special gift."

"Can I get a dog now?" Barley had begged for a dog for years.

"No way." Nelson Lick laughed.

By twelve, Barley was so far ahead of everyone else in his geography class that his teacher, Mr. Dawson, had taken to consulting him during lessons. "Barley Lick," he'd say with an extra roll on the "l" of Lick. "Can you please tell us the capital of Djibouti?"

"That's easy. Djibouti City." Barley could list all the countries of the world and their capitals. Although he sometimes stumbled on pronunciations. It was a monumental day when he mastered the pronunciation of the capital of Slovenia. "Ljubljana" became a word of exclamation and affirmation in the Lick household.

"Did you see Colin today?" his mother might ask.

"Ljubljana!" Barley would exclaim.

"Do you like the ice cream?"

"Ljubljana!"

"Want to go see a movie?"

"Ljubljana!"

As long as "Ljubljana" was the answer, life was good.

8

Barley's Fifteenth Birthday

For his fifteenth birthday in 2004, Barley's parents presented him with a small rectangle wrapped in a hiking map. Barley shook the box. "What is it?" He figured it was a signed hockey card in a plastic display case or something else hockey related. He was wrong.

"Open it." His mother sat alongside him on the couch. She wore her pink housecoat and a silly grin.

He tore off the paper to read the words Garmin eTrex on a little black box. "It's a… Global Positioning System?" Barley had never touched one before.

"Yes," said his father, adjusting his recliner. "Now no matter where you are in the world, in the middle of the desert or at the top of a mountain, this thing can tell you your coordinates. It just needs a clear view of the satellites." Nelson Lick's smile was so big, his eyes scrunched into slits.

Barley tried to mask his disappointment. It was indeed a sleek-looking gadget, but he had been hoping for a kayak so he could go out on the Fraser River with Colin. His mother, who always seemed to know his emotions, put a hand on his arm and he turned to her.

"You know how your father's GPS tells him his exact

position on earth to within eight metres?"

"Ljubljana," said Barley, to show he remembered.

"Well, when he first started using one for work, they weren't nearly as accurate as they are now." Barley's mother looked to his father and nodded.

"That's right, the first one I had wasn't accurate at all."

"How come?"

Barley's mother passed Barley scissors to cut through the tough plastic encasing the tiny machine.

His father continued. "Because all the information from the satellites regarding latitude and longitude was scrambled."

"Why?" Barley had wrestled the Garmin out of its package, and it sat in his hand like a bright blue Walkie Talkie, but without an antenna.

"So, people wouldn't be able to know the exact coordinates of things."

"That doesn't make sense. That's what a GPS is for, isn't it?" Barley tried to open the battery door. His mother could see he was getting frustrated and showed him how to pull up on a small round metal loop and twist. Then, like a personal assistant, she passed him the double As; he inserted them one by one.

"Yes, that's what a GPS is for, but governments didn't want terrorists knowing the exact coordinates of important infrastructure, like airports, hospitals, or factories." Barley's father stroked his jaw.

Barley bunched up his lips so his mother continued. "Anything they might be able to direct a missile towards, the White House, other government buildings."

"You're talking about the US, not here in Canada?"

Barley's father took over again. "That's where the rulings came from, yes. But in May 2000, President Clinton did away with the intentional degradation of all civilian GPS signals..."

"Degradation?" Barley's brow furrowed.

"He did away with the system that scrambled satellite information. It was called Selective Availability or SA. And with SA turned off, a handheld GPS can lead a person within eight metres of a set of coordinates. Before it was eighty metres. That's a quantum leap."

Barley's mother prodded his arm. "Why don't you turn it on."

Barley poked the *on* button and the grey screen came to life.

"With SA satellites, it'd be like a novice hunter searching for a moose in the woods. Every tree would look like a rack," Barley's mother said. "But when things aren't scrambled, the antlers stand out clearly."

"Mo-om, we're not going hunting." Barley was getting frustrated with both his parents.

"Not for animals, but you can use the GPS to hunt for hidden caches." She smiled and hugged Barley into her side.

Barley scrolled through the various screens. "Caches? What do you mean?"

His father held up a copy of *Outside* magazine. He opened it to a page titled: "Geocaching: International Hide and Seek".

"When Clinton turned off the satellite scrambling system and people could get more detailed satellite information, someone in Oregon came up with a game. He hid a bucket in the woods and used a handheld GPS to find the coordinates."

"And?" Barley's left eyebrow lifted. "What happened then?"

His father scanned the article. "This other guy named Mike Teague got the coordinates and used his GPS to find the bucket."

"That's it?" Barley scrunched up his face.

"Not quite." Barley's father reread a couple of paragraphs, his eyes quickly moving from line to line. "Then this third guy came along." His father read a bit further. "Jeremy Irish was his name... he created a website called geocaching.com. And he invited anyone to post coordinates of a hidden bucket so other people could find it."

Barley looked at the screen. "Nothing is happening."

"That's 'cause it needs a clear view of the satellites," said his mother. "Why don't we get dressed, take it outside, and let it hook up."

It was a hot August day. Barley went out to the backyard barefoot and pointed the screen at the sky. That's when he heard Colin. He laid the GPS on a bench and ran to open the gate. Colin tumbled into the yard holding what was obviously a paddle wrapped in newspaper. "What kind did you get?" He scanned the yard for signs of a kayak.

"Uh..." said Barley. "I didn't get a kayak." He swallowed.

"Oh... oops." Colin laid the paddle on the ground. "You can use my kayak and I'll use the paddle board."

"Christmas is coming though," said Barley's mother. "Maybe Santa will bring you one."

Barley felt badly then, and led Colin to the blue Garmin sitting face up on the bench. "I got a GPS."

"A GP what?"

"A global positioning system." Barley picked it up.

"Oh yeah, Dad uses one on the sailboat, but it doesn't look like this."

"This is a handheld version," said Barley's father. "Has it synched with the satellites yet?"

Barley stared at the screen. "I don't think so. How long does it take to hook up?"

"The first time, it can take about twenty minutes," said his father. "But after that, it does it right away as long as it has a clear view."

"Why wouldn't it have a clear view if you're outside?" asked Colin.

"Sometimes tree branches or rock walls or even dense fog can interfere." Barley's father came closer. "I think it's ready to go. Look." Magically the latitude and longitude displayed on the screen.

"Now for the fun part," said Barley's mother. She passed Barley a slip of paper. On it was written: "At the pond, use this to stay afloat."

"Must be a life jacket," said Colin. "Does it say anything else?"

"Just a set of numbers," said Barley. "Coordinates, very close to the ones on the screen."

"What are you waiting for?" his mother said. "Go get 'em."

"How?" asked Barley.

"All you have to do is move with the machine and you'll be able to see if you're getting closer or farther away," his father explained.

Barley held up the GPS. He walked a little left and then right until he saw the geographical seconds move. "How do I know which way I'm supposed to go?"

"Are the coordinates your mother gave you more north than the ones on the GPS?"

Barley looked at both. "Yes."

"Which way is north?" asked his father.

Barley turned to face the sun and pointed left.

"Then you have to move north to get to the new coordinates. In a bit, I'll show you how to upload coordinates so the GPS can lead you to them. For now, just see what happens when you get close to the spot on the paper."

Barley held his arm stiffly before him, and he and Colin watched the coordinates change on the little grey screen. If they stopped, the machine stopped working, but as long as they were in motion, the numbers changed. They came to the fence but hadn't yet reached the correct place, so they hopped it and continued through the small grove of trees behind the house.

"Let me have a turn," said Colin.

Barley passed him the machine. "That's sick," he said, watching the numbers move along with them. "How do we know when we're there?"

"Not sure. Here, pass it back." Barley followed the machine another thirty metres or so until they came to the tiny pond where Barley and his parents used to have picnics when he was young.

"I think it's stopped working." Barley looked up at the thick branches overhead.

"How close are you to the coordinates your mother gave you?"

"Almost right on them."

"Well, let's start looking for a life jacket," said Colin, beginning to dig through the tall grass.

"I see something," yelled Barley. There among the reeds in the water was a kayak. Not the new yellow Pyranha white-water one he had seen at Mountain Equipment Co-op and asked for, but a slightly battered orange P & H Capella touring one.

"This is way better than the one you looked at," said Colin to make Barley feel better. "It's like mine. Look, there's something in it."

Barley pulled out a plastic bucket with a green handle and pried off the lid. In it sat a red envelope.

"Open it," said Colin.

Barley grabbed it and pulled out two movie passes and a folded piece of paper.

"Hey, we can go see *Harry Potter and the Order of the Phoenix* in 3D," said Colin.

"Or *Superbad*."

"What does the paper say?"

"Every fifteen-year-old boy needs a skirt."

"Really? Let me see." Colin took the paper. "Is there something you're not telling me?"

"No, I'm not sure what it means. I guess I have to go to the next coordinates to find out. They look far away."

79

"Well, come on. Let's bring the kayak back to the house and get your father to show us how to get the machine to tell us where to go."

Barley shoved the GPS in his pocket and hooked the bucket over his arm. Then the boys hoisted the kayak out of the water and portaged back to the house. Barley called to his father.

"So, you found it," said his mother from behind the fence. "What do you think?"

"It's pretty rad," said Barley. "Thanks Mom and Dad. We're going to lift it over the fence. Can you take it?"

"Sure. Then we'll have some breakfast while you learn how to put in the new coordinates."

Barley's mother had made their special family breakfast of chocolate chip pancakes, bacon, eggs, and guacamole toast.

"Wahoo," said Colin. "You should open a diner, Mrs. L."

"Lujubljana," mumbled Barley, his mouth full of pancake.

Over breakfast, Barley's father showed them how to upload the coordinates on the paper and press Go To. It was awkward manipulating the tiny joystick to put in the numbers. Once in, Barley brought the GPS to the windowsill. It told them the next coordinates were over thirty kilometres away as the crow flies.

"That's too far to walk. How are we gonna get to them?" asked Colin, syrup drooling out the corner of his mouth.

"We'll take you," said Barley's mother. "But you have to direct us."

"Make sure you bring the bucket," said Barley's father, passing the plastic container to Barley. After breakfast, they piled in his father's rust bucket of a truck, the 1999 Ford SuperCab he had bought second hand, and headed downtown. Barley held the Garmin up to the window and whenever his father asked him which way to turn, he followed the little arrow. They only made two wrong turns and when they were almost at the destination, the tiny needle on the screen started spinning.

"There's something wrong," said Barley. "It's not working anymore."

"Let me see," said his father. He pulled into the nearest parking space.

"When the needle does that, it means you're so close, the machine can't help you anymore."

"Really? So, it's somewhere around here. What street are we on?"

"West Broadway."

"Let's get out and start looking," said Colin. "I can't wait to see Barley in a skirt." He elbowed Barley in the ribs.

"You're a riot, Colin." Barley got out of the car, and Colin and his parents followed. "Hey, we're at MEC." The Mountain Equipment Co-op sign was across the street.

"Is it in there?" asked Barley.

"Don't know." His mother shrugged her shoulders. "You'll have to go in and find out."

Barley felt timid entering the store. "What am I supposed to do?"

Colin pushed him towards the cash counter. "Ask them if they have anything for you?"

Barley took a breath and got in line. When it was his turn, he asked the cashier if she happened to have anything for Barley Lick.

She made an announcement over the speaker and all the staff in the store began to sing "Happy Birthday." Colin and Barley's parents joined in with other shoppers. Barley shrank into his shoes. When they had finished, the clerk smiled and passed Barley a large bag.

"Thanks," he mumbled, and moved away from the counter. "Mo-om."

"Go ahead, open it."

Barley opened the bag and pulled out a Farmer John kayaking neoprene suit and a spray skirt.

Colin cracked up laughing. "That's the best present ever."

On the way home, Barley's mother said they had one more surprise. "We're going to look for a geocache on the way home."

"How do we know where to look?" asked Barley.

"I looked on geocaching.com and found this one called 'Hockey Night in Cloverdale,'" said his father. "Here are the coordinates. You plug them in to the GPS and tell me where to go."

Once again, Barley struggled to toggle the tiny joy stick around the letters, but it was easier than the first time.

They piled back into the truck and Barley played navigator as his father drove the forty minutes back to Cloverdale.

"There's a clue," Barley said. "But it looks like you have to decode it or something."

His mother leaned over the seat to show them how to transpose the numbers for letters to read the clue. "Look for Toronto players," said Barley. "What the heck does that mean?"

"Hmmm," said Colin.

They pondered what that might mean all the way to Cloverdale while Barley kept an eye on the GPS instructing his father which way to turn.

"We've got less than 500 metres to go," said Barley, pointing to the right. "Pull in."

"Where?" asked his father.

"Into the parking lot."

They had arrived at the Cloverdale Arena where Barley had played hockey since he was five. The boys tumbled out of the cramped back seat and took turns holding the Garmin as it led them into the grove of trees behind the rink. The trees weren't too big so the Garmin could still communicate with the satellites.

"You see anything?" asked Colin.

"Nope," said Barley. "But the needle started jiggling again."

"Why does it do that?"

"I think it's so close to the coordinates that it has trouble latching on or something."

"Tell me what the clue says exactly," said Colin.

"Look for Toronto players."

"OK, what are Toronto players?"

"Maple Leafs," both boys said in unison.

"It must be near a maple tree," said Colin.

He ran one way through the grove and Barley went the other, until Barley screamed. "I see something."

"Where?" Colin ran to where Barley was pointing.

"There in that maple tree." Barley pulled a Tupperware container covered in camouflage tape from a branch of the small maple. His parents arrived just as Barley pulled off the lid to expose a few packs of hockey cards and a dozen of those little ceramic hockey mugs. There was also a tiny notebook and pencil in a plastic baggy.

"What's that for?" asked Barley.

"That's so the people who find this cache can write in the little book and when the owner comes to check on it, they'll be able to see who's been here."

"So, we're supposed to write our names?" asked Colin.

"Not your real names," said Barley's father. "You're supposed to invent online names."

"What name are you going to use, Barley?" asked Colin. "I'm going to be River Otter."

"I think I'll be Billy G."

"What does that mean?"

"It's short for Billy Goat." Barley opened the book and saw that someone else had found the cache that morning. And the day before and two days before that. "Wow, there are lots of geocachers out there."

"Did you say we get to take something out of the bucket, Mr. Lick?"

"Yes, you can take one thing as long as you put something else back in."

Colin picked up a mini mug with Colorado on it. He dug his hands into his pockets and drew out a candy covered in lint. "This is all I have."

"That's OK," said Barley's mother, holding up two round silver discs. "We brought some Geocoins."

"What are they?" said Colin.

"They're coins with numbers on them. You can get metal tags too. They're called travellers. When another geocacher finds one, they can take it and move it to another cache. Once we register the number, we'll get an email telling us where your coins have gone."

Barley and Colin examined the coins. "These are better than the loot in the bucket," said Barley.

"It'll be fun once you start getting messages tracking their journey," said his mother. "It'll be like when you did Flat Stanley in Grade 5. Remember he went to Paris?"

"Oh yeah," said Colin, "we wrote letters to that class of French kids for a whole year." He dropped his coin into the container. Barley did the same and took a pack of hockey cards. He opened them and held up a rookie Marcus Näslund.

"No way," said Colin.

"Yep," said Barley, a smile forming on his face. This was turning out to be the best birthday ever and he hadn't even tried out the kayak yet.

★

Barley and Colin messed around with the GPS until the sun faded on the horizon. They didn't master all its intricacies, but they quickly became proficient with most of its main features.

Between geocaching and kayaking, the last few days of

summer melted away. Labour Day came and went, and the first day of school snuck up on them. Before long, the hockey season started. Barley put away the GPS and didn't think much about geocaching until the following spring.

9

Thieves Work Here

N 49° 22.207, W 121° 21.891

Back at the Othello Tunnels, Barley slid his phone into its leather sheath on his belt. Why had he answered? Grumbling, he stood up quickly and misjudged how close he was to the granite wall. "Ugh." He whacked his forehead on an overhanging stone. He crouched again, rubbing his forehead. Warm blood trickled down his temple.

Stanley hovered over him like a protective nanny. He licked the cut.

"Thanks, buddy." Barley picked up the bungee attached to the Great Dane's collar and slowly got to his feet. He had to get back on track, erase the phone call from his mind.

"OK, Stanley," he said. "Let's see how fast you are." Barley began sprinting through the last two tunnels. Stanley lagged. Barley assumed it was the heat. Or maybe it was because the dog hadn't had a proper lunch. Or breakfast, for that matter. He slowed up and gave Stanley another Milk-Bone from his pocket. How often did Great Danes need to eat? There was a lot Barley had to learn.

Out in the parking lot, Stanley began whimpering; Barley slowed down enough to see he was favouring one of his front legs. A few hundred feet from the Corvette, Stanley came to an abrupt stop. That's when Barley noticed a trail of blood. It was coming from Stanley's front left paw. The poor dog. Barley felt terrible.

But how could this be happening now? What else can possibly go wrong?

Barley took Stanley's paw in his hand. Stanley pulled away, but not before Barley saw a small cube of glass between the pads. Barley grabbed the paw again, held it tight, and spoke to the dog in soothing tones. "It's OK, big guy. Let me see."

Stanley whined low and haunting when Barley touched his foot. Stanley was not aggressive, but he was strong. Barley took the Swiss Army knife from another sheath on his belt and extracted the tweezers, then put Stanley in a headlock. "Stanley, you gotta stop pulling away from me. I know..." He kissed the top of the dog's head. "I would, too, if I had a lump of glass stuck between my toes."

It only took a minute to remove the tiny square of glass from between the tender pink pads. Blood trickled onto Barley's pants leg. The glass measured about one square millimeter. Barley slipped it into his pocket to investigate later.

"There. It's all gone." Barley cooed and dropped the paw. "That mean old glass won't hurt you anymore." Holding his paw off the ground like a show horse, Stanley looked unconvinced. When Barley pulled the bungee, the dog jolted, but didn't lower the injured paw.

Barley took off his hiking boot and transferred his sock from his foot to Stanley's. Stanley still refused to walk. In fact, he stood as still as a statue. Barley tugged forcefully on the bungee; Stanley began walking sideways, his socked leg moving like he was pushing a pedal around on a bike. Under less urgent circumstances, it might have been comical.

Barley gave him another dog biscuit. Stanley wolfed it down and slobbered. Brown this time.

"Come on, Stanley buddy, you can do it." Barley dragged the injured dog with his socked foot towards the car; he tried to steer him clear of any more broken glass, but it was futile. The entire parking lot was littered with the bluish cubes.

What Barley saw next made him gasp.

Shards of bluish glass pointed up out of the Corvette's window frame. Like transparent stalactites. *No. No. No, no, no!* How dare someone break into his father's Corvette? It was like pissing on his grave.

He kicked one of the back tires. "Pigs," Barley yelled, just as an elderly couple got out of their Oldsmobile. The woman's eyes widened.

Barley pointed at the blue shards on the ground, but before he could speak, the man and woman jumped back in their car, belted up, and tore out of the lot, their Olds practically airborne.

Barley wondered what could have been visible in the car to make someone want to break in. Except for a bunch of his father's topo maps shoved behind the back seat, there wasn't much.

He covered the passenger seat and floor with an old towel his father kept under the driver's seat in case the windshield fogged up. "Load up," Barley said, and four feet of beige fur stepped delicately into the passenger side. Barley was amazed at the Great Dane's bendability. Once he installed his butt in the bucket seat and arranged his front paws on the floor, his upright ear again touched the roof.

Barley went around to the driver's side, opened the door, and covering his hand with his shirt, banged out the remaining glass stuck in the frame. He swept the cubes off the seat so he could sit down. Right next to the vehicle was a sign that read: *Thieves Work Here. Do not leave valuables in your car.*

"Argh."

Barley couldn't recall seeing anyone in the parking lot when they arrived. The thieves must hide in the bushes, he thought. Then he remembered the guy on the bike, the way he watched to make sure they went in the tunnel, the earpiece. It all made sense now. Once visitors were in the tunnels, the guy with the earpiece must notify his partner back on the parking lot that it was safe to break in. Barley clenched his teeth as he sat down; his pants still wet from the puddle.

At least there was no damage to the ignition. He put the car in gear and began to drive slowly across the lot, dodging the larger sections of broken glass. This day was not going well, not well at all.

Barley tried to think of what his father would do. He'd say: 'Just start again. Forget whatever's happened, and simply pick up where you need to.'

Barley was almost out to the road when he noticed a yellow Mini turning in the lot. Phyllis. That meant she had already finished her first cache and was on to the second. She smiled and made motion for Barley to roll down the window, her hand twisting as if rotating a handle. He didn't need to roll down the window—it was busted. He should warn her about the thieves, he knew, but he faked a smile and kept going. Phyllis looked surprised. Barley didn't care. She was enemy number one.

Barley began the five-kilometre drive back to Hope swearing at every gush of wind that ripped in through the broken window. At least it was warm and not raining. In fact, the sun was hot enough to split the rocks. After months of cool rain, that should have made Barley happy. But today wasn't going smoothly, and Barley liked things to go smoothly.

Turning west on the Trans-Canada Highway, he got stuck behind a slug of a driver in a Chrysler LeBaron. He revved the engine to show he meant business before roaring around the geezer. Stanley jolted forward and Barley's arm flew out instinctively to keep him from hitting the windshield. "I might have to get you a doggy seatbelt," he said, watching Stanley right himself in the seat.

In the left lane, Barley picked up speed. He had to make sure he finished ahead of Phyllis at every stage. He couldn't risk her getting ahead. The speedometer reached 110 kilometres an hour, and Barley gulped in the wind. Stanley squinted; his ears pinned to the sides of his head; his short fur blew back like he was in a convertible commercial.

How could Phyllis have checked in and be all the way out here already? Damn her. Damn the thieves. Damn Hope. Barley's next cache had better be an easy one. He gunned it and watched the speedometer needle jerk to the right.

Think, Barley. Prioritize. That's what his father taught him whenever he got overwhelmed with an assignment or exams at school. *First thing—get to Colossus and log the Geocoin number. Get the second cache and move on. Forget Phyllis. She wouldn't be tall enough to reach up in the rafters either.*

After logging his second cache, he would find a place close to home to get the car window fixed before his mother saw it and found out about his little joyride. He racked his mind trying to think of a windshield repair place in Cloverdale. He had no idea how much it would cost. He had saved $238 so far from his Big Bite job.

One thing at a time, Barley. Relax your breathing and think. What is your biggest priority?

The most important thing he had to do was make sure he was faster than Phyllis Henderson.

"Hang on to your hat, Stanley," he said. He put his foot to the floor.

10

Benjamin

Benjamin dreams about spirit bears. In the dream a Kitasoo elder dances with eleven bears around a campfire; one is white. "To remind us that this land we inhabit was once covered by ice," he says, his words disappearing into the flames. A raven flies over, and wherever its shadow falls, the land below turns a vibrant green. "So, the animals can remember how pure it was after the ice receded."

The elder continues to dance with the bears. "No harm will ever come to this spirit bear," he says. "It will be safe in this paradise forever."

Then the elder and the bears rise into the sky, lifted by the flames, except the elder is Benjamin's father and two of the bears are Benjamin and his mother.

Benjamin wakes up in a sweat. He is in a sleeping bag. But is it his sleeping bag? He is woozy and finds it difficult to think clearly. He knows he should be at camp, but there, they sleep on wooden bunks in cabins. Here he is alone in a tent and doesn't seem able to move. He struggles to piece together how he got here. He sort of remembers a long car trip, maybe a ferry ride. But where did he go and who with? Not his parents. Where are his parents? He wishes he could see them now, especially his mother. He would tell her about his dream.

She had first told him the legend of the spirit bear when BC Lions Society for Children with Disabilities had started their fundraiser and spirit bear statues popped up all over Vancouver. They had driven downtown to visit his father at work—his parents were still together then—and then he and his mother spent a wet afternoon traipsing around Gastown to see all the fibreglass statues of bears wearing jeans and sunglasses or Team Canada jerseys. Bears painted with peace signs and rainbows, even Van Gogh's Starry Night. Benjamin's favourite was playing a traditional First Nation drum. His mother was on the board of Easter Seals, and the auction raised hundreds of thousands of dollars for BC Lions and two other charities. Benjamin enjoyed the afternoon, but he'd caught a cold and that night had gone to bed with a fever. His mother came into his room and rubbed his back and told him the legend of the Kermode bear. He remembered relaxing under the touch of her fingers and falling asleep listening to her voice recount the story of the raven in the forests before man started hacking down the trees.

She was the only one who knew exactly how to make him feel better.

How he wishes he could feel the warmth of her hand on his back now.

11

Mastering the GPS

2005

During the spring of 2005, Colin enrolled in a paddle-boarding camp. Barley wasn't into it as much as Colin, so once hockey ended, during the weekends that Colin was out on the water, Barley went geocaching. It took Barley a while to get a handle on all the GPS functions. He had mastered locating coordinates the previous summer, but figuring out how to mark waypoints took a while.

Recording waypoints was like making note of a big rock or bridge or radio tower on a map. If you marked these points on the GPS as you went along, it made it easier to follow a specific trail, especially if you wanted to take the same route back, or wanted others to come the same way after you've gone.

"Once you master waypoints, you can be the one to choose the next geocaching destination," said his father. "We'll go wherever you want after my next rotation." Nelson Lick's field work was usually two weeks on, one week off.

With that enticement, Barley was on it. He practiced every morning, and by the time his father had finished his two weeks in the field, Barley had mastered the GPS.

"Where do you want to go?" asked his father.

Barley's mother had to work, so he and his father went camping near the North Cascade Mountains in Washington, just the two of them. Barley looked up a cache in the Cathedral Spire rock formation.

"What's it called?" asked his father.

"Stay-Puft Marshmallow Man," answered Barley. "What's that icon there mean?" Barley pointed at a small brick-like object with a green top that was on the screen just to the left of the cache name.

"I thought you said you knew everything there was to know about geocaching." Nelson Lick gave his son a knuckle noogie. "That indicates it's a traditional cache. A normal-sized container like a plastic bucket or Tupperware. There are other icons to tell you if it's a microcache or mystery cache."

All the clue said was "Volcanic rock." Barley couldn't wipe the smile from his face when he spotted an eight-foot crag that looked exactly like the Stay-Puft Man. They scrambled up and found the bucket hidden behind a scraggly bush. Barley opened it up to find action figures from *Ghostbusters*. He took Slimer, the green ghost, and dropped in a billy goat. He signed the book, and was on such a high, he wanted to search for another one right away. That afternoon they found their first microcache at the dam. It was called Cathedral Rock and the tiny container was full of holy medals and attached to a metal sign with a magnet. It was better than Christmas.

When school got out in June, Colin came with them on a trip to Whistler, where after a lazy swim in Lost Lake, they set up their own cache—a beef bucket full of one hundred plastic billy goats.

"What are we gonna call it?" asked Colin.

"How about 'Billy Goat's Gruff'?" said Barley.

"That's perfect," said Colin, tossing him a Sharpie. "You gotta write that on the lid."

Barley wrote that along with the words *Geocache: Please do not remove* in black ink.

"Now we have to hide it," said Colin.

"Don't forget to take the GPS," his father added. "We need to list the coordinates on the website so other people can find it."

Barley's parents followed the boys into the forest.

"Maybe we can bury it," said Colin.

"No, you can put a cache in a tree or under a rock but you're not allowed to bury it," said his mother.

When they got home, Barley's father helped them post their cache on the geocaching website.

And then they waited.

They didn't have to wait long. While Barley and Colin took their kayaks out on the Fraser River, somebody called "He Who Cannot Be Named" logged onto geocaching.com to say they had found the cache.

That afternoon!

Barley was hooked.

Even now the Billy Goat's Gruff cache was still popular, and every time someone logged it online, geocaching.com sent Barley an email. He got a little rush of adrenaline with every email saying someone had found one of his caches; not a big rush like when *he* found a new cache for the first time, but a pleasant injection of energy all the same.

The first weeks of that summer of 2005 disappeared. Afternoons when Colin was available to hang out, Barley would drag him into the woods and teach him all he had learned about GPS functions. It was mid-July when Colin and Barley went down to White Rock to sign up for the new Geocaching Club. Barley was amazed that the geocaching world had been chugging along without him, and he hadn't even been aware of it. It was like he had been asleep and just woken up.

Barley had never heard of GeoFind before Phyllis Henderson mentioned it to him. She was the queen of geocaching, even before they both signed up to compete in Seattle at the end of July. Barley's father drove him down in the Corvette. They stayed in a Travel Lodge a few streets east of the Space Needle. Phyllis went with her mother and little sister.

The competition took them to all the parks along the ocean and Lake Union, as well as Volunteer, Interlaken, and the Arboretum. Barley wasn't familiar with any of the locations, but his father drove him to each place. Once they arrived at a park, Nelson Lick wouldn't help his son find the caches, and although Barley thought he was making good time, he had no idea how he was doing compared to the others until the last day.

The award ceremony was at the Children's Museum. Barley felt like he had swallowed a squirrel. That's how wound up he was. It came as no surprise to anyone when Phyllis Henderson won, but Barley threw everyone for a loop when, as a first-time competitor, an unknown, he came a close second. He and Phyllis stood together on a podium, each with a $50 gift certificate for the geocaching store, two Travel Bugs and an invitation to the 2006 GeoFind competition in BC.

His father was over the moon. "You can win next year, Barley," he said on the drive north back home to Cloverdale. "I know you will."

Next year had come, and Barley wasn't going to let him down. That's why he couldn't be off gallivanting with Newton finding caches for God-knows-what. He had to beat Phyllis and win GeoFind for his father.

12

Speed Demon

It wasn't until the speedometer hit 130 that Barley was aware of the siren. It was loud enough to hear over the Black Sabbath song blaring out of the radio. He glanced in the rearview to see the flashing lights of the ghost car.

Barley had never been pulled over before. He had never even been with anyone else who got pulled over. Sweat was forming on his back; it began to trickle down his spine. His hands were shaky on the steering wheel as he indicated right to change lanes and slowed to a stop on the highway shoulder near the turnoff to Agassiz. He wiped his sweaty palms on his pants and glanced in the rear-view to see what he was up against. The officer was a woman— that was a relief. He couldn't help but catch a glimpse of her butt in her tight blue pants as she leaned in and took something out of the squad car.

When she came alongside the Corvette, he saw her take note of the broken window. He knew it looked bad. He knew what she was thinking. *She's thinking I'm some low-life and I just stole this sweet Corvette. Well, I've got news for her; although I love the 'Vette, if I was going to steal something, I'd get myself some rigged-up four-by-four. And since*

when do car thieves travel with Great Danes as sidekicks?
He wanted to ask her all this, but he realized it was best to
keep his mouth shut.

The sun was behind her and he had trouble discerning
her facial features. He could tell she was attractive though.
He could make out the outline of her nose and lips. As it
turned out, her voice wasn't as pleasant as her face. It was
husky—like she drank a bottle of whisky every day—and
it made her sound mean.

"Good afternoon, sir and..." She glanced over at
Stanley who had a foot-long string of green drool hanging from his whiskered jowls. She blinked. "That's one
large canine."

Barley nodded, too intimidated to speak.

"Where's the fire?"

"No fire, officer. I'm just going to Colossus."

"What's the hurry? Late for the matinee?"

"No, I'm in a contest and we're ranked on time."

"That's a shame," she said, not even asking what kind
of contest. "You're not going to do very well now. License
and registration, please."

Stanley outweighed her by at least a hundred pounds.

Barley willed himself not to speak. When he was
stressed, his mouth always got him into trouble. He steadied his hand and reached over, pushing Stanley's big head
out of the way, and opened the glove box. *Maybe she'll let
me go with a warning if I'm a good boy.* He felt around in
the back of the glove compartment—his hand came out
empty. That's when the realization hit him. His wallet. The
thieves had stolen his wallet.

"Damn," he said. "It's stolen."

"The car is stolen?" She smiled slightly; a nasty smile
that made Barley want to throw up. Stanley made a noise
in the back of his throat to show his empathy.

"No, someone broke into my car at the Othello Tunnels;

they must have taken my wallet."

"And you're just noticing this now?"

"Yes, I was in a hurry."

"I noticed. Who is the owner of this vehicle?" she asked, now frowning.

"I am," Barley answered.

"What's your name?"

"Barley Lick." He waited for the inevitable look of incredulity when she heard his name. For almost seventeen years, teachers, neighbours, anyone Barley met for the first time, got that same look. The cop didn't let him down. The corners of her mouth curved up into a slight smirk, but she caught herself and bit her lip before turning away to write something on her pad.

"Do you have *any* ID, Mr. Lick?"

He shook his head.

"Stay here, sir."

Barley clenched his jaw and looked at Stanley, who wore an empathetic expression. This can't be happening. Why did he have to speed?

Demon cop was back in no time, looking as menacing as a crocodile. She told him what he already knew.

"The car's registration has expired, but it used to be registered in the name of a Nelson Lick."

"That's my father." Barley could see the winch lowering the dark wood coffin into the ground. The first spade full of soil hitting the brass plaque with his father's name. It was horrible thinking of the worms that were waiting. But Barley had begged his mother not to put his father into an oven to be burned into ashes. That creeped him out. His father had never specified what way he'd like to go. His mother had favoured the crematorium and wanted to take his ashes to Ireland to sprinkle in County Clare, where they had gone on their honeymoon. But Barley had just studied "The Cremation of Sam McGee" in school and had vivid images of the oven. "Please, let's bury him," he begged. "We can put a special Travel Bug in his coffin."

Stanley nudged Barley's cheek again with his nose. Barley blinked and remembered he was on the side of a highway with a cop asking questions.

"I thought you said you were the owner of this vehicle?"

"I am the owner."

"How can you be the owner if it's not registered in your name?"

"My father died and left it to me. He didn't have a chance to get down to Motor Vehicles after his heart exploded." God, if he only could have prevented his father from driving that day... he would do anything to be able to rewind the clock. *I promise to be well-mannered and think before I speak. I won't be nasty to my mother. I'll even forgive Phyllis... if only I can have Dad back.*

Her cheeks got tight with this news. She looked him over before continuing. He could tell she was trying to figure out if he was telling the truth or if he was a psychopath.

"What was the date of your father's death?"

He knew the answer to that question. How could he forget? The surreal look on his mother's face when she told him. The rain that began to fall and didn't stop for weeks on end. The emptiness that filled their house that night. And every night since. "December 6, 2005."

She scribbled some more on her notepad.

Barley couldn't help but feel angry with his mother. If she had just remembered to take care of the insurance and registration, this wouldn't be happening. Phyllis was definitely going to get ahead of him.

But he knew his mother was having a hard time too.

What does this cop know about how much effort was required to do anything since his father died? How long it took some days just to drag himself out of bed. How long it took to write a ten-page assignment for some idiot teacher. How long it took to fall asleep every night. How Barley could hardly bring himself to play a game of pick-up, let alone a league match. How he had fallen off his game. How he only had ten points all spring.

Demon Cop looked right through him as if she could hear his inner thoughts but didn't care. "Mr. Lick. This vehicle is uninsured."

Tell me something I don't already know.

Then she did tell him something he didn't know. "And..." she paused for effect. "It was reported stolen thirty minutes ago."

"What? No! It couldn't be."

"I assure you it was."

"By who?" It couldn't have been his mother. Did Mr. Jewer somehow see him leave?

"That is not information I am able to share. Now if you'll step out of the vehicle, I will escort you to the police station."

"Bitch." The word escaped his lips before he had time to take it back.

The officer stopped and cocked her head.

"What was that?"

"Which..." Barley gulped. "Which police station?"

"Mr. Lick, you just got yourself three demerit points on top of the speeding ticket and whatever else you get for driving with no insurance or registration."

"You can't."

"Indeed, I can." She smiled a beautiful lopsided smile, scribbled something on her pad, and handed him a ticket for a whopping $300.

"What about the car? We can't just leave it here."

"A tow truck will be here shortly to transport it to the impound yard."

Barley felt a tickle in the back of this throat and tried not to tear up. I will not cry, he thought.

"Keys." The cop held out a manicured hand.

Barley passed her the keys and got out of the car. Stanley stuck his head out the broken window. "What about my dog?"

"I guess he'll have to come too."

Stanley hopped out and had a quick pee on the highway shoulder; Barley took up his makeshift lead, and together they did the death march back to the patrol car where Demon Cop loaded both of them into the back seat behind the Plexiglas barricade.

I'm doomed, Barley thought for the second time that day.

This was worse than Colin texting to say he couldn't drive. This was worse than Stanley's cut foot or the Corvette's broken window. It was even worse than losing his wallet. This was big. This was "Doom" with a capital D.

Worse than facing his mother was knowing that Phyllis would beat him in GeoFind.

Why did I have to call her a bitch to her face?

The fact that he had brought this upon himself by speeding down the highway in an uninsured, unregistered Corvette with a broken window didn't enter his mind. He hoped his father couldn't see his prized sports car abandoned on the side of the highway. He would be so disappointed.

How could I have screwed up so badly?

He would never win GeoFind now. Barley repeated his mantra. *I will not cry, I will not cry, I will not cry.* When he looked at Stanley, one tear rolled down his cheek. Stanley licked it away and Barley dug in his pocket for a Milk-Bone. Stanley leaned into his shoulder as he crunched the biscuit. They stayed like that in the back of the police car all the way down Highway 10 to Surrey.

13

The Corvette, Kootenay Lake

N 49° 27.060, W 116° 45.466

Barley remembered the day his father bought the Corvette. It was about a month before he joined the Geocaching Club. Barley had stumbled upon an intriguing cache on the geocaching website. "You know you said I could find a geocache to do for my birthday? I think I found one. It's inside a singing horse."

"I wonder what he sings?" said his father.

"Maybe Leonard Cohen." His mother laughed.

"I can hear it now... a horse singing 'Hallelujah,'" said his father, putting down the newspaper to come look at the computer screen. "Let's see where it is."

Barley brought up a map. "Uh, Boswell."

"Boswell? Isn't that in the Kootenays?" His mother's eyes got wide.

"Yep, east shore of Kootenay Lake." His father looked from his wife to his son.

"What's wrong with that?" asked Barley. "You said I could choose where we go as an early birthday gift."

"I hate to break it to you, Barley, but Boswell is almost nine hours from Cloverdale. With the truck acting up, we were thinking of somewhere closer to home."

"Come on, Dad. Has the truck ever failed us before?"

"No, but I fear she's on her last legs."

Barley still wasn't sure how he convinced them, but at the beginning of July, they piled into his father's F150 and drove east for what seemed like forever. It was stinking hot, the hottest summer in a decade, and the truck had no air conditioning. They spent the first night in dusty Osoyoos when the truck overheated.

"Uh oh," thought Barley.

But they had pulled in right next to the lake where they set up their tent, and Barley and his mother went for a swim while his father poured water on the engine to cool it. The truck was good to go the next morning, but the engine overheated again in Grand Forks. And in Salmo. They inched their way down the highway as far as Creston, where the Ford let out a wheeze and finally gave up the ghost about five kilometres outside Boswell.

The sun was just beginning its descent in the western sky when Barley's father opened up the hood and poured on the water.

Crack.

Barley's father backed away. Then both his parents moved close to the front of the Ford to peer under the hood.

"Sweet be to Jesus," said his mother.

Barley knew things were serious. His mother never swore, at least not in his presence. This was truly unprecedented. Maybe they wouldn't get to see the singing horse after all.

"What happened?" he asked.

"The water split the engine block," said his mother, her head still under the hood.

Barley moved closer so he could see; a jagged fracture line ran across the engine casing like a fissure in rock.

"This is beyond my capabilities," said his father. "I need

to find a garage; I'll get them to call a taxi to bring you to the rental house."

"That's good," said his mother. "Even if you could fix it, I'd implode if I had to drive another minute in that rattle trap."

Barley and his mother settled into the taxi; their bags safely stowed in the trunk. The log house they rented had open beams and a second-storey balcony facing the lake and deer antlers above the door. The view from the balcony looked over the west shore of Kootenay Lake with a tiny bit of the Kokanee Glacier behind the Selkirk Mountains.

Barley and his mother ate sandwiches from the cooler and settled on the deck to watch the sun set over an osprey nesting on wooden pilings that held up a pier.

They were starting to worry when Barley's father hadn't turned up by 9:30. When he did arrive around 10:00, Nelson Lick wasn't driving the truck; he was driving a 1985 forest green Corvette with white-rimmed tires and a racing stripe down the front.

"Did they give you that," his mother gestured from the balcony to the sports car in the driveway, "as a loaner?"

"Nope, I traded the truck for it." Barley's father had talked about trading in the truck for something more reliable for over a year.

"You what?"

He nodded.

"Nelson, you were supposed to get something newer than the Ford."

"Too good a deal to pass up," he said.

"But honey, we can't drive home in that?"

"Why not?"

"I'll tell you why not; it's only got two seats, and I'm not sure if you noticed, but there are three of us."

His father smiled showing all his teeth. It was what Barley's mother called his oops-I-did-it-again smile.

Barley was down the stairs in four strides and jumped in the 'Vette. "Ljubljana," he said, knowing his awe would be adequately expressed in that one word.

"She's got 9.5-inch wheels front and back," said his father. "And 205 horsepower." He beamed like a toddler after his first-ever taste of ice cream.

"Does it drive well?"

"She handles like a cockroach."

"Nelson, if this is a mid-life crisis, hurry up and get over it. You'll have to take it back in the morning."

"No can do. It's a done deal, M.J." His lips turned up in the smile he reserved for bringing bad news.

That night his parents had a hushed conversation in their bedroom, but by morning, their little world had righted on its axis. "We have a reached a deal," his mother said. "We'll keep the Corvette, but I get to buy a vehicle too. I'll follow behind you on the way home."

That was the first time Barley's world had been shook up. In a good way, but wow, this was big. He knew they weren't poor, but he had never known his parents to spend frivolously.

"How can we afford two cars?" asked Barley.

"Don't you worry your little noggin over that," said his mother, rubbing his hair.

So, that day while his mother went car shopping in Boswell, Barley and his father went to scout out the Singing Horse geocache. The only clue said: "Follow the praying goat."

The GPS led them to what appeared to be a farm. A massive creature—its species not immediately evident to Barley—greeted them at the front gate. Brown feathers fanned out behind and to the sides of a round body the size of a large beachball. Its head was a mix of light blue and red and its wattle had the consistency of male genitalia.

"That's the ugliest bird I've ever seen," said Barley.

"You insulting my turkey?" A voice that sounded a hundred years old came from behind a Colgate-coloured truck, even rustier than the one his father had just traded. A wrinkled man wearing a white t-shirt, blue jeans, and a white ten-gallon hat appeared. "Name's Bill. Turkey's name is Elvis. Why don't y'all come on in and I'll show you around?"

"We're actually looking for a geocache," said Barley.

"I suspected as much," said Farmer Bill, nodding towards the blue Garmin in Barley's hand.

"Is the geocache on your farm?"

"Yep."

"Can we look for it?" asked Barley.

"I dare say that's what you come here for. All you need to do is find Boswell saying his prayers." Bill moved out of the way; Barley shot a look at his father, who nodded and led the little party down a mucky path to the barn, where a brown-and-white bearded goat knelt next to a barn door.

"The needle's spinning." Barley glanced inside the door, where a homemade, life-size horse sat on wheels. Barley's stomach did a flip. Strains of electronic dance music emanated from the horse's belly.

"Gadzooks," said Nelson Lick. "The cache description wasn't lying."

"Uh, you like Britney Spears?" Barley asked Bill, recognizing the song as "Toxic."

"Sure do. She's a spunky young thing, idn't she?"

Barley nodded, hoping Bill wasn't going to comment on the video.

"What's it made of?" asked Barley's father.

"Peat sod covered with papier mâché," said Bill, as if it were a normal thing to fashion an ungulate out of earth.

Barley touched the horse's long face, and as he did, Britney Spears's "Toxic" suddenly changed to Chubby Checker singing "The Twist."

Barley got down on his knees to check out the horse's underbelly and found a hole had been cut in the sod to expose a speaker.

"Go on, don't be shy. Put your hand in, see what you find."

Barley was reluctant, but he forced his hand in beside the speaker. His fingers lighted upon an open wooden box.

"Go on, put your hand in and take the first thing you touch," said Bill.

Barley slid in his hand, dug around, and pulled out keychain with a little Colonel Saunders attached. That was the first time he had ever found a Travel Bug.

"That there is a genuine Travel Bug," said Bill, pointing out the metal dog tag attached. "Ordered it from the online geocaching store and decided to attach it to the Colonel. I've eaten a lot of his chicken in my time." He patted his belly. "You're the first one to find it. You can take it and bring it to a cache wherever you're from. Just make sure you log it online so I can follow the Colonel on his journey into space."

"Did you say space, as in outer?" Barley was perplexed.

"Yep, the Colonel is going to be the first geocache item to go into orbit. Mark my words."

"Uh, I don't think I'll be in space anytime soon."

Bill laughed. "No, but you can start him on his journey. Now go on, young man, hop up on her back."

Barley passed his father the Colonel and put his foot in the stirrup. Farmer Bill hoisted him up. "The Twist" changed to the Crazy Frog song that had become all the rage that June.

"You have an eclectic taste in music," said Barley's father.

"That I do. You're all welcome to stay for lunch and I can show you something a lot crazier than a singing horse."

After a feed of farm-fresh scrambled eggs and his wife's homemade bread, Bill drove them up the road to a house made entirely out of glass bottles. Bevelled glass windows trimmed in red looked out from round towers in the castle-like structure. Even the bridge was made of bottles.

By the time Bill dropped them back to the lake house and said good-bye, Barley's mother was laid out on a chaise longue in her bikini doing a cryptic crossword. She was amazing at cryptic crosswords. Barley couldn't even figure out which word to make an anagram out of, and his mother would already have the answer written in. A tall glass covered with condensation sat next to her, an inch of brown liquid settled in the bottom. It had to be 38 degrees. Her gastrointestinal music CD played in the boom box she had brought outside.

She smiled lazily. "Hi honey," she said to Barley. She looked at her husband. "Come rub sunscreen on my back, will you, baby?"

Uh oh, who is this and what have they done with my mother? Barley thought.

"I take it you found a car?" said his father, picking up the plastic squeeze bottle.

His mother flattened the chaise and flipped over onto her stomach. "Yes," she purred.

"And...?" Nelson Lick's head swung back to the driveway where there was only one green Corvette parked.

"It's a surprise. I pick it up tomorrow."

Two new cars, thought Barley. It was too much to take in.

That next morning his mother insisted she wanted to pick up the car on her own. After all his father had purchased the 'Vette "without assistance," she said.

Barley and his father tossed a few snacks into a day pack with a bottle of Gatorade, dropped Barley's mother at the dealer and went by Farmer Bill's to accompany him on a hike up Haystack Mountain. When they climbed aboard Bill's Colgate truck, they saw the praying goat kneeling in the truck bed wearing bags over his back like a Saint Bernard.

"Is the goat coming on the hike?" Barley asked.

"Boswell? Yeah, he wouldn't miss it for the world," said Bill.

The last bit was so steep, the humans had to crawl on all fours. Boswell had no trouble, but Barley's knees were bludgeoned from the sharp rocks. At the summit, the GPS indicated more than nine hundred metres of elevation.

Barley's father peered into a narrow crevasse. "Wouldn't want to fall down there," he said. "Especially alone. I imagine it'd be some time before anyone found you."

Farmer Bill looked pensive. "I think we'll see the day when humans are outfitted with microchips, just like Boswell here." He grabbed Boswell by the leg and showed them the tag clipped to his ear. "That way if someone goes missing—God forbid—we'll be able to find them fast."

"That's pretty sci-fi," said Barley's father.

"I'm a forward thinker," said Bill, patting the goat on the head before opening one of the saddle bags strapped to his back. He pulled out several tins of smoked oysters and a container full of boiled eggs. "From Maisie," he said, offering them around. He pulled a bladder bag of water from Boswell's other saddle bag; he poured some into a collapsible bowl for the goat and shared the rest with Barley and his father.

"I think I'll visit the little boy's room," said Barley's father, walking a few feet behind them to relieve himself.

Barley opened a tin of smoked oysters, something he never would have considered eating, but after seven kilometres almost straight uphill and another seven to go to get back to the Colgate truck, he was happy to have anything. The Gatorade and granola bars were long gone. "I'd never make it down again without Boswell's snacks," said Barley.

"Yep, he's a good hiking companion. Always senses bears before I do too."

"Bears?" said Barley. "Around here?"

"Yes, Kootenays are crawling with them, especially in the west, but you're all good as long as you know what to do if you meet one."

Barley gulped. "And what's that?"

"Well first..." said Bill. "You need to know the difference between a black bear and a grizzly."

"How do you tell?" asked Barley.

"Well, if you climb a tree and the bear climbs up and eats you, that's a black bear. But if you climb a tree and the bear shakes you out of it and eats you, then that's a grizzly." Bill laughed then until tears ran down his weathered cheeks.

"What did I miss?" asked Barley's father.

"I was just telling tales," said Bill. "We'd better start back, see what kind of machine yer wife's gone and got herself."

It was mid-afternoon by the time they got back to the log cabin. When he stopped to let them out, Bill got out, let down the tailgate, and invited Boswell to ride up front. They could hear Pink Floyd's "Comfortably Numb" coming from somewhere. They had just said their thank-yous and turned to walk down the driveway when Bill whistled.

"Well, would you look at that? I think that might be the Mustang the mayor just traded."

"Oh no," said Barley's father.

"Oh yes," said Barley.

"You'll have to tell me all about it before you go home," said Bill, laughing and backing out.

Barley called out to his mother and began running all over to find her. "She's not in the cabin," he called out.

"She's not on the balcony or the beach," said his father. "Maybe she's next door." They had met the woman renting the cabin next to theirs; she was younger, a bit of a modern-day hippy. "M.J.," he called. "Where are you?"

"Up here." A voice, like his mother's but not quite hers, came from high above. Where the roof flattened over the porch sat his mother with the hippy neighbour, who raised her fingers and gave them a royal wave. The smell of pot wafted down to where Barley and his father stood in the driveway.

"Uh, M.J. There's a Mustang here." Barley's father squinted into the sun.

"Yes, it's from this decade too. You like it?"

"Ljubljana!" said Barley.

"You always said you wanted a convertible," said his father.

And that was how the Licks went from a family with one old beater truck to a family with two sports cars.

Hours later, once Barley's mother came back down to earth, she noticed his legs. "Barley, what in heaven's name did you do to yourself?"

Barley had forgotten the dried blood curdled on his shins. The view from the top of the mountain had obliterated any pain.

★

For ten days that July the three of them hung out in the Kootenays like they were all teenagers. Barley's mother caught a five-pound rainbow trout and his father fried it up while his mother sipped rum and Coke on the patio. His parents were kissing and nuzzling like they were on a date and Barley was their chaperone. He didn't mind. It was fun watching them. They were so in love.

Like all good things though, the vacation came to an end. They drove back to Cloverdale, Barley switching from the Corvette to the Mustang every couple of hours.

14

Newton Takes Over

Federal Operations Building. That's what the plaque said at the entrance to the parking lot. Demon cop opened the back door of the patrol car and held it while Barley and Stanley stepped out in front of high black cast-iron bars that surrounded the huge building. Like a fancy prison.

She gestured towards a yard at the back of the building. "That's where your father's car will be until things get sorted."

Barley gulped and tried to ignore the knots in his intestines. The impound lot was surrounded by high shrubs; a pedestrian on the street would never know that it was filled with hundreds of delinquent cars.

Demon Cop waited while Stanley discreetly peed on the back tire of the ghost car, then walked Barley and Stanley towards the RCMP station. Barley took one last breath of summer air before passing through the door of the cop shop. Inside the marble floors and walls smelled of Javex, and a giant buffalo head peered down at them from a balcony.

In the main lobby, a big man with a mustache did a double take when he saw a Great Dane being led by a teenager down the echoey halls of the police station. He looked hard at Barley's face and stopped dead in his tracks. "Excuse me, Constable, can you tell me what this young man is here for?"

"Picked him up doing 130 on the T-Can near Agassiz. In a stolen sports car with a broken window; no license, no insurance, no registration"

"The car?"

"Green 1985 Corvette with a white racing stripe. On its way to the impound lot."

"Thank you. If you don't mind, Constable, I'll take it from here," said the man.

"Whatever you say, Sir." She handed over the paperwork. "You know where to find me if you have questions."

What's up? thought Barley. *Some guy in civilian clothes takes me away from Demon Cop. What's next? The stretching rack?* Barley sized up the man from the side. He was wearing jeans and a plaid button-up shirt. He looked like he was going to the rodeo, not working for the RCMP.

"You got yourself into a bit of trouble, I see." He looked from Barley to the dog and back.

Barley cringed.

"Barley, it's Fred Newton. I called you this morning."

The salt-and-pepper mustache, the receding hairline. *Oh my God, it's the arsehole who was all over my mother the other night, the guy who called me in Hope.* Barley's mind raced. Could it get any worse?

But Barley was confused. Demon Cop had called him Sir. *The man my mother brought home can't possibly work here. He's not wearing a uniform.* What did his mother say that guy did? Who knows? Barley had blocked all that out.

But it was hard to block out the man now that he was in front of him, chewing gum like a masticating cow and reading through the file folder from Demon Cop.

Barley blinked. It really was the big man Barley had seen molesting his mother.

The man tried again. "You like the dog?"

Barley wrapped the bungee cord tight around his hand, as if he wanted to establish possession. "Yep."

"Are you going to try and show him?" asked Newton.

"No, he has a gimpy ear." Barley hoped his tone showed his irritation.

"Oh right, from the tracking chip. I didn't expect to see Bailey again so soon." He patted the Great Dane on the head.

"His name is *not* Bailey."

"Oh, the woman called him Bailey."

"Well, he's not Bailey anymore."

"OK, Barley and Not-Bailey-Anymore, why don't we take a trip up to my office and try to sort out this mess." Newton took Barley by the arm and led him down a corridor to the right. Stanley paraded alongside; head held high. Ears at alert.

Newton stopped at an elevator and the door magically opened. He held out his hand to allow Barley to go first. Barley started to enter, but Stanley was having none of it. Barley pulled on the bungee. For his size, this dog was turning out to be quite the wimp. Newton put his knee to Stanley's rear end and pushed him into the elevator. Then he took a card attached to his waist and swiped it against a dark screen. When the doors opened, they were inside an office with two glass walls, overlooking all of Surrey and Langley to the east. Barley could see Cloverdale High and in the distance Colossus Movie Cinema, where he was supposed to be checking in and getting his next clue. He would never catch up with Phyllis now.

Newton motioned for Barley to sit in the chair in front of a huge metal desk, on which sat a neat stack of paper files, a see-through blue Apple computer, and a black telephone.

Behind a swivel chair hung a mounted map of Scotland.

Barley did as he was told. Stanley began to sit on his lap, but Barley pushed him off. The dog rested his head on the desktop and began sniffing at a ceramic bowl shaped like a pig.

Newton pushed the pig-shaped bowl away from the black padded nose and closer to Barley. "Candy?"

Barley might hate Newton, but he loved candy. He stretched out his hand to take a foil-covered chocolate. The bowl grunted. Stanley barked and Barley jumped. Newton laughed. *What a jerk.*

Newton leaned forward until his elbows rested on a mouse pad with an aerial photo of the ruins of some big church, three spires sticking out of the rubble like a kicked-over sandcastle. Looked like something out of *Harry Potter.* "I have to make a phone call." Newton gestured to the bowl. "Help yourself while I'm gone." Newton entered an oversized, sound-proof phone booth in a corner behind his desk and made a call from a landline.

Barley gently reached in and removed a chocolate covered in green foil. The bowl snorted again, but he was ready and didn't jump. Stanley, however, let out another bark. Barley unwrapped the foil and popped the dark ball into his mouth. Stanley stood at attention near his elbow. Drool swung from his gums, then slipped to the floor. Barley dug around in his pocket and pulled out half a Milk-Bone covered in lint. "That's all I have, buddy." Stanley took it gently and looked adoringly at Barley. Barley rubbed his gimpy ear.

After a minute or two, Newton reappeared. "Where were we? Oh yes, this morning; we lost connection when you were at that cave."

"I was not in a cave; it was a tunnel."

"OK. OK." Newton held his hands up as if to ward off an assault. "Why don't you tell me a bit about geocaching."

Newton sat back in his chair and audibly chewed his gum. "I don't really have time right now. I have to get back to the contest." Barley looked at Stanley, who lay down at the side of the desk and began shamelessly licking his private parts.

"Ah yes, M.J. mentioned you were competing in..." He picked up a red file folder off the top of the stack and opened it. "GeoFind, is it? Against your ex-girlfriend, no less." He smiled.

Barley inhaled through his nose and glared at Newton. He had hated this man the other night, but he hated him even more now. He hadn't known that hate came in degrees.

Barley removed his hand from Stanley's head. "How did you even get my number?"

"Your mother provided it."

"I'll have to tell her not to give it out. To anyone." Barley did his best to sound mean.

"She'll be here shortly. You can tell her then."

"What? She's coming here?"

"Yes, I just called her to join this meeting, seeing as she was most concerned about a certain sports car missing from her garage."

Barley let out a sound like a wild cat. Stanley's ears wiggled and stood upright.

"Listen, son..." began Newton.

"I am not your son."

"No, you're not, but you are in a bit of a pickle here." His voice took on a serious tone. He flipped through the red file folder. "I can help you with that, but you have to help me in return."

"Sorry, not gonna happen."

"Well, here are your options. You can help me. Or you can stay here in a holding cell and explain to a judge why you were speeding on the TransCanada with no insurance and no registration in a stolen car with a smashed-out window."

"It was not stolen."

"Save it for the judge." Newton consulted the file. "You can also explain why you insulted a police officer."

Barley gulped and looked at Stanley. He was in deep. Newton's jaws chewed like his life depended on it. "So, how about we start again. Can you tell me about geocaching?"

Here we go, Barley thought. He may as well get it over with. He had given this spiel a hundred times if he had given it once. Now he had to give it to this imbecile, while Phyllis was out winning GeoFind. Barley sighed audibly. "It's like a treasure hunt," he said, without emotion.

"In what way?"

"Someone hides a bucket, usually in the woods. They post the coordinates on the Internet, and someone else uses the posted coordinates to find the bucket." Barley kept his eyes trained on Stanley, as if he were talking to him rather than the butthead sitting in front of him chewing gum like a cow.

"Using a GPS."

"Yes, using a GPS." Barley looked out the window at a crane moving tilt-up walls into place on a new building.

"What's in a cache?"

"Could be anything, but usually just junk."

"Junk?"

"Yeah, like key chains, golf balls, McDonald toys." Barley spit the words.

"Hmmm." Newton rubbed his chin. "So, you don't know in advance what you're looking for?"

"No, not unless it's listed on the site. They do tell you what type of bucket it's in."

Newton looked puzzled. "I'm still not clear on how you know where to look for one of these buckets?"

"You log on to geocaching.com and it shows you the coordinates of caches."

"How many caches are there?"

"Hundreds of thousands all over the world."

Newton chewed furiously for a few seconds. "That's quite a large number. When you go on the website, how do you know how to find buckets close by?"

"You can key in a postal code and ask the computer to supply you with the nearest caches, say, within a two-mile radius."

"From anywhere?"

"Anywhere. Belfast or Baffin Island. Singapore or Shanghai. Why don't you just cut to the chase, or we'll be here all day."

"I want you to find the location of a set of coordinates."

"I told you, I can't. I'm in the middle of a contest."

"And I told you that this is more important than any contest."

Barley stood up, rage showing on his face. GeoFind was the most important thing in his life. "I can't help you."

"Have it your way. I will call Constable Hynes, and she'll take you down for fingerprinting." He looked directly at Barley. "Or..." He sniffed. "I can make the demerit points and speeding ticket disappear."

Barley's head slumped. "What about the registration and insurance? Mom forgot to do it."

"I can take care of that too."

"And the report of the stolen car?"

"Never happened."

"A new driver's license to replace the stolen one?"

"Done."

The elevator door opened. Mary Jane Lick stepped out, wearing three-quarter length yoga pants, a blue t-shirt, and a jean jacket. The Great Dane ran over and bumped into her. His weight pushed her off balance, and for a second, she lost her footing. She caught herself, straightened up, and noticed the white cotton sock on the dog's foot.

"Why – is – the – dog – wearing – clothing?" She shot daggers at Barley.

"He cut his foot on glass in Hope."

"Hope?" Mary Jane Lick collapsed into a chair.

"Yes, Hope, you know, out near Agassiz."

"I know where Hope is." Her jaw was set so tightly he thought it might snap. "Did you have an accident?"

"No, I didn't. Honestly, Mom. Someone broke into the car. There was glass all over the place. Stanley cut his foot."

"Stanley?"

"The dog. That's the name I gave him." Three sets of eyes looked to the Great Dane, who was stepping up into Newton's vacated leather office chair. Despite his amazing ability to turn himself into a canine pretzel, he didn't quite manage to fit his body in. He gave up and lay on the floor, his head resting on his paws, one eye looking up at them.

Mary Jane Lick turned back to her son. "Barley, why did you take the Corvette?"

"Colin couldn't drive because he had to cover my shift at Big Bite. I had no way to get to Colossus, Mom. I wouldn't have been able to compete."

"Why didn't you ask me?"

"'Cause you had to work... How could you report the car stolen, Mom?"

"I came home to pick up an extension cord in the garage, and it was gone." His mother's cheeks reddened, and she inhaled deeply and loudly through her nose.

Barley swallowed a dry lump of nothing. He thought about how things could go from bad to worse really fast. "Why didn't you call my cell?"

"I did call your cell. You didn't pick up."

"I was in a tunnel."

"Fred got through to you."

"Yeah, I had service then."

"Didn't you see my number? I am not paying for your cell phone if you won't answer when I call."

"When he called…" Barley refused to look at Newton. "I thought that it was you calling back from a different line."

"But it wasn't me, and you still didn't call me back."

"I had a lot going on. Stanley cut his foot; someone broke into the Corvette…"

"Barley Lick. I don't know what to say. Your father would be disappointed."

"If he was still around to be disappointed, I wouldn't be in this mess."

"How so?"

"He would have had the car insured by now. And registered."

"I told you I would do that."

"Yeah, when? You said you'd do it last week and then this week. You're always too busy with your… your boyfriend." Barley had crossed a line. Before his father died, he would never be rude to his mother. To other people, yes, but never ever to this mother. Now it seemed like he was always nasty to her. It was like someone else had taken over his brain.

Newton cleared his throat. "M.J., I think I may be able to help sort things out." He leaned over Stanley and opened his top desk drawer with a key. He withdrew a Ziploc bag and passed it to Barley. "Don't worry about prints," he said. "I've already had it dusted."

"Dusted? Where did you get this?"

Newton didn't answer, just gave Barley's mother a look as if he were asking for permission.

Barley took the blue Garmin eTrex Legend out of the bag and turned it over in his hand. It was the size of a fat cell phone and sat comfortably in his palm, the same model he had received for his fifteenth birthday. You could pick one up for $130 at any Walmart or Canadian Tire. He walked to the floor-to-ceiling windows and pressed the "on" button.

While Barley waited for the satellites to hook up, Stanley roused himself and began trying to remove the sock from his leg. Barley's mother took it off and sized up the cut. The blood had dried, and it looked OK. Stanley licked it.

Barley turned his attention back to the GPS. He took note of the awkward mouse button above the screen. When he entered the machine's history, one lone set of coordinates appeared.

"Can you tell if it's a cache?" Newton chewed frantically.

"No, not just by looking at the coordinates. Did you check to see if they're posted on geocaching.com?"

"No."

"Did someone say it's a cache?"

"No."

"So, what are you looking for?" Barley spit the words.

"I'm not sure. But whatever we find is confidential. You're not to breathe a word of it to anyone, you hear me? Not anyone."

"Why? What are we gonna find? A dead body?"

Newton straightened up as if he had been burned.

Barley's mother touched his arm. "Barley, honey, do you have any idea where these coordinates are located?"

Barley paused a moment to visualize the location. "Vancouver Island."

"You can tell just like that?" asked Newton.

Barley saw he didn't believe him. "Yep."

"I told you," said his mother.

Newton steepled his fingers. "I didn't doubt you for a second."

The GPS brought up the coordinates. "It's in MacMillan Provincial Park. Can I use your computer to check on geocaching.com?"

"Of course." Newton entered his password.

Barley opened geocaching.com and plugged in the coordinates. "This cache isn't listed on the website."

"No, I didn't think it would be."

"Where did you get the coordinates?"

"Sorry, classified. Will you be able to find the site?"

"I'd say. IF I was on Vancouver Island."

"Today is your lucky day." He indicated out the window down to a helicopter landing pad that Barley hadn't noticed before; it was behind them, to the south towards the border with Washington.

"M.J., is it OK if I bring Barley on a helicopter ride? We'll pick up a sandwich downstairs before we leave."

"But..." Barley began.

"No 'buts', Barley; I'll take the dog home and if I'm not there when you get there, I'll leave something for you in the fridge; I may have to work late tonight." Mary Jane Lick gave her son a stiff hug and kissed Newton on the cheek. She appraised the bungee attached to Stanley's collar, and all four of them descended in the elevator.

15

Cathedral Grove

N 49° 17.530, W 124° 39.727

Barley stared at the AS 350 B3 helicopter. It was like a streamlined cigar that could sit five people plus a pilot. A long flagpole tail stuck off the back with two rotor blades on top. How the hell did he get here? How was he ever going to get to Vancouver Island and back to Colossus in time to get the next clue and find today's second cache before 4:00?

"Ballyhoo," roared Martin, the pilot, through his headset, as they lifted off the landing pad, leaving behind Barley's mother and Stanley standing inside the glass doors of the RCMP Federal Operations Building. Mary Jane Lick blew a kiss before turning and walking away with the dog.

The smell of fuel was overwhelming. "That's just av gas," said Martin. "Shouldn't be that strong, but it's not dangerous."

The machine was deafeningly loud. Barley adjusted his headphones to better block out the noise and tried desperately to ignore the funny feeling in his stomach as they gained altitude.

"You all right?" asked Newton. "You're looking a bit pale." He flipped through a green file folder he had taken from his desk.

"I'm good," Barley lied. No way he would admit feeling queasy to Newton. The sandwich he had eaten had better stay where it was and not fly up in his lap.

"All right, I'm going to mute my mic for a bit while I catch up on this file," he said, and lowered his face.

Barley turned to the pilot and tried to think of something intelligent to say. "Is the noise coming from the top rotors or the two smaller ones on the tail?" he said loudly into his headset.

"Mainly the top," said Martin. "They're thirty-five feet long. But try to forget about the noise. Look down. You're the king of the world."

It was true. The Eurocopter had lots of Plexiglas that offered an almost panoramic view of the Coast Mountains to the north, a dragon-shaped cloud behind them, and the mighty Fraser River snaking its way westward toward the Pacific. But looking down made Barley nervous. He decided to keep his eyes straight ahead, which for the moment, meant he was looking south towards Washington. "I can see Mount Baker."

"Always reminds me of ice cream," said Martin, turning to offer Barley a smile.

Barley took deep breaths and his stomach calmed. "My father spent lots of time in helicopters for work."

"Oh yeah, what did he do?"

"Field work. Geology."

"Who'd he work for?"

"Geological Survey of Canada."

"I've done some work for them. Maybe I've met him. What's his name?"

"Nelson Lick." Barley did not offer the fact he was dead.

"Oh yeah, I remember him. Big beard. Always telling me about his son, the geographical Wunderkind. Hey, that must be you."

Barley felt his cheeks redden and glanced away.

Newton still had his head in the folder. A small bald patch exposed scalp on the left side of Newton's head.

"What happened to his hair?" Barley motioned towards Newton with his chin. "He have a fight with a pair of scissors?"

Martin laughed. "Forgot to take his gum out before he went to sleep as I understand it."

"That is truly disgusting."

"What's disgusting?" Newton had unmuted his headphones and was wrestling with the plastic wrapping on a package of Mackintosh's creamy toffee. He held out the red box to Barley. *Give your Mack a Smack*, it read. It had a green, blue, and red tartan pattern on the front. What was it about Newton and tartan? Barley shook his head, but Martin took a piece.

"What's disgusting?" Newton repeated.

"Oh nothing," answered Martin. "Barley here was just saying how when I swoop down..." He sent the chopper into a deep dive. "It makes his stomach turn over."

Barley had to close his eyes to tell the contents of his stomach to stay put. When he opened them again, he saw they had left the Coast Mountains behind and were already navigating across the channel towards Vancouver Island.

"Gosh, Martin, you don't mean to make the boy sick, do you?" Newton closed up the box and slid it into a jacket pocket.

"No, sir," he straightened the chopper. "MacMillan Provincial Park where we're headed, isn't that Cathedral Grove?" Martin glanced over at Newton.

"I think so. Why?"

"That's where the tree huggers are protesting."

"Oh yeah, I saw it on the news," said Newton. "There were hundreds of them."

"Might be dicey landing with crowds everywhere," said Martin, looking serious.

Barley consulted the Garmin in his lap. "That means if it's a normal cache, it's going to be something small like a film canister."

"How do you know?" Newton peered over at the tiny screen.

"Because it's hard to hide something big in a place that's full of people without getting noticed. A Muggle might find it by mistake."

"What do you mean? A Muggle?"

"A Muggle... a person like you. A non-geocacher."

"Hmm." Newton pondered for a moment. "So, you think whatever we're looking for is small. Not a person, for example."

"A person? A geocache can't be a person." Barley looked at Newton and shook his head. The man was an idiot through and through. "Naw, this cache will be tiny and well hidden."

"If there are protestors, there can be trouble." Deep lines formed in Martin's forehead. "We can't risk anyone messing with the chopper."

"You stay with it once we land," said Newton, still chewing the toffee. "Call me if you need to."

"OK. I'm going to switch channels and talk to air traffic control." Martin's voice clicked out of the headset, leaving Barley and Newton on the other channel.

"If it's small, will you be able to find it using the GPS and the coordinates?" asked Newton.

"Don't see why not, but you have to remember a GPS receiver has a margin of error. We might need to search a fairly large area. It'd be better if we had a clue." Barley could now see the huge blue swath of Cameron Lake below them. "Did the person who hid the cache give you a clue?"

Before Newton had a chance to answer, Martin clicked back over: "The protestors have blocked off Highway 4," he said. "That's the only route between Qualicum Beach on the east coast of the island and Port Alberni in the interior."

Newton pulled out a paper map. "What does that mean for us?"

"Air traffic control says my only option for landing is the parking lot."

They were close enough now to skim the tops of the virgin forest. Douglas fir stood so tall, it was like they could touch the stars. Barley had never even imagined trees could be so big. He had seen huge trees in Olympic Park in Washington, and in Chilliwack, but they were nowhere near as big as these. These were like something out of *The Lord of the Rings*.

Martin navigated west towards the parking lot. "Whisky. Tango. Foxtrot," he said, drawing strange looks from both Barley and Newton. "I can't bring it down there. Too many people." People were indeed everywhere, like little ants, getting bigger and bigger as they descended.

"God, look at them all," said Newton.

Barley couldn't believe what he was looking at in the middle of a majestic old-growth forest. It looked like an army base with skids of food and supplies, and what appeared to be solar-powered battery packs. He felt a knot forming in his stomach, not from motion sickness. This was something different altogether.

Martin brought the chopper around to the roadway, which was eerily empty of motorized vehicles because the conservationists weren't letting any cars through. "I can set her down along that wide stretch there. There'll still be enough room for cars to pass if traffic resumes," he said.

"That doesn't seem likely any time soon," said Newton. "Yes, bring her down, Martin."

The big machine jostled in a cross wind as he landed, last year's leaves flying up and dancing across the road. A huge toppled hemlock stood about seven feet on its side, an orange slash spray painted on its bark.

"Ljubljana," said Barley, under his breath. In the distance, at least a hundred sign-waving tree huggers formed a human barricade across the highway. When Martin cut the engine and the rotor blades slowed, Barley could make out what the protestors were chanting. They were singing really. Some off-key. Some perfectly tuned like a Sunday school choir.

It was Joni Mitchell's "Big Yellow Taxi." Barley knew it; since his father had died, his mother had taken out his old record player and they spent some nights listening to all his old vinyl. She said the song was about appreciating what you have while you have it.

Martin sang along with the crowd, until Newton gave him a look, and he clammed up. "I'll stay with the chopper, sir."

Barley followed Newton, jumping out of the helicopter, careful to stay away from the rotors. Two protestors wielding placards that said *Save the Trees* were busy smashing out the windshield out of a Ford F-350 truck, a $50,000 machine. Barley flinched, thinking of the Corvette. He swallowed. "You sure this is a good idea?"

Just beyond, a more peaceful group sat on colourful blankets around a small totem pole; others danced to the rhythm of a skin drum. A cloth banner proclaiming *First Nations of Vancouver Island* swayed behind them, held up on poles cut from dead wood.

When a banana peel came flying out of the trees above them, Barley put his hands up to protect his head. Dozens of environmentalists were camped out on platforms built into the canopy of the massive Douglas firs surrounding the parking lot. Some trees had orange slash marks spray painted on their trunks like the fallen western hemlock next to the helicopter.

"Woah." Newton pulled up the collar of his coat. "Stay close to me, Barley. We'll be all right."

"Why are they protesting?" Barley suddenly felt scared. What was he doing in the middle of a violent protest with this man who threatened to wreck his family?

"They call themselves Friends of Cathedral Grove. They're angry because trees are being cut down to make room for a new parking lot."

"I wonder how long they've been up there?" Barley motioned towards the tree dwellers.

"Who knows?" Newton put his hand up to shade his eyes and scanned the trees. "Don't worry about them," he said. "We'll just do what we came to do and get out of here."

Barley discretely pointed the screen of the Garmin heavenward to take a reading.

"Maybe you should wait until we're in the trees and out of sight," said Newton.

"I can't get a reading if there's tree cover," Barley explained. "A GPS needs a clear view of the sky to work. Once we're under the branches, we'll have trouble getting a signal."

"I thought you were using your GPS in a tunnel?"

Barley shook his head. Why didn't people get it? "I used the GPS to get to the tunnel. Then I had to rely on clues to find the cache. Do you have any clues?" he asked again.

Newton did not answer the question. Instead, he asked a question of his own. "Is it far to the coordinates?"

"Five hundred and eighty metres southeast." Barley indicated with one finger towards a path through a thick stand of Sitka spruce.

"That's only half a kilometre," said Newton.

"Yes, but that's as the crow flies. The GPS doesn't follow trails. If there's a 200-foot-long rock wall in the way, we have to go around, and that distance isn't counted by the GPS."

A woman in her thirties with green hair held a painted placard blocking their way. The placard read *Say no to clearcutting* and had pictures of trees lying dead on the ground. They had arms and legs and faces like people in pain. "You are not one of us," she said. "What brings you here?"

Barley's throat was too dry to speak. *What are we doing way out here?* Barley had no idea.

Newton said, "We support your cause."

She let them pass. The woods smelled of rot and cotton candy all at once.

Barley was relieved when the needle on the RCMP Garmin pointed away from the woman with the sign.

"We're going the right way," he whispered, as they reached a sign reading *Oldest Tree Trail*. "We're down to three hundred and eight-seven metres."

"That's good," said Newton, who did not sound good at all; in fact, he sounded more nervous than Barley felt. They continued walking until they came to a tree stump as wide as two parking spaces. Seven adults stood shoulder to shoulder on top. The stump appeared to have been dragged from somewhere else to block the path, although Barley couldn't imagine how they could have moved it.

"I am the Lorax," announced a man with a huge walrus mustache glued over his top lip. "I speak for the trees, for the trees have no tongues."

"What the hell is he talking about?" said Newton. He pulled Barley away from the man.

"It's from the Dr. Seuss book," said Barley, still whispering so that the protestors couldn't hear what they were saying.

"Can't say I know that one," said Newton.

"You have to know *The Lorax*. It's the one where the Once-ler cuts down all the truffula trees."

"Nope." Newton shook his head.

"He makes Thneeds and the brown Bar-ba-loots are forced to move away?"

Newton shook his head again. How could this guy have grown up in the twentieth century and not be familiar with Dr. Seuss?

"You mustn't have children."

"You are correct." The man sounded like a robot.

"My dad told me Dr. Seuss wrote the story after Walt Disney wanted to set up a resort at Mineral King Valley in the High Sierra. People didn't want a resort there and someone took Disney to Supreme Court. The judge who ruled against the proposal said: 'Who will speak for the trees?'" Barley glanced at Newton, who didn't appear to be listening, and then back to the mustachioed protester.

"I'll decapitate any person who tries to get past," said the Lorax.

"Don't worry," said Newton. "We'll just double back a bit and cut through the trees."

They made their way around two teenagers about Barley's age holding a huge cloth banner of a Grumpy Stump stamping out Government and Industry.

Barley tried to steal a glance at the GPS. No reception. They skirted a small waterfall that whooshed over a moss-covered fir. Here they found a parallel trail, and Barley was able to get a clear signal. "We have to go due south."

"How do you know where south is. I can hardly see the sun through the canopy."

"I have a compass." Barley strapped his orienteering compass onto his thumb. After ten minutes of scrambling through a labyrinth of deadfall, they reached another clearing. The path veered right, and a sign announced *The Oldest Tree*.

Barley noticed Newton was sweating like a sumo wrestler in a sauna. He pointed at a Douglas fir that measured at least nine metres in circumference. A plaque on the base read *This tree is over 800 years old*. The tree was so tall it made Barley dizzy to follow the branches up towards the sky. He felt the skip in his heart that indicated they were close, and even though the Garmin had no clear view of the satellites, he knew the needle would be spinning if it did.

"We're within metres of the cache," he told Newton. "Start looking for something out of the ordinary."

"What do you mean 'out of the ordinary'?" asked Newton, peering up at the towering forest.

Barley turned his eyes earthward and started at the ground and worked his way up, looking for a nook where it would be easy to hide something. The site wasn't as infested with Muggles as Barley had expected. The psycho Lorax might actually be helping their cause.

"Something unnatural, something that's not supposed to be..."

Before Barley had a chance to finish his sentence, a placard came out of nowhere and clocked Newton on the back of the head. He went down.

"Are you out of your mind?" Barley yelled at the Lorax, who had turned back on, jabbing his placard at a family of tourists.

"That's what happens if you cross the line," he said. "You must show respect for this tree. It was growing here before white man even set foot on this continent." With that, he turned without checking what kind of damage he had inflicted.

Barley crouched to see if Newton was OK. He might hate the man, but he didn't want him killed. Blood was oozing out from under Newton's head, staining the leaf-covered ground reddish black.

Barley gulped; he took his muddy jacket out of his backpack and tucked it under Newton's head to mop up the blood. He had no idea how bad the injury was. Several people came over to look at him, and a man offered to get a wagon that he'd used to tow his children from beyond the barricade where they had to park. He ran off giving the Lorax a wide berth. Someone else said she was a nurse. While she gave Newton the once over, Barley looked around and caught a glimpse of silver in one of the lower branches of a young fir about two metres off the path. He crept over and discreetly placed what looked like a cigar case engraved with a palm tree inside his shirt and under his jeans.

Barley felt sick. He knew they couldn't wait for the wagon. He sat Newton up—no easy feat considering his size. He tied his jacket around Newton's head wound, then dragged him as best he could over logs and roots back to the chopper. It was slow going. The man was no lightweight, that's for sure. By the time they arrived, Newton was ghastly white, and blood had soaked through Barley's jacket wrapped around his head. Martin saw them approach and jumped down to help ease Newton into his seat.

"What happened?" he asked, helping Newton fasten his seatbelt. He looked at Barley.

"Some lunatic dressed like the Lorax hit him with a wooden sign."

"Are you OK, sir?" He put the back of his hand to Newton's brow.

"I'll be all right, but we didn't get the cache."

"Yes, we did." Barley held up the cigar case.

"You found it," said Newton, trying to sit up straighter. He grimaced with the effort.

"Yep." Barley smiled and opened the lid. Inside sat a folded piece of beige paper. It was thicker than regular paper; it looked like it had been made of lots of bits of paper somehow glued together.

When he unfolded the sheet, a small plastic baggy dropped out. He held it up to the window and squinted. "Looks like somebody's hair."

"Hold on!" said Newton. "You shouldn't be touching that without gloves."

The smile disappeared off Barley's face. For a moment there, Barley had actually thought they were bonding. Now, he knew better. "Gloves? Why do I need gloves? It's not a crime scene or anything." Barley went to touch it, but Newton waved frantically and slowly dug in his vest pocket for some of those thin rubber gloves that doctors wear.

Newton handed a pair of gloves to Barley and slid the second pair on his own hands before taking the silver case. Barley watched as he examined the sheet of letter-sized paper. It was embossed with a tree in the lower left corner.

"Bravo. Nice to know you care," he read aloud. "If you reach the chapel, you best say a prayer, because you have gone too far."

"Is that all it says? No coordinates?" asked Barley.

"No, there are numbers too." Newton held up the paper for Barley to read. Under the clue and above the tree were two rows of numbers. Barley closed his eyes and erased the day's events from his mind. Instead of thinking about Newton and gloves, GeoFind and Phyllis, his father's car and his angry mother, and the forest full of protesters, he imagined the topo maps he and his father used to study on the dining room table. He breathed in slowly. When he opened his eyes, the two men were watching him closely.

"Well...?" said Newton.

"It's somewhere around Kamloops," he announced.

Martin was staring at Barley as if he had just encountered ET in his shed. "Kamloops? How do you know?"

"I dunno. I just do. It's like I have a built-in GPS."

Martin shook his head and smiled. "Tell me the coordinates."

As Barley read them out, Martin plugged them into his console. "My God, that's amazing. It's Sun Peaks, about half an hour north of Kamloops by car."

"The ski resort?" asked Newton.

"That's it." Martin's smile was so big, he looked like the Joker.

Barley was relieved. Although he was intrigued by what might be at Sun Peaks, he had had enough excitement for the day and was anxious to get back to Colossus and explain to Mr. C. what the heck had happened to him. Maybe, he'd let him catch up once he heard about the police investigation.

"Martin, do you have enough fuel to take us there?"

"Take YOU there," said Barley. "I have to get back. You can just drop me off at the airport and..."

"You can't go yet." Four eyes burrowed into Barley's skull.

Barley looked from Newton to Martin to the coordinates and back again. "Listen, Newton..." Oops, did he call him Newton to his face? He swallowed. "I said I'd help you find some coordinates. I've fulfilled my end of the bargain. And now I'd like to get back to Langley. I might have time to get the next cache before 4:00."

Newton looked worse than when he had got clobbered with the sign. "You've got to come with me. I won't be able to find something hidden in a forest. I'd be bumbling around for days."

"You said it, not me." Barley smiled without showing his teeth. He sat back and crossed his arms.

Newton looked at Martin. Martin began to speak. "Maybe if you fill him in...?"

"I can't." Newton's words came out loud. He had regained some colour, but he was still perspiring heavily.

"Well, you also can't kidnap me and drag me around freakin' war zones where you... you get beat up and find chunks of someone's hair, and not explain what's going on." He pushed the GPS towards Newton's chest.

Newton looked at Martin, who blew out through his lips.

"Listen, Barley, it's not that I don't trust you, but the details of the case are confidential."

"Why don't you come to Sun Peaks?" said Martin. He smiled, the corners of his eyes crinkling. "Then we'll get you back as soon as we can so you can continue with your contest. Maybe Sergeant Newton can talk to Mr. Czanecki and explain that you were helping with an investigation."

"How did you know I was in a contest?" asked Barley.

"I saw your big maw on the front page of the paper the other day," answered Martin. "You're famous."

"Tell me what we're investigating. Who owns the hair?"

"That I don't know. But I know it's important we find out. In fact, it could be a matter of life or death."

"Are you serious?"

"Yes, unfortunately," said Martin.

"OK, if I do one more, then will you take me back to Langley?"

"Yes," said Newton. "One more and we'll take you home."

"And you'll call Mr. C.?"

"Yes, I will call Mr. C."

"And take care of all that other stuff with the car?"

"Yes."

"OK, then. Let's go skiing."

16

Sun Peaks

N 50° 53.624, W 119° 54.184

Two hours and a sub sandwich after leaving the protestors on Vancouver Island, the helicopter was hovering near the base of a mountain on which several ski runs cut through a swath of trees. They had arrived at Sun Peaks, located fifty-six kilometres northeast of Kamloops and featuring sixteen square kilometres of ski runs. The highest peak is over two thousand metres, and the longest ski run over eight kilometres.

Barley had never been to Sun Peaks, and although he was still pissed with Newton for dragging him away from GeoFind, he couldn't deny it was exciting flying around with Martin. His stomach did much better on the second flight. He also figured if Newton didn't go right to a hospital to get his head stitched up after getting beaten with a wooden sign, whatever he was working on had to be pretty serious. His head had to be throbbing and the gash was about two inches long. Martin bandaged it as best he could. Barley couldn't let himself pity the man though, he had to defend his father's rightful spot in the family unit. He glanced over at him. His jaws were working purple Thrills gum. He offered Barley a piece, but when Barley put it in his mouth, it tasted so much like soap, he had to spit it out.

Martin brought down the chopper near a medieval-style turret and pastel-coloured rental units that joined up in the shape of an Irish harp. Across the road from the village, a new-looking golf course lay virtually empty.

Barley consulted the Garmin before he descended from the chopper. Martin had used the helicopter's GPS system to get them as close to the coordinates as he could. Barley pressed the Go To command and the arrow pointed him on his way. He wished he knew what the heck they were doing. If the first cache contained a hair sample, what would the next one have—a tooth? Who would put things like that in a geocache?

Newton deposited a fresh piece of gum in his mouth and followed Barley out of the chopper. "How far is this one?"

"About a kilometre that way." Barley pointed.

"That's not too bad."

"I hate to tell you this, but geocaching coordinates also don't include altitude." Barley looked at the summit of what the sign said was Tod Mountain.

"You're saying it's up the mountain?" Newton grimaced.

"Afraid so," said Barley. "Looks like it's on a ski run called Sunburst. At least there's no snow on the slopes."

"Maybe we can take the lift?" Newton raised his eyebrows.

"I don't think it runs in June." Barley indicated toward the deserted chair lift. "Unless there's a mountain biking event on the go, it's not likely."

"You should stay here, Sergeant," said Martin. "I can go with Barley. You're not looking too good."

"No, I'm fine. The bleeding has stopped." Newton turned his head to exhibit a matted mass of hair at the back, covered with a mishmash of Band-Aids, not far from the bald patch. "Let's go."

Barley hopped out of the chopper, ignoring the rotor blades deafening roar. He stopped at the Sunburst trail sign. Top elevation was 1,850 metres. He wasn't too sure Newton, who was already blowing out air through his mouth and then loudly inhaling through his nose, would make that. They had only just begun.

But the GPS showed the cache located partway up Sunburst Mountain at an elevation of 5,596 feet. The GPS always used imperial instead of metric.

Maybe he can make it. It's not my problem, Barley thought and started up the steep incline. Everything smelled woody, like when his father used to come home from a mapping trip. Newton trailed behind him, stopping every ten metres or so to catch his breath.

It took forty-five minutes to reach the north coordinates. The air was considerably cooler. Barley owled his head around to see how far behind Newton had fallen. He was about thirty metres back. Barley decided to wait once they reached the proper elevation for the cache.

"How much higher do we have to go?" Newton's breathing was rapid and jagged.

Barley double-checked the elevation on the Garmin. "We're as high as we have to go, 5,596 feet."

Newton removed a cigarillo from his pocket and put it in his mouth.

Barley's sympathy faded fast. "That's disgusting. No wonder you can hardly walk uphill." Why would his mother even speak to this guy? She was dead set against smoking. She told Barley if he ever took it up, she'd inject cancer cells into him herself.

"I don't smoke them. I just chew on the end."

"Aren't you already chewing that soapy gum?"

"Yeah, so?" Newton paused. "Is it around here then?"

"Not yet, we have to head that way." Barley pointed west towards a thicket between the Exhibition and Cruiser ski runs. He started walking where the arrow pointed, checking the GPS every minute or so.

A bald eagle flew overhead, something white in its talons. Barley watched as the eagle landed on the top of a fir tree and turned its head to follow the movement of Newton's hands putting away the cigarillo pack. A moment later it took flight, soaring gracefully to a higher tree about forty feet up the slope, where it eyed them like an avian spy ready to dispatch news to the enemy before lowering its beak and tearing fleshy pieces out of its dinner.

Barley paused to consult the screen. "Can you read the clues?"

Newton removed the unlit cigarillo from his lips and reread the piece of stationary he had pulled from his pocket. "'If you reach the chapel, you'd best say a prayer because you have gone too far.' I wonder what the chapel bit means?" Newton's voice sort of echoed in the open space. "There can't be a church up here."

Barley pointed fifty meters across the mountain from where they were standing. A tiny A-frame with a cross over the door was silhouetted in the sun. Barley had seen a couple who had just got married in Banff once. The bride wiped out while skiing down the mountain in her wedding dress. The groom tried to help her, and went head over heels too. At least he had been wearing a tux. She was strapless.

"I think it means if we reach the chapel, we've overshot the coordinates," Barley called. "Here, why don't you hold the GPS." As vile as Newton was, Barley felt a bit sorry for him, standing there wheezing and bandaged. Everyone should experience the excitement of the hunt.

Newton took the machine and focused on the screen. "Nothing's happening."

"You have to be moving for it to work."

Newton walked slowly towards the chapel with Barley

following. Steps from the front door, he stopped. "Something is wrong. The needle is flicking left and right. It's not leading me anymore."

Barley felt the familiar skip of his heart. "That's because you've entered the zone of uncertainty. It's time to start searching for something out of place again. Maybe in the trees." He nudged Newton into a small, yet surprisingly dense copse of evergreens in the middle of the ski run. Barley had already spotted a blue-and-white Krinos Feta Cheese container tied to a tree. It was hard not to grab it, but Barley knew the thrill of finding your very first geocache. In his life to date, he had experienced nothing remotely similar to the rush, except maybe kissing Phyllis. He quickly blocked out those memories. "Try looking around waist height."

"I see something." Newton jogged towards the three-kilogram bucket. He jammed the cigarillo in his pocket and fumbled for his rubber gloves. He detached the bucket from the rope that held it to the tree and pulled off the blue lid. Then, much to Barley's surprise, Newton dropped the bucket. It wasn't the reaction Barley had expected. He thought Newton would share the excitement of locating Ground Zero.

"What is it?" Barley reached into the bucket on the ground and removed a baseball cap, white with the Vancouver Canucks retro hockey stick logo embroidered on the front. "What's wrong with a hat?"

"I told you not to touch anything without gloves." Newton pulled a large Ziploc from his pocket, snatched the hat from Barley, and zipped it into the bag.

"It looks new."

"Yeah, the kid is apparently a Vancouver fan. His father took him to all the games." Newton caught himself before he said more.

"What kid?"

Newton shook his head. "I've said too much already."
He unfolded a piece of beige homemade paper, embossed
with the same tree as the one in Cathedral Grove. You could
see where the individual bits of pulp came together. He
stopped chewing his gum and read: "How far will you go?"

He passed Barley the paper so he could decipher the
new coordinates listed below the cryptic message. Barley
plugged the coordinates into the Garmin.

"It's south of Williams Lake," he said, after taking one
look. He dropped the note back in the bucket on top of the
bagged hat. "Who's the Canucks fan?"

"I told you; I can't say." Newton inhaled loudly and
puffed up his chest.

"It's too late to head up there now." Barley looked at the
trees, their leaves dappled by the dipping sun.

"You're right," said Newton. "There won't be enough
daylight by the time we get there. Can you meet me at
Langley Airport tomorrow morning?"

Barley had to admit he was curious, but the pull of
GeoFind and beating Phyllis was stronger than that of riding in a helicopter to find out who owned a stupid Canucks
ball cap. "Sorry, I have to get back to GeoFind."

"Right." Newton sounded resigned.

"Newton, we all agreed I would help you today. Today
is now over, and tomorrow I'm going back to GeoFind."

"GeoFind. Pfff. Can't you think of anyone but yourself
for once?"

"If you tell me who I'm supposed to be thinking about,
maybe I'll change my mind."

"I told you I can't do that. What I can do is pay you
double what they pay you at Big Bite."

"I'm not in the contest to win money."

"What are you in it for then?"

Barley shook his head and started down the mountain,
leaving Newton standing there holding the bucket.

When Barley climbed aboard the chopper, Martin asked, "Where's Sergeant Newton?"

"He'll be here soon."

"Did you find the cache?"

"Yes."

Martin must have known Barley was not in the mood for talking. He nodded and they waited in silence for Newton to appear. When he did, he laid the bucket by his feet and heaved his sweating form aboard the chopper.

"Where are we going, boss."

"Back to Langley, please, Martin. The next cache is too far to get to tonight."

They flew home in silence, each to his own thoughts; Newton probably thinking about what he was going to do tomorrow morning when Barley went back to GeoFind, and Barley also thinking about getting back to GeoFind, about how he had to win the contest for his father. He had no allegiance to Newton. His allegiance would always lie with his father.

17

Phyllis Drops By

It was 8:39 by the time Newton's silver Mercedes pulled in front of the stucco house on 62A Avenue and Barley hopped out. He was pissed off that Newton had made him miss the Stanley Cup final. What an asshole. Not only that, but he was hungry and tired—hangry his mother called it. All he wanted was to get inside, away from Newton, grab something to eat, and vegetate. He had to think things through. What was he doing out there today? A lock of hair and a hat. Whose were they? And why were the police helicoptering all over creation looking for them?

As the Mercedes pulled away from the curb, Barley noticed there was someone on the porch. It couldn't be his mother; when Newton called her to say they were on the way, she confirmed she wouldn't be home for at least another hour. Plus, it wasn't her shape. But definitely female. The person stood up, but her face was partially obscured by one of his mother's hanging plants. He wondered who could be lurking on his porch at almost 9 p.m.; it was the legs that gave her away. Shapely and tanned. Shoot, he didn't have to look at the long brown hair with blonde streaks to recognize her:

Phyllis Henderson. What was she doing here? Come to rub his nose in the fact that he had screwed up GeoFind and that she would win?

Barley gulped. This was the first time she'd been at his house in eight months, the first time since Hallowe'en weekend.

Phyllis was wearing khaki shorts and a plain black top covered by a Reebok jacket. Barley realized he'd never seen her wear pants. He wondered how he could still find her attractive, after what she did to him.

"Hi, Barley. What's up?"

Barley felt a light sweat building under his arms. "Nothing much." Thoughts of hair and baseball caps flitted through his mind.

"I didn't know you had a dog. I saw him in the car when I passed you in Hope."

Yes, a dog to replace my dead father. Barley had forgotten all about the fact his mother had brought home a Great Dane. That seemed like a lifetime ago. Barley could see his big hairy face in an upstairs window. A loud woof sounded from above, followed by an unmistakable four-footed thump, thump, thump, thump, thump, as Stanley whipped down the stairs. Poor dog. How long had he been locked indoors? He must be about to burst.

"Barley, I think he's got to pee." Phyllis indicated to Stanley's big mug in the living room window.

Stanley's massive head disappeared and reappeared in the window in the front door. He whined and rubbed his nose against the glass. He didn't look like he could last much longer. Phyllis crouched down and began calmly cooing to him through the beveled glass.

"Hurry. He's in a frenzy."

Stanley responded with another guttural woof.

"He's all right." Barley knew full well he wasn't, but he was afraid Phyllis might invite herself in.

"He is *not* all right, Barley Lick. Let the poor animal out, or I'll report you to the Humane Society."

Barley looked from the dog who had magically appeared in his life to Phyllis who had disappeared out of it, and debated what to do.

Reluctantly he made a move towards the doorknob. Stanley was beside himself with anticipation. I will die if you don't let me out soon, he whined. Barley opened the door and Stanley barrelled through like a hurricane. The sheer momentum of two hundred plus pounds of beige fur knocked Phyllis off balance. Stanley beat his way to a rhododendron and relieved himself.

"Holy hankies," she said, getting up and brushing herself off. "What's his name?"

Before the word "Stanley" was out of Barley's mouth, Phyllis had proceeded up the steps and into the house. By the time he caught up with her, she was hanging her jacket on the back of a chair. Stanley seemed disappointed to be going back in so soon. He looked at Barley, lifted a rear leg a second time, this time over the wooden grizzly carving's feet.

"You can't pee on Hope!" said Barley. The dog gave him a guilty stare, then resignedly followed him up the steps and back into the house.

Panic turned the juices in Barley's stomach to acid at the thought of Phyllis Henderson inside his house. He looked at the hardwood floor and wished he had swept it like his mother always pestered him to do. Popcorn kernels were visible under the couch. At least it was better than the orange shag carpet that used to cover the floor back in October. Barley's father had always threatened to pull up the carpet and expose the hardwood underneath. In January his mother had called some contractors to come in and do just that. She had been given grief time from work. She couldn't concentrate on reading, so she started to renovate with a vengeance. What a mess it was when the contractors exposed the floor. What his mother assumed would be gleaming intact hardwood was really four- and five-foot square patches of dirty maple covered with the sticky gum of underlay glue. The contractors had to rip up everything and relay the whole surface. It had cost a fortune.

Phyllis was talking. "Earth to Barley. I asked you what his name was."

Barley blinked. "Oh, he's Stanley."

"You've changed things," she said, moving past Stanley whose rudder-like tail sent the black floor lamp dancing. Barley steadied the lamp with one hand and removed a pair of grey socks hanging off the rim with the other, praying Phyllis hadn't noticed. He felt a flush in his cheeks.

"It looks good... looks a lot bigger than the last time I was here," she said, as if her last visit had been a pleasant evening. She was right about the space though. When Barley's mother renovated, she hadn't stopped at the floors. She had the guys take out a few walls to open up the kitchen and living areas. Barley thought the whole ceiling was going to come toppling down, but they must have known what they were doing, because that hadn't happened yet. For a month that winter, their house was a construction zone. With so much chaos at home, Barley was happy to go to school. The change was amazing though. It hardly looked like the same house. The new living room/kitchen was off-white with dark wood accents and a marble island.

Phyllis stopped in front of Barley's computer. A framed topo map of the Lower Mainland hung on the wall behind the screen. She examined it before sitting down. He was happy to note that he was a few inches taller than her now. He hadn't realized how much he'd grown since last year.

She picked up a can of SPAM from next to the monitor and began to read the ingredients. Before Barley could protest, she had pulled the tab, removed the little key and started twisting off the lid. Liquid fat began oozing out.

"Got a spoon?" she said.

"You can't eat that." Barley looked at her suntanned face. It was always a creamy colour and had tanned to a deep brown in only a couple of days. Her teeth looked amazing without braces, and he wondered what she would do if he kissed her right now. *Get that thought out of your mind, Barley. Always remember that Phyllis Henderson is a she-devil.*

"Why not?" she asked, moving to choose a small spoon from a jam jar standing on the counter next to the toaster.

"Because…"

"Because why?" It was always like this with Phyllis. He was so intimidated in her presence his mind didn't work properly.

"I dunno." He did know. His father had given him the SPAM as a joke about a month before he died.

"Well, I'm half starved. Tell you what. I'll pay you for it." She stepped around Stanley, who had followed her to the computer and moved to the kitchen. She dumped a pocketful of change on the counter, and moving one coin at a time with her finger, counted out $3.50. "That should be enough to get another tin." She put the rest of the coins back in her pocket, moved to the sink, and poured the fatty liquid down the drain, before installing herself on a stool at the island.

Barley was incensed. He straightened his back and tried to calm his mind. He had forgotten his own hunger. All he wanted was to be alone and eat whatever leftovers he could find. What could he do to get Phyllis out of his house?

Stanley sat at attention in front of Phyllis while she wolfed down the meat. Desperate to get at whatever yummy pork by-products were in that tin, he began intermittently flinging up a front paw.

"Can I give him some?" she said, about to feed Stanley from her spoon.

"No," Barley almost shouted. "That stuff would make him sick. He's got a very sensitive digestive system." Barley knew nothing about Stanley's digestive system. What he did know was that he did not want Stanley eating his father's SPAM. Barley couldn't explain why. It hurt his head to think about it.

Determined not to show Phyllis how upset he was, Barley went to the propane fireplace and flipped the switch. The artificial logs crackled to life. He patted the huge doggy bed his mother had bought. But Stanley wouldn't budge from Phyllis's side; a glob of gelatin had fallen on the floor and the huge canine licked it up with his eager tongue.

Phyllis began rubbing her bare feet back and forth on Stanley's back as she polished off the rest. Stanley tipped over sideways to optimize the foot massage.

Barley's breath was coming in short spurts. He had to sit down. He made his way across the room to the couch. "Phyllis, what are you doing here?"

Phyllis followed, speaking between mouthfuls. "After I saw you in Hope, you didn't show up at Colossus to get your next clue."

"How do you know?"

She paused. "I asked Mr. C. when I checked at the end of the day. He said he had no idea where you were. No one else knew what had happened either. So, I called your mother and she said you were geocaching."

"And?"

"Well, how could you be geocaching if you didn't check in at Colossus for your second clue?"

"What's it to ya?"

"I was worried."

"Worried? You weren't worried. You were just keeping tabs on me."

"I admit I keep tabs on you, just like you keep tabs on me."

"I don't keep tabs on you." Of course, it was a lie. He always kept tabs on her. Stanley looked at him as if to say fess up. There was no way Barley would admit any interest in Phyllis Henderson. "Is that all you came here to say, Syphilis?"

Slowly she laid the SPAM tin on the coffee table and stood up to face him. "I told you to never call me that."

"Well, Syphilis, I didn't listen."

The fist that hit Barley's nose was as hard as a boxer's. Barley couldn't believe it belonged to a girl. It sent him sprawling. Blood poured out, as if from a hose, all over his shirt and pants. Tears spring to his eyes making it difficult to focus. Stanley woofed three times in a row and stood protectively over him.

"You broke my nose!" Barley gagged on the blood running down the back of his throat. He ran to the stove and grabbed a hand towel off the front. He sat on the stool Phyllis had vacated, put his head back, and pinched to stop the flow of blood.

"I'll break more than that if you ever disrespect me again. Now, tell me why you didn't go back to Colossus."

"I was busy in Sun Peaks." The words came out nasal, s's becoming th's. "...bithy in Thun Peaks."

"Sun Peaks? Where the hell is that?" she asked.

"Not very ladylike language, Phyllis," he said through the towel.

"Sorry, Barley, I forgot I was in the presence of a gentleman. Where is Sun Peaks?"

"Near Kamloops." Blood pooled in his throat. He wanted to vomit.

"Is there a new cache there?"

"No, I mean yes, but it's not part of GeoFind."

"Did you find it on geocaching.com?"

"No."

"So why were you looking for it?"

"I was helping a cop."

"A cop?"

"Yeah, a cop. His name is Fred Newton." He couldn't bear to tell her that the horrible gum-chewing cigarillo-chomping man was dating his mother. He took down the towel to check the blood. It was still running out like thick red wine. He replaced the towel quickly.

Stanley had his nose in the empty tin of SPAM. Barley jumped to take it away before he cut himself on the sharp metal.

"Why?" Phyllis asks.

"I can't answer that."

"You can't or you won't?"

"Listen, Phyllis. You come barging in here, break my nose, and bombard me with questions. Who do you think you are?"

"The real reason I came, Barley, is to tell you about Selective Availability."

"What about it?" He mumbled through the towel.

"Pfff, you think I'm going to tell you now?" She grabbed her jacket off the chair back and poked her arms through the sleeves. Stanley's worried eyes followed her every move.

Through his own watery eyes, Barley could see Phyllis pulling her ASICS on over her bare feet. She didn't stop to do them up.

"You're a bastard, Barley Lick." She patted Stanley on the head and was out the door without another word.

18

Flashback, Barley Meets Phyllis

The first time Barley Lick met Phyllis Henderson, he had to hold his breath. It was the day he and Colin had gone down to White Rock to sign up at the geocaching club. The morning sun streamed in through the window, highlighting her high cheek bones and dark brown eyes. She was wearing a tiny green t-shirt and cut-off jean shorts; ragged bits of white string accentuated her thighs. Her legs were long and tanned with well-defined muscles. Barley had seen her before at school—she was on the cross-country team. To him, she was this hot older girl; he'd been eyeing her since Grade 10. But she was a year ahead of him and he never had the guts to approach her. That morning down at the beach, he felt like if he exhaled, she might disappear. He couldn't formulate words when she introduced herself.

"I'm Phyllis," she said, extending her hand.

Barley remained mute. She looked at him and raised her eyebrows. Colin came over and rescued him. Colin was always rescuing Barley. "Hi, I'm Colin. This here is Barley Lick. I think we all go to Cloverdale High."

"Barney, I think I've seen you play hockey," she said, her eyes locked on Barley's.

"Not Barney, Barley—B-A-R-L-E-Y," said Colin. "I know, unique name." Colin shot Barley a quick look as if to say calm down, this is not the time for an outburst. Barley gave him a look right back. How old did he think he was? Ten? He had to admit that when he was less mature, he would sometimes get a bit bent out of shape when people gave him a hard time over his name. It seemed like no one could get it straight. At that moment, Barley didn't care if he was called Cucumber. All he cared about was keeping this girl here.

"Barley? Like the grain?" she asked.

"Yes, like the grain," said Colin. "And he can talk; just not to girls." Colin elbowed Barley in the ribs, cackled out a laugh, and walked away.

"Well, Mr. Barley Lick. You know how to geocache or what?"

Barley found his voice. He was afraid it might crack, even though it hadn't in two years. "I... I know a bit."

"Grapevine says you know more than a bit. You have a partner yet?"

Barley had told Colin he'd be his partner. "No," he squawked.

"Excellent. We can make a team." Phyllis began writing on a card, then left him standing there and went to slide the card over the counter to one of the organizers.

Older members of the club had set up a geocaching extravaganza where teams of two had to try to find up to twenty-five caches in one day. Barley didn't have his license yet. Phyllis drove a yellow Mini Cooper with Union Jacks on the mirrors and roof. Barley thought that riding in that car was the coolest thing. Colin was not so thrilled when he found out he had been abandoned, but he told Barley to go on, he'd find someone else to partner with.

They were in North Van in Lynn Valley. They had just crossed the suspension bridge and Barley was deep down in a patch of ferns looking for a cache. Phyllis was out on the path keeping guard against Muggles when a couple spotted Barley and began to snicker, no doubt thinking he was squatting in the woods because he couldn't make it to a toilet. He was mortified. Phyllis was laughing so hard she couldn't breathe. She sounded like a machine gun. She left the trail and came through the bushes and crouched down next to Barley. When she saw the look on his face, she stifled her laughter and said: "Oh, Barley, don't get your knickers in a knot." And before he knew what was happening, she hip-checked him into the ferns, retrieved the cache, which had been right in front of him all along, and began running through the thick undergrowth taunting him to follow.

He sat stunned for a couple of seconds trying to figure out why his brain had stopped sending signals to his limbs.

"Come find me." Her voice was sing-song-y. She wasn't far, but she was out of sight.

Barley had to talk to his fluttery stomach to make his legs cooperate. He ran cautiously through the ferns. The ground was uneven and covered in exposed tree roots. Where was she?

"Gotcha." She came out from behind a huge redwood and tackled him. Pushing him back into the ferns, she straddled him. She held the cache, a flat silver box over her head. Her shirt rode up a little exposing a diamond stud in her naval. Barley had seen it before when she competed in races for Cloverdale High. But never up close. Her belly was flat and brown and…

Oh my God, what's happening? Barley felt himself harden, and Phyllis pushed him farther down into the undergrowth.

"Would you like to see… what's in here?" She laid the metal box on his chest.

"Um…" That's all that came from Barley's lips.

"Cat's got your tongue, hey. I'll tell you what we'll do. First, we'll turn off your GPS. Don't want to waste the batteries." Phyllis removed the Garmin from Barley's hand, turned it off, and shoved it in her bra. Barley felt his Adam's apple bob dryly in his throat.

"There now. Shall we open the case?"

Barley tried to raise his head, but she lowered her forehead to his. He felt her breath on his face. Her hair fell around her shoulders, tickling his cheek. It smelled like strawberries. "You're pretty cute now that I get a good look at you."

She shifted her weight on his pelvis. He felt blood throb in his nether regions and knew she could feel it too. She lowered her lips to his ear. "Are you ready?" She pulled up the clasp. The case made a tiny click. She opened the lid and her eyes widened.

Curiosity helped Barley find his voice. "What... what is it?"

"Tell me who the best geocacher is, and I'll tell you what's in the box." She crossed her arms behind her head and stretched her torso back and forth, revealing more of the diamond stud. Barley saw it was a star with a clear center outlined in tiny pink stones.

"I uh... I dunno."

"Bzzz. Wrong answer." Phyllis dipped down as she spoke, and her lips brushed his cheek.

"Um..." Barley couldn't think about anything except what was happening in his pants. "I uh..."

"Incorrect again, Barley Lick. You have one more chance to answer the question or...," she shut the case and licked her finger rubbing it along the perimeter of the lid, "... you'll never find out what's in here."

"Um... what's the question again?"

Phyllis rose up off him and lowered herself down again. "Who is the best geocacher on the Lower Mainland?"

He was going to explode. "Uh, is it you?"

"Correct." Her words were muffled because her lips were on his. They were cool and tasted minty.

Barley had never had a girl kiss him before. His body seemed to know what to do. He closed his eyes and parted his lips.

The first kiss had only lasted a few seconds, but the second one felt longer than a third overtime. Barley forgot about the competition. He forgot what might be in the silver case. He forgot to breathe.

19

The Kidnapping

After Phyllis barged out of his house, Barley removed the hand towel from his nose to assess the damage. The bleeding had slowed, but the pain was excruciating. He felt woozy, like he might be sick. He should eat, he knew that, but he had no appetite. He got up unsteadily and Stanley followed him to the bathroom. His nose was bent and swollen, and his left eye quickly turning black. Stanley whined. *I can't believe she gave me a shiner. I suppose I deserved it, but who does she think she is, just showing up at my house like that?*

He pulled off his shirt and filled the sink with cold water. Blood dripped on the tiled floor; he'd best clean it before his mother got home. She'd have a cow. Stanley stood, chin over the counter, overseeing Barley's chore. When he was finished, he stuck the bloody hand towel deep into the garbage bucket, went to his room to find a ratty t-shirt and pulled it over his head. Stanley followed his every move.

Back in the living room, Barley collapsed on the couch. TV would take his mind off things. He would find out who won the Stanley Cup. He couldn't believe he had missed the final. Stanley's ears stood at attention when he heard the click of the remote. He sat directly on Barley's lap.

"What do you think I am? A doggy chair?" The weight of the animal on Barley's legs caused the Blackberry sheath to cut into his skin. He pushed Stanley off and removed the sheath. He clicked off the phone and plugged it into the charger he kept on the side table. Once again Stanley backed himself into his Barley's lap. It was like parking a car. Barley rolled his eyes, but it was sort of comforting really, feeling that big hairy warmth so close. So, craning his neck around Stanley's giant head, Barley channel surfed until he came to highlights of the game. This was not how he imagined watching the Stanley Cup final. He put a hand to his nose and cursed Phyllis and Newton.

Frantisek Kaberle scored the winning goal in the second period and Carolina went on to beat Edmonton 3-1. Carolina's goalie, Cam Ward, was MVP.

Coverage of the game wrapped up and the news was starting. Barley moved to switch off the TV but stopped when he heard the top story.

"Kidnapping on Vancouver Island. For details, we go to Bonnie Landells at the scene."

The image switched from the host to a reporter standing in the forest near a sign that said *Sleeman's Outdoor Extreme Camp*. "It's been six days since nine-year-old Benjamin Fagan was snatched from this outdoor wilderness camp near Cathedral Grove on Vancouver Island," she said.

Barley sat up straight to turn up the volume, sending Stanley sliding sideways on the couch.

"Early speculation pointed to an animal attack, but no evidence has been found. Then the boy's father, BC logging magnate Phonse Fagan, found a note left by kidnappers. CTV News learned of the story this afternoon when Mr. Fagan dropped off a video pleading for his son's safe return."

The image switched to grainy home video. A tiny man wearing a pressed white shirt, a plain blue tie, and a lightweight tweed sports jacket sat on a chair looking straight at the camera. The man's head was bald and smooth as a baby's bum. The prominent cleft in his chin was deep and defined.

"Please don't hurt my Benjamin." Phonse Fagan's face filled the screen. Barley recognized the teary-eyed fifty-five-year-old logging millionaire immediately. He was more recognizable than the premier.

"How can I give you what you want if you don't contact me? How can we make a deal if I'm the only one communicating? Somebody out there has to know something. Please, if you know anything at all, call the number at the bottom of the screen. Please cooperate. I'll give you whatever you want. Just bring Benjamin home safe."

"Holy jumpins," said Barley.

The TV switched back to the reporter.

"Adding to the mystery surrounding the abduction is the fact that no ransom has been demanded," said Bonnie Landells. The video now showed Cathedral Grove where Newton had got beaned by the Lorax.

"Mr. Fagan's company, Fagan Contracting has been criticized recently for the controversial logging of old growth forest near Cathedral Grove on Vancouver Island. They were the successful bidder in a contract to double the size of the parking lot at the popular tourist stop."

The camera zoomed in on a photo of a red-haired boy wearing a white Vancouver Canuck's ball cap. The cap, which featured the blue oval with a white hockey stick inside, was pulled back slightly revealing a unibrow with a scar through the left half. Barley gaped at the photo. The hat the boy was wearing was the same one Barley had pulled out of a bucket at Sun Peaks today.

"Police refuse to comment on this case, saying divulging details might hurt their investigation."

"Frig," Barley said.

"No need for profanities. What's up?" His mother had come in and laid her purse on the island. Barley turned so his nose stayed behind Stanley and out of her line of sight. Stanley unfolded himself from where he had tumbled off Barley's lap and began scooting across the hardwood on his belly. Once he got to Barley's mother, he rolled over in an obscene pose. She began giving him a vigorous belly rub with her foot.

"This kidnapping case on the news. That's what I was helping Newton with today." The words came out: Thith kidnapping cath on the newth. Thath what I wath helping Newton with today.

"What's wrong with your voice? And it's *Mr.* Newton, Barley."

She took her foot off the dog and straightened her back as she got her first view of Barley's face.

"Mary, mother of God, what happened to your nose?"

"I ran into a tree."

"Barley, you are incorrigible." His mother went to the fridge and took an ice-cube tray from the top freezer. She filled a baggy with ice and passed it to Barley.

"What was *Mr.* Newton thinking? Sending a teenager out searching for a kidnapped kid."

"He couldn't tell you it was a kidnapping."

"Don't tell me you knew?"

"I wasn't supposed to. But Fred needed my permission to let you help."

"Mom, there could have been some maniac in the woods waiting to kill us."

"Fred would never have let you get hurt."

"He's an asshole."

"Barley Lick. If you weren't almost 17, I'd redden your

rear and send you to your room."

Barley held the ice to his nose. He wished this day was over.

"Are you going to help Fred in the morning?"

"No, Newton is going to call Mr. C. to explain why I didn't show up to register this morning's first cache and get clues for the second one. I wouldn't be in this mess if it wasn't for your boyfriend."

"Barley, it's not Fred's fault that you missed the contest. He didn't force you to take your father's car and speed down the highway."

"But it's his fault that I didn't make it back to Colossus to explain."

"Was he the one who caught you doing 130 kilometres an hour on Highway 1?"

"No, but…"

"It's my understanding that if Fred hadn't rescued you, you'd probably still be at the police station facing a string of charges. In fact, you and I still have to discuss the fact that you took your father's car without permission, knowing full well the registration and insurance had expired. I have to decide whether you are ready to have a car of your own at all, but…" She finally stopped to take a breath. "If you help Fred, I'll be a bit more understanding."

"Aw Mom, that's not fair. I need a car to compete and your boyfriend doesn't need me. I'm sure there are plenty of RCMP officers capable of using a GPS to find coordinates. It's not rocket science."

"I know, but no one on the force has the experience you have. They can get close to the coordinates, but they need someone who's an expert at figuring out clues." She sat in the chair at the end of the couch. "Someone like you."

"But what about GeoFind? If Dad were here, he'd want me to compete. He always said I could win. I want to, for him."

"I know you do, honey. But your father would want you to help out with this police investigation more."

"You think Dad would want me to help your boyfriend?"

"Yes, I do." She crossed her arms.

Barley inhaled deeply and looked at his mother. He wanted her to be happy. He just wanted her to be happy alone.

"Barley, please, they need you. Think of that poor father losing his son." She wrapped her arms around Barley's neck and gave him a hug.

Barley remembered Phonse Fagan's tortured expression on the news. But it didn't make him think of a father losing a son as much as a son losing a father. He sighed. Helping would mean giving up on GeoFind, which he didn't want to do, but he realized his mother was right. "OK. I'll do it."

"Excellent. Fred said he's leaving Langley airport at 7:00."

20

Wednesday, Selective Availability

When Barley woke up the next morning, his nose throbbed like a base drum and his feet were pinned under a great warm weight. He opened his eyes to see his mother standing over him, one hand holding a glass, the other rubbing the Great Dane who was curled up like a massive cinnamon bun on the bottom of the bed, contentedly snoring.

Barley had been dreaming about his father. He was searching for him in a dark old-growth forest filled with moss-covered tree trunks and towering limbs. *Protect the trees, Barley,* came his father's far-away voice. *You have to be their protector. You have to preserve the forest. It's urgent.* A stream trickled through a valley, a large blue butterfly flying over it, seeming to show Barley the way. But the way to what? His father?

Barley tried to hold onto the details of the dream, but they were fading, getting vaguer with every second he was awake, until finally they disappeared.

Barley yawned and pulled his feet out from under Stanley. He sat up enough to take the water his mother held out to him.

His mother nodded at the blood stain on his pillowcase; it was in the shape of a cloud. "You'll have to put that in cold water to soak," she said, kissing him on the forehead. "Take care of yourself today, Barley. No more banging into trees."

Wasn't she a barrel of laughs this morning? Barley swallowed the pill she presented and passed back the glass. From the end of the bed, Stanley's stomach sounded as if it had springs.

His mother started for the door. "I have to go in early, but I'll see you this evening."

Barley's mother had been working long hours lately on a movie about a house decorated with so many Christmas lights that you could see it from space. It was supposed to be Massachusetts at Christmastime, but they were filming it in Cloverdale in June. It was 28 degrees outside by 9 a.m., and Danny DeVito and Matthew Broderick were downtown wearing winter coats and scarves. Roses were poking through the fake snow. Barley thought it was hokey, but his mother was proud. At least she was back at work. When she took bereavement time back in December and January, Barley never knew what to expect when he came home. One day, she'd have the floor torn up. The next, there'd be no front door. At Christmas, their lives were a shambles. By January, their house was too.

Barley had bought his father's Christmas present near the end of November. It was an old metallurgical map of Vancouver. It was still in the tube in his room. He never did get a present for his mother. She gave him a new hockey helmet and chest protector. The holiday was a blur. They went to his father's parents for Christmas dinner. He didn't know why they bothered. It was exactly like the wake and funeral. Except Barley could remember more of it. His grandparents and aunts and uncles snotting and crying. Everyone patting him on the back and hugging.

He couldn't wait to get out of there.

He and his mother were invited to Colin's house for New Year's Eve. Barley's mother begged off, but Barley went and appreciated the fact that Colin's parents didn't dwell on the fact that Nelson Lick was dead. They just treated Barley like they always did. It helped a lot.

Barley dragged himself away from the nest of blankets and down the stairs into the kitchen. Stanley followed. It was like having a canine shadow. Barley could imagine Stanley using the toilet and brushing his teeth. Weird. He shook that thought out of his mind.

The Cloverdale Reporter was laid out flat on the island. Barley was about to flip to sports when he noticed a picture of Phonse Fagan and his son, Benjamin, staring up at him from above the crease on the front page. Barley grabbed the milk carton from the fridge and began to chug. No need to use a glass. His mother drank almond milk.

The kidnapping story reiterated what he had seen on TV. It continued on the second page, where the same photo of Benjamin wearing the white Vancouver Canucks hat was printed in colour next to interviews with his friends saying how he told them he didn't want to go to the wilderness camp and was mad at his parents for sending him to the island when all his friends got to stay home and hang out.

He had to call Colin. He grabbed his phone from the charger.

"You sound funny. You got a cold, or what?"

"Phyllis sucker punched me. She came over last night."

"To your house? Wow."

"Yeah, I called her 'Syphilis' and she went a bit ballistic."

"Not again. No wonder she punched you. You know, Barley, I've had a lot more girlfriends than you, and not once did I ever consider calling one of them a venereal disease."

"I know, it just comes out. I can't control it."

"Of course, you can control it."

"I dunno, my mouth works faster than my brain. Speaking of which I got into a bit of trouble with the police yesterday too."

"What happened?"

"I got caught speeding on my way back to Colossus after the first cache."

"Oh no."

"Oh yes, and it gets worse. Mom didn't know I took the 'Vette, and when she came home and it was gone, she reported it stolen."

"That's bad."

"Real bad. It's still not insured, and the registration is expired."

"Uh oh."

"They impounded it, and I got three demerit points when I called the officer a bitch."

"You definitely gotta learn to control your mouth, Barley."

"You sound like my mother. Did you hear about the kid who was kidnapped?"

"Yeah. I heard the Amber Alert on the radio. They're asking people to watch out for anyone travelling with a red-headed boy between the ages of eight and thirteen."

"My mother's boyfriend..." Barley choked on the word.

"The wrestler guy with no muscles?"

"Yeah, it turns out he's a cop at the Serious Crime Unit and he's working on the kidnapping case."

"Really? He's an RCMP officer?"

"Sergeant. And the kidnapper has left clues to find the boy in geocaches."

"Get outta here."

"Yup."

"Kidnapping by geocache. That's sick."

"I know. Anyway, I missed yesterday afternoon at

GeoFind because I was helping him."

"What? Back up a second. You missed GeoFind, but not because you were arrested for speeding in a stolen Corvette with no license and registration?"

"That too." Barley filled Colin in.

"I have to help the police again today. I'm rotted. Phyllis is going to win." Barley opened a tin of dog food and winced. Stanley woofed.

"What's that?"

"Oh yeah, my mother brought home a Great Dane."

Stanley inhaled the slop as soon as it hit his bowl on the stool.

"No friggin' way. A Great Dane! More happens to you in a day than to me in a year. But listen, I've got to get to Big Bite. Mr. Franklyn has me working a ton of shifts while you're off. Apparently, Samantha quit, so now he's short two people."

"When will I see you?"

"Probably not till Friday. I managed to get tomorrow off for my paddle-board competition."

"Where's this one?"

"Fraser River around Fort Langley."

"Don't drown out there."

There was little chance of that. Colin was talented on the water like Barley was talented on land. He had been competing in paddle board since he was thirteen.

Barley hung up the phone and picked up the newspaper. Through the throbbing, he tried to make sense of it all. What kind of sicko would kidnap a kid and then leave clues in geocaches? Why not just demand a ransom and be done with it?

And where did Newton get those first coordinates? Barley wished he had more details. They could be on a wild goose chase. Or worse, there could be a bomb or something waiting for them in one of the caches. Mr. Fagan had forestry operations all over British Columbia. Maybe the tree huggers kidnapped his son.

Closing the paper, Barley headed to the bathroom to see if he looked any better. His reflection was not encouraging; the left eye was almost completely swollen shut, but the pill his mother had given him was starting to kick in. The pain was down to a dull throb. He would grab some breakfast and head over to Langley airport to meet Newton for 7:00. He still couldn't believe Newton hadn't told him they were looking for a kidnapped kid. It wasn't right. He hated that man.

But he had to try and help the boy. *What kind of person would I be if I didn't? Forget that; what kind of person would take a kid? Was Benjamin Fagan even alive? And if he was, how much longer did he have?*

Barley thought back to the hair clipping and the hat. Whoever had Benjamin sure got around. From Vancouver Island to Sun Peaks and now Williams Lake. It was way up north. Barley's father had done work up there. It had to be hundreds of kilometres from Sun Peaks. It would take a few hours by helicopter even. How was the kidnapper getting around? Did he take the boy with him while he set up the caches? How much time did the boy have left?

Barley ran upstairs to dress, shoved a bagel in one pocket, a bottle of water in the other. He grabbed an old boy-scout wallet out of his drawer. It had been a birthday present from an aunt years ago and it still had the twenty-dollar bill that she had given him inside. He hadn't even begun to think about replacing the cards in his stolen wallet. At least he didn't have a credit card to worry about. Still, what a disaster.

At the door, Stanley waited eagerly. Argh, the beast! Barley let him out to pee. He couldn't take him with him. He couldn't possibly leave him at the airport. Plus, he was going to have to ride his bike.

Barley poured a scoop of dry dog chow into the bowl to lure him back inside, and avoided eye contact. "I can't take you today, big guy," he said. Before Stanley had a chance to protest, Barley quickly slipped out the door to the garage shutting the big hairy face inside the house.

Barley lifted his mountain bike from the hooks and pulled on his helmet. He could hear whines emanating from behind the wall. It wouldn't take long to whip down the Langley By-Pass.

Barley turned left on Fraser Highway, and began peddling faster. Ten minutes later, he came to a halt at Langley airport, which was only the size of a small school with two short runways. He locked his bike on a metal pole. The parking lot only held fifty cars, and he spotted Newton's silver Mercedes right away. Barley tried not to think about Newton and how much he disliked him. Instead, he thought about the kid with the unibrow and how scared he must be. He also thought about how cool flying in a helicopter was. Maybe he should consider flight school.

Barley had to go inside the airport building to access the airfield. He checked his watch. Two minutes to 7:00. He hoped he wasn't too late. He glanced out the window towards the chopper and what he saw stopped him dead in his tracks. Looking splendid in black jean shorts and her Reebok jacket was sucker-punch Phyllis Henderson walking to the chopper alongside Newton. Her brown braid was so thick it looked like a coil of rope down her back. Newton wore khakis and a golf shirt. The two looked relaxed, as if they were heading out to play eighteen holes.

Phyllis Henderson. How could Newton call her? What a witch. First, she shows up at Barley's house unannounced and uninvited, thwocks him in the nose, and leaves him bleeding. Then she grinds his face back into the dirt by replacing him on the police case.

Barley had trouble swallowing. He needed to drink something. He pulled out his water and took a swig. *How did Newton even know where to find Phyllis? And how could she have left GeoFind? She'd never give up. What does it matter now? It's obvious my help is not needed anymore.*

As Barley turned to leave, an employee stopped him, sizing up the black eye and swollen nose. "Can I help you with something?" The man did not disguise his disgust, like Barley was some riff-raff and not a vital aide assisting on a police case.

"No, I think I'm in the wrong place." Barley took a deep breath, turned around, and re-envisioned his day.

I should be happy, Barley thought. *Just last night, I wanted out of helping Newton; now I have an excuse. I can go back to GeoFind. I just have to see if Mr. C. will let me log yesterday's first cache and find the second one today as well as the two new ones. Maybe Newton called him like he said he would.*

Barley pedaled as fast as he could. The traffic was bad on 200th, but he made it to Colossus in plenty of time.

As soon as he entered the cinema, he knew something was wrong. The alien helpers weren't in costume. Their rubber head gear lay limp on the countertops. Only four other competitors were there. Where were the others?

Mr. Czanecki was looking dour in a dull-grey, pin-striped suit. Even his black-framed glasses looked sad.

"What's going on?" Barley asked the first person he saw.

Larry Lobez's eyes widened when he saw Barley's battered face. "Holy shebangers! What happened to you?"

"Nothing, ran into a tree. Where is everyone?"

"Haven't you heard?" Larry's eyes opened even wider.

"Heard what?" Barley cocked his head. He wasn't sure if he should believe anything Larry Lobez said.

"Selective Availability, they're turning it back on."

"Yeah right, and I'm Wayne Gretzky."

"I'm serious. President Bush gave a press conference last night. GPS precision will be gone as of ..." He paused and looked up to the left towards the alien that was like St. Paul. "Five o'clock tomorrow."

"What? No. You must have heard wrong."

Selective Availability was the system the US military used to use to scramble satellite signals so that wackos couldn't home in on a building and blow it up. But they had lifted it in 2000. When 9-11 happened, geocachers were sure George Bush was going to reinstate the scrambling system, and they wouldn't be able to geocache anymore. It didn't happen. So, if they didn't turn it back on then, why turn it back on now?

Barley had seen a news piece on Saudia Arabia a couple of days ago. The Saudi government was up in arms over some sanctions the US had imposed. But the American government couldn't bring back SA now. Barley had a niggling feeling that that's what Phyllis must have come to tell him last night. What had she said? He could hear her words. "The real reason I came, Barley, is to tell you about Selective Availability."

Damn. I am such an idiot, Barley thought. *That's why Phyllis was able to help Newton.*

Mr. Czanecki had moved to the microphone, his trusty assistant, Keiko, alongside.

"Ladies and gentlemen geocachers, we made every attempt to reach all of you before you came here this morning. As you all know, geocaching became possible in 2000 because the government of the United States eliminated a policy called Selective Availability, allowing people like us to enjoy much greater precision using a handheld GPS." He paused. "In an unforeseen move this morning, the government announced it has decided to reinstate SA restrictive satellites as of 5:00 p.m. tomorrow."

"Why would they do that?" Chase called out, his usual quiet voice a few decibels higher.

"I only know what the news has reported. That is, in response to a threat from the Middle East, the government will once again scramble satellite signals so that, with a handheld GPS, we can only accurately get within eighty metres of a designated set of coordinates."

"What about GeoFind?"

"Because the government has intentionally degraded these satellite signals, adding fifty metres of error horizontally and one hundred metres vertically, I am forced to make the unfortunate decision to cancel GeoFind until Selective Availability is turned off."

Chase sat down on the floor. A wave of verbal protests travelled through the atrium. Mr. C. held up his hand to quiet them.

No, this is not happening, thought Barley. *I am trapped in a nightmare. On second thought though, maybe this is good. I can start again with a clean slate. No missed caches. Hmm.*

"Excuse me, Mr. Czanecki, sir." This was Marcie Redding, the girl from Bellingham. "Will you determine a winner based upon the two days?"

"Impossible, my dear. All competitors need to attempt all clues in order to determine a winner."

Imagine being the president and having the power to flick the switch and screw up not only the GeoFind competition but also the hunt for a kidnapped child. Barley had come here worried that he wouldn't be able to explain what had happened to him yesterday. Now the whole contest was off.

And what about the boy, Benjamin? What would happen to him?

21

Green Lake, Call from Phyllis

Barley went back out in the humid summer air and turned on his phone to see if he had a missed call from one of Mr. C.'s assistants. Sure enough, there was a message from last night explaining exactly what he had just heard in person. This was too much to take in. He had to go home and try to digest it all. He put his phone into its sheath and unlocked his bike. He was about to get on when he heard the flock of seagulls squawking. He pulled the phone back out and saw Phyllis Henderson's name on the identification panel. Couldn't she just leave him alone?

Barley leaned the bike against his leg and clicked to answer. "What the frig is it, Phyllis?"

"Barley, uh listen, how's your nose?"

He practically spit on the phone. "It's broken, you psychopath."

"Oh, well think about what you're gonna say next time you speak." She paused. "I'm here with Fred, and…"

"You're on a first-name basis with that loser now? How'd he know to call you?"

"Pardon?"

"I said: how did Newton know where to find you?"

"I don't know, Barley. He's a cop. That's his job. Plus, we were in the newspaper, remember?"

Oh yeah, he had forgotten that. "Where is he now?"

"He had to make a phone call. He knows I'm asking you for help."

"If you think I'm helping him, forget it. He's got Miss Reigning Champ with him now. Why are you helping him, Phyllis?"

"GeoFind was called off so, I dunno... He spoke to Mom and she said it was OK."

"How did you know about GeoFind getting cancelled?"

"One of those weird alien assistants called and told me last night. I asked if she had got through to you. She said she hadn't reached you yet, and that you hadn't even checked in after your first cache. She worried you may have fallen... That's why I came to your house, to see if you were all right and to tell you..." She paused. "Anyway, after I left your place, Fred called and asked me to help. I figured you were helping too. I wanted to ask you what it was all about, but..." She paused again. "I'm not sure what I'm doing really. It's all so weird."

Curiosity suddenly got the better of Barley, and for a minute he couldn't help but think of the hair clipping and the hat, and wonder what they would find next. "Weird in what way? Where are you? What did you find?"

"We're at a provincial camp site on the south end of Green Lake."

"Green Lake? I thought the cache was near Williams Lake?"

"It is. It's not too far from where I grew up actually. Between Clinton and 100 Mile House. Anyway, we found this piece of plumbing pipe. About five inches long with heavy caps screwed on either end. It was hard to get the end off, but when we did, a slip of homemade paper fell out. It had a note that says: 'Gold equals Greed' and a black-and-white postcard with these two men standing on springboards coming out of a massive tree trunk. There's a crosscut in the tree between them with a third man lying on it. On the back, besides new coordinates, a note was written in red pen. It said: Hi, Dad. Wish you were here.'"

"No homemade stationary with a tree?"

"No, just a postcard, but when Fred saw it, he lost his mind. I have no idea what's going on."

Barley's mind churned. First a hair clipping. Then a hat. Now a postcard. Gold equals greed? He hoped the boy, Benjamin, was OK. He swallowed.

Then he remembered that he was talking to his arch-enemy. "So, you found a postcard. What do you want me to do about it?"

"The next coordinates are in Barkerville, Barley, but we're stuck here. A storm came through last night with lots of lightning. Everywhere lightning hit, fires broke out. It's so dry up here compared to Surrey; the trees are all dead because of the pine beetle infestation. Now there's a forest fire. Two actually. One north of 100 Mile House and another south towards Clinton. The helicopter can't take off 'cause there's zero visibility with all the smoke."

"Can't you drive? Isn't there an RCMP detachment up there?"

"Yes, but they've closed Highway 97 to the north and south. They've even closed down the road to Little Fort. We're really stuck. It's scary."

She paused again, waiting for Barley to offer assistance.

Barley thought of his mother's words. 'Fred would never have let you get hurt.' This same Fred had dragged Phyllis into the middle of a raging fire. But why should Barley care?

"Barley, we can't get to Barkerville, but you can." Phyllis's voice jolted him back to earth. "Fred says these caches are very important. And we've only got till tomorrow to find the rest."

"What do you mean tomorrow? Is that what the kidnapper said? Newton never mentioned any time limit for finding the caches."

"Kidnapper?"

"Yes, a boy named Benjamin was kidnapped from a camp on Vancouver Island."

"Oh my God, is that was this is about?"

"Yes, Newton likes to keep his slaves in the dark."

"OK, Barley, listen to me; if this is really a kidnapping, then we have to find all the clues before 5:00 tomorrow when SA comes back."

"Did Newton tell you how many caches are left?"

"No, he doesn't know. No one seems to know. I heard him asking on the phone. Will you go to Barkerville?"

"Ask Newton if he's taken care of the things we discussed."

"You mean the demerit points and speeding ticket and the fact that you were driving a stolen car?"

"Nice to know my private affairs are kept confidential."

"I've been with him all morning, Barley. I can hear everything he says on the phone. He's working on it. You did a lot of damage yesterday."

"The biggest damage yesterday was you breaking my freaking nose."

"You deserved it. And like I said, if you ever compare me, or any other female on the planet, to an STI again, I will cause more damage than a broken nose. You need to show more respect, especially to women."

Barley swallowed. "You done?"

Phyllis cleared her throat. "Yes."

"In that case, how do I get to Barkerville if you're stuck in Green Lake in the helicopter?"

"Fred's got another chopper waiting in Langley."

"Give me the coordinates. I'll see what I can do."

"N 53° 03.34 W 121° 31.119. Did you get them?"

"Yeah, I got 'em." He repeated them back to her.

"And the clue, 'Gold equals Greed'?"

"Got that too."

"Thanks, Barley. Call me back as soon as you find the cache."

22

Barkerville

Martin took one look at Barley's shiner and whistled. "Whoo-wee, someone got you good."

Barley sighed. He was tuckered out—physically, from all the peddling, and emotionally too. "Yeah, a girl."

"No kidding? She knows how to throw a punch."

"You don't have to tell me."

"Didn't think I'd see you back on board."

Barley shrugged. "And I thought you were in Green Lake." .

"Nope, another pilot was on the early shift. This bird was in for maintenance until ten minutes ago." Martin patted the console. "Got that av gas smell taken care of."

"That's a relief." Barley did up his seat belt.

"Yep. The weather's not good in Barkerville though. Hope you packed a rain jacket," said Martin, looking at Barley's light shirt and cotton pants. "I've got an extra one if you need it."

Barley thought of his jacket soaked with Newton's blood. The incident with the Lorax seemed like it had happened in another lifetime.

Except for the roar of the rotor blades, they flew along

in silence. Barley picked up a copy of the *Cloverdale Reporter*. "Is it OK if I read this?"

"Sure," said Martin. The front page had a new picture of Benjamin Fagan. It looked like one of those school shots with the fake background. He appeared to be wearing a school uniform. "One of the largest criminal investigations in the history of Surrey," read the pull-out quote. "More than sixty police officers are working around the clock to find Benjamin Fagan, son of logging magnate, Phonse Fagan." The rest of the article talked about how the more-than-one-thousand tips that had been left on an anonymous tip line had not brought police any closer to finding the kidnapper. There were also a few quotes from Benjamin's friends, and one from his father saying: "Please don't give up. If you know anything at all, please come forward. One detail, no matter how small or inconsequential, may be the one that brings Benjamin home safely."

Barley folded the paper and reviewed the facts. The kid, Benjamin, disappeared from a camp not far from Cathedral Grove on Vancouver Island. Phonse Fagan, his father, owns the company that's doing the clearcutting at Cathedral Grove. Some of the protesters at Cathedral Grove had been violent. Maybe it was the protesters who abducted Benjamin Fagan from the camp.

Barley had learned about syllogisms at school. He knew enough to know that his reasoning didn't follow the rules of logic. But it seemed to him that the Lorax or one of his friends could be crazy enough to kidnap a child. Was Newton investigating them?

Martin's voice came through the headset snapping Barley out of his thoughts. "Look at the forest," he said. "Beetles have completely decimated the lodge-pole pines."

Barley looked down at the trees; they were evergreen, but they looked deciduous, yellow as if showing off fall colours. That's what Phyllis was talking about, why the fire had spread so quickly around Green Lake. "What a shame. All those trees."

Martin nodded. "I know. They say sometimes fire is a good thing for the forest, helps it regenerate, but it sure doesn't look that way from up here, does it?"

Barley shook his head. "Are we getting close?"

"About twenty minutes away. You ever been to Barkerville?"

It was Barley's turn to nod. "When I was eight."

One summer Barley's parents had taken him on a five-day canoe trip to the Bowron Lakes, just north of Barkerville. The trip is rated one of the top ten canoe excursions in the world, and it didn't disappoint. One their last day, they visited Barkerville, which had been a boomtown until the gold died out in 1870. The fortune seekers drifted away leaving a ghost town. In the late 1950s the provincial government decided to restore about a hundred of the old buildings and turned the site into a tourist attraction.

Just before their descent, Martin spoke up again. "Sergeant Newton told me the cache is apparently smack dab in the middle of Barkerville, but the airport is about two kilometres out of town. That means you're going to have to run from there, I'm sorry to say."

The sky had darkened considerably. Barley could see the mucky puddles pooled on the dirt road as they touched down. It was going to be wet, but he shouldn't get lost. The run looked fairly straight forward. Plus, he had plugged the coordinates into the GPS.

"Here, put this on." Martin handed him his rain jacket.

Barley donned the coat, and hopped down from the helicopter into the chilled air. Barkerville was nowhere near as warm as Cloverdale. Barley began running as fast as he could through the pounding rain. Playing hockey gave him excellent cardio, but he always found running hard. Different muscles. By the time he reached the main gates, he was not only absolutely drenched, but also gasping for air—his bent nose wasn't functioning at full capacity. *Damn that Phyllis.*

He entered the reception area to buy a ticket. Despite the rain, the old gold mining town was swamped with tourists. Weather had no bearing on the number of people coming through the site. Barkerville is the end of a long road, so families were not going to turn back because of a little rain. Inside the main gates, Barley took out his boyscout wallet and paid the ten-dollar entrance fee. The clerk passed him a site map. He needed to get in and out as quickly as possible. He was so cold and wet he was actually shaking. People were staring at his face, which he was sure did not look pretty with its black eye and swollen nose. At last view, his cheek was turning purple.

The air stank of burning brush and a group of fire fighters wearing neon orange shirts gathered outside the door drinking from thermoses and a large water dispenser.

Barley approached the closest firefighter, who had a gas mask hanging below his soot-stained face. "Is it safe?" Barley nodded towards the billows of smoke rose up from the fires, which were scattered all around the perimeter of the site.

"Oh yeah, no worries. We're doing controlled brush fires to create a buffer zone between the trees and the heritage buildings."

Ah, so it wasn't like the forest fires that had trapped Phyllis and Newton. Barley took out his father's GPS and followed it past the gift shop where a group of children panned for gold under an overhang that protected them from the pounding rain. They shifted tin bowls in a water trough, and one young boy was hopping around with a huge grin showing off a miniature glass bottle full of water topped with a cork. He shook the bottle in front of his face, mesmerized by the twirling gold dust inside. Barley remembered doing the exact same thing with his parents. Afterwards his father had taken him into the saloon where he pretended to pay for drinks with the gold dust. Barley remembered protesting. He wanted to keep his gold. His father laughed and told him not to worry, they'd get some more on their way out. Barley drank his root beer but wasn't happy until his father admitted he was joking. He bought Barley a coonskin cap to make up. It was still hanging on the corner of the mirror in his bedroom.

Barley made his way past dirt mounds; several groundhogs popped out of holes, scurried a few feet, and disappeared down into others. They smelled like Colin's hamster when he got wet. Barley was surprised he could smell anything with his damaged nose.

A horse-drawn carriage stopped to take on passengers. A morose-looking man wearing a black hat and vest sat atop a red wooden stagecoach with bright yellow wheels. "Whoa Nellie," he said, tugging on the reins. Barley hopped aboard to travel down the brown sludgy street past two banjo-playing interpreters strumming out Hank Williams tunes on the wooden boardwalk under the shelter of an awning. The whole town was grey. Or brown. With patches of dull green grass and dark green trees in the distance. It was like an old black-and-white picture that someone had colour enhanced just the tiniest bit. Rain pinged off the canvas covering. Barley didn't want to leave the shelter of the buggy, but when the GPS told him to veer right, he hopped off into the relentless rain and stood before St. Saviour's old wooden church which was covered with faded grey clapboard, a bell tower on the roof.

From there, Barley followed the black Magellan to the steps of the Richfield Courthouse. The needle started spinning, and Barley felt something take hold of his heart, but it wasn't the same feeling of excitement and anticipation he felt with normal caches, caches that didn't involve kidnapped boys with red hair. He opened the heavy door, water dripping off Martin's jacket to the old oak floorboards. The wooden benches were full to overflowing. There was some sort of judicial re-enactment happening. The number of visitors probably had more to do with the rain outside than actual interest in judicial proceedings. A young actor dressed like a judge in black robes with red trim and full white wig glared at him. "What is the reason for this intrusion?" he bellowed.

Barley gave no answer.

"Well, sit down then," said the judge.

"What an ass," he heard himself say. The judge was too far away to make out the words, but he understood the gist of them. "I will not have you make a mockery of this court." He came and dragged Barley to the front of the room. Powder flew from his wig.

"This man has no respect for authority," the judge announced to the seated audience. "I hereby sentence him to ten years hard labour." A cheer ran through the crowd. The people looked as if they would be happy to see Barley lynched. He was like Alice trapped in Wonderland.

The judge's eyes began giving him the once over. The black eye. The swollen nose. Then his eyes lowered to the GPS. "And what is this treasonous weapon?" He grabbed it like a gull stealing a French fry from the garbage.

"Give that back." Barley attempted to extract the machine from his grasp.

"You'll get it back after you serve your debt to society." He let out a maniacal cackle and banged his gavel—thwack—on the wooden podium. The sound resonated through the small building. "This court is adjourned." The smiling audience applauded and began moving from their seats and grudgingly pulling up hoods and zipping jackets before they filed out into the rain. Some hung back to take photos of the inside.

The judge came out of character to return the GPS. "That's probably the last time you'll interrupt court proceedings in Barkerville, hey. What is that thing anyway?"

"It's a global positioning system," said Barley. "And next time you think about touching it, I'd recommend you take a long look at your fingers first because you may lose them." *God, where had that come from?*

The stragglers averted their eyes. The judge looked embarrassed. Barley walked over to the east wall of the building and realized that the cache was outside, maybe underneath the building. The judge followed him out the door and down the steps into the driving rain. Barley took a reading: the GPS directed him about thirty feet to the right. He got down on all fours and looked under the courthouse, which was raised on wooden beams. The judge started to say something but was interrupted by a family asking him to pose for a picture. Barley was relieved to get rid of him.

A small green-and-white Export A tobacco tin lay in the scrubby grass near a concrete support. A faded Zellers price tag was still stuck to the side near the tiny round picture of the Scottish lady. $5.86. This tin had been around a while. Barley twisted off the lid. The thick odour of tobacco filled his nostrils. It reminded him of Newton on the ski hill.

He pulled a Polaroid from the tin, careful to shelter it from the rain. The picture showed Benjamin Fagan in what looked like the door of a tent. It was definitely the same boy from the news. He had same dark eyes and a scar through his bushy unibrow. His face was turned away from the lens, looking at something outside the frame.

Once Barley established that new coordinates were listed on the same paper embossed with the tree, he shoved the photo and paper back in the tin and took off.

On his way back towards the main entrance, Barley

passed a bakery next to the blacksmith's shop, and hunger hit him like a kick to the ribs. He had no time for food though. He wondered if Phyllis and Newton were still stuck at Green Lake. He ran all the way through town, in and out the gift shop packed with stuffed groundhogs and miners' hats, and back to the chopper. Fifteen minutes after Barley set out, Martin pulled him aboard. "Change into this," he said, handing Barley a dry hoodie. He also gave him a thermos filled with turkey soup. "Wife made it," he said, smiling.

Barley didn't bother with a spoon. He brought the thermos to his lips and felt the warm fluid gush all the way to his stomach. He sighed. "Tell her thank you. She saved me."

Barley was happy to leave Barkerville with its puddles and smoke and rain. It wasn't until they were airborne, headphones installed, that he opened the tin again.

"What's in this one?" Martin asked, his tone sober.

"It's a picture of the boy, Benjamin." Barley held up the Polaroid. "I can't explain it, but he sort of looks dopey."

"I see what you mean." Martin breathed in over his teeth. "Coordinates?"

"They're south. Down near the border. I'll look them up." Barley pressed several buttons on the GPS and used the tiny mouse to find the proper map. "Yep, White Rock."

White Rock, back where it all started with Phyllis.

"I'm gonna call Phyllis. She's with Newton."

"Hopefully, you'll get service. I find it iffy out here."

Barley went to his contacts and found Phyllis's number. He had no idea why he kept it. He'd have to get Newton to pay the long-distance bill. His mother was going to have a conniption.

Newton answered Phyllis's phone. "Barley, are you ok?"

Barley gritted his teeth. He explained about the photo. "Do you know if the kidnappers set up the caches ahead of time or as they went along."

"We don't know."

"Well, do you know how many are left?"

"No idea. Is there a clue?" Newton sounded weary.

"Yeah, it says: 'A line has been crossed.' The coordinates are near the border at Peace Arch Park."

"Good work, Barley. Please ask Martin to take the chopper back to Langley. He's needed elsewhere. Once you land, go over there right away." He sounded like an army colonel.

Yes, Sir, Colonel, Sir. That's what Barley felt like shouting into the little phone. Of course, he wanted to help find Benjamin, but he would have appreciated being asked. He should tell Newton where to go. "Are you still at Green Lake?" he said instead.

"Yes, the roads are blocked. Not just to the north. The one to the south too. And we can't fly because of the smoke. Plus, we didn't know where the next coordinates would be. They could have been farther north than Barkerville, so we wouldn't have driven south even if we could have."

"That makes sense. Any leads on who the kidnappers are?"

"I can't discuss that with you, Barley."

"Do you think it's one of the tree huggers on Vancouver Island?"

There was a shuffling sound for a few seconds, and then Phyllis's voice cut in. "Hi, Barley. Thanks for finding that cache."

"Mm." Barley grunted. He was still fuming about his nose, but he couldn't help but think about what Phyllis had said earlier. He probably shouldn't have called her a venereal disease.

"A simple 'you're welcome' would suffice. Do you know where the next cache is?"

"Right at the border in White Rock."

"What are the coordinates?"

"You don't trust me?"

"It's not that. I just..." Phyllis paused. "I like to double-check things."

"N 49° 00.103 W 122° 45.377."

"You're spot on. They are at the border."

"Imagine that."

"Barley. Listen, when Fred and I get out of here, when this thing is over, we'll sit down and talk. For now, though, can you just help without being nasty?"

"Why should I?"

"We're friends."

"If punching someone in the nose is what you do to your friends, I'd hate to be your enemy." With that, Barley slid the Blackberry into its sheath, thinking how nice it was to be able to obliterate someone so easily.

23

Benjamin

Benjamin lies on the floor of the tent. It is dark and rain pounds on the nylon fabric; the fly sticks to the walls, and water drips on his face. He feels groggy and has trouble sitting up. A mental fog envelops him. He tries to fight his way out of it, but he feels so heavy. There's a topo map folded in the front mesh pocket of the backpack. He wants to take it out, find out where he is.

But he's been warned not to touch anything.

Or else.

24

Illegal Alien

N 49° 00.103, W 122° 45.377

Back in Langley, the sun was still high in the sky, a flaming ball that the area had not seen for months until its re-emergence earlier that week. Barley still had a chill from the rain up north, however, and Martin suggested he hold on to the hoodie until he got home.

"Thanks, Martin. I'll make sure my mother gives it to Newton."

"Take care of yourself," called Martin, as Barley mounted his bike and headed home for a change of clothes.

Stanley's whole body shook with glee when he saw his new friend. He brought his wet nose over to Barley's face and touched his cheek. How was Barley going to abandon the dog again?

After a change of clothes and a snack, Barley had made up his mind. The Douglas border crossing wasn't far by bike, less than twenty kilometres. He would take Stanley with him. He was a big dog with long legs. He could jog alongside the bike. Barley shoved a handful of Milk-Bones in his pocket, found a proper leash on a coat hook, and took the dog and bike outside. For the first hundred metres or so, Stanley hopped along like a kangaroo. But then, he slowed to a canter.

It turned out that twenty kilometres was extremely far for a dog. Stanley might look like a racehorse, but he was not a runner. That was established within minutes. Although Barley let him off the lead, Stanley sort of ran on an angle rather than straight on. As Barley pedaled down Highway 99 to reach White Rock, drivers turned their heads to see the lunatic who took a pony-sized dog for a run on a highway.

Barley's Blackberry rang with its chorus of seagulls. He paused to let the dog catch up but didn't bother to take the phone from its sheath. "Phyllis will just have to wait," he told Stanley. "She's not my friend. In fact, I hate her." Stanley raised an eyebrow. He was not convinced.

By the time they arrived at Peace Arch Park, the dog was moving sideways like a crab. Barley poured some water into his hand and gave Stanley a drink. This seemed to revive him sufficiently to continue.

Barley had a jittery feeling in his stomach. He assumed it was because he was worried about the boy, but it was something else too. For months before he died, Barley's father had talked about going to the border with Barley to find the exact place where the GPS would lock onto 49 degrees north, zero minutes, and zero seconds. And now Barley was here, albeit without his father. Would 49 degrees be right on the line between the US-Canada border?

Barley always thought it would until now that he realized the American crossing and the Canadian crossing lay east to west and not north to south. They were also about a football field apart. He had never really taken note the dozen or so times he had driven to Washington with his parents.

Barley and his father had watched a movie about the surveyors who marked the original Canada-US boundary in the mid-nineteenth century. Some of them started just west of the Great Lakes in Ontario and the others near the Red River settlement in Manitoba; their goal was to draw a straight line across half a continent using rudimentary instruments. They had no roads, no electricity, and most importantly, no satellite precision. Barley couldn't imagine how they managed. They forged along the 49th parallel across rivers and streams, down into valleys, and up over mountains. When they finally met, one group was just a few metres north of the other. Barley knew he was a geography geek, but he thought their precision was amazing—astounding, in fact; they had strayed off the line by such a small margin.

He remembered his father quoting a Canadian diplomat named Hugh Llewellyn Keenleyside. "The boundary between Canada and the United States is a typically human creation; it is physically invisible, geographically illogical, militarily indefensible, and emotionally inescapable."

It fascinated Barley, and today he wanted nothing more than to lock onto 49 degrees north, zero minutes, and zero seconds. It would be like communicating with his father.

He gently tugged on the leash, telling Stanley it was time to move on. Stanley would have none of it. His new best friend was a snack vendor wearing a huge red hat in the shape of a maple leaf.

"OK, OK, I'll get you a hot dog." Barley lined up behind a man who had emerged from a purple pick-up truck with an outhouse strapped to the back.

A big electronic sign next to the hot dog stand warned people heading to the US to expect a forty-five-minute wait. Barley was relieved they wouldn't actually have to cross the border. The coordinates were north of the 49th parallel in Peace Arch Park. He would just pick up the cache and move on. By then Newton and that spaz should be on their way home. And Barley would be off the hook.

But the boy... he kept thinking of the boy. Benjamin. He had left the Export A tin with Martin to deliver back to the police station.

In each lane, at least fifty cars were snaking slowly towards the US, every one stopping several minutes at the check-in booths. Some cars were directed to pull in for further inspection. "That's a lot of cars for a weekday," Barley said to the hotdog vendor.

"Yep," he said. "Tomorrow's the first of July. Be even worse then."

A quick glance at Barley's watch confirmed that the next day, Thursday, was indeed July 1st. *People must be getting a head start on the Canada Day long weekend. Good thing we don't have to wait in that line,* thought Barley, as he opened his cub-scout wallet and passed his last ten-dollar bill over to the man. Stanley wolfed down the foot-long, bun and all, in three chomps. He belched and took a long pee on a huge crimson king maple.

Barley dragged the sheet of homemade paper from his pocket; it was crumpled but he could still read the words: "A line has been crossed." He double-checked the coordinates on his father's Magellan against those on the paper. The cache was straight to the east. Stanley had other ideas and began pulling to the west, towards the flower beds and cherry trees and the Pacific Ocean beyond. Barley looked towards the forty-foot drop to the mud flats; the tide was coming in, and the salty ocean smell mixed with the early summer flowers. A horizontal white sign said *USA Canada Border: No Trespassing* in bold black letters, train tracks just beyond. He pulled Stanley south past a gardener dispensing some sort of noxious chemical from a big pack on his back. He looked like a Ghostbuster. Stanley sneezed, then stopped to relieve himself yet again on a small obelisk commemorating the Treaty of Washington.

"Man, Stanley, do you have to leave your mark everywhere?" They walked alongside the line of vehicles until they reached the sign that said *Welcome to the United States of America.* Barley took a reading hoping he'd lock in on N 49° 00.000.

No go. The GPS screen read N 49° 00.122. *If I had put up that sign, I would have made darn well sure it was right on 49,* he thought. He'd try to lock on to 49 again after he had the cache. The sun was beginning its westward dance towards the horizon. Barley realized he had to get a move on.

The arrow on the GPS pointed southeast. It looked like it might be past American customs. *But it couldn't be. Or could it?*

Barley hoped it was wrong. He took a few more steps towards a stylized *Welcome to the United States of America* sign showing the Statue of Liberty and Mount Rushmore and another standard sign telling pedestrians to check in on the east side of the building. Barley certainly couldn't cross an international border. He didn't have any ID on him thanks to the thieves in Hope. Even if he did have his wallet, Stanley would probably need papers too.

What to do? He certainly wasn't going to peddle home for his birth certificate. It would take an hour—maybe two with Stanley—to ride home and then back to Peace Arch. Forget that, Stanley would keel over belly up if he had to run that distance again.

Even if he had his license, he didn't have time to wait in that line. Mr. Czanecki said Selective Availability would be back at 5:00 tomorrow. Thursday. Canada Day. They had to find Benjamin Fagan before that. After 5:00 tomorrow, scrambled satellite signals would render the GPS useless. It would be like finding a creased treasure map that was wet and falling apart; you wouldn't be able to read the clues.

Barley figured his only choice was to sneak across the border, get the cache, and scoot back before anyone noticed. A high hedge separated the line of cars from the railway tracks and the Pacific Ocean. According to the GPS, if he ducked behind the hedge, he'd have to run about seventy-five metres. As long as the cache wasn't too hard to find, it should only take a couple of minutes, max. He could do it.

Then he remembered Stanley. Three children were pointing and calling, "Here, Giant Puppy Dog," from the side door of a van, which was open to let in air while they waited in line. That's when Barley realized it would be impossible to sneak across an international border with a Great Dane in tow. He took another look at the snaking line of vehicles before making up his mind. He led Stanley behind the twenty-foot hedge and tied him on near the railway tracks, far from prying eyes. Before he left him, he nuzzled his forehead, took a Milk-Bone from his pocket, and deposited it into Stanley's eager mouth. He would run the last bit on his own.

When Barley reached the end of the hedge, the arrow on the screen veered left, east towards the blue-topped US Customs Building. In order to reach the site, Barley still had to navigate through some painful-looking black-berry bushes. A chain link fence separated him from the US side of the border. Four American customs officials in dark blue uniforms were busy interrogating people who had been instructed to pull in under a shelter and pop their trunks.

Barley took a deep breath and jumped the fence. Then he meandered as nonchalantly as he could across the road separating him from the border patrol officers. He could see their gun holsters. Glock 17s. He wouldn't have known that except he saw a news piece about the Canadian border guards whining about not having guns like their American counter-parts. The GPS led him to a small landscaped area to the south of the guards, a rock garden with low-lying bushes and red berries. Barley started to dig amongst the shrubbery, pushing leaves out of the way to see if a bucket could be hidden underneath. He got down on one knee and ... felt something touch his shoulder.

"Where're you headed?" said a southern accent. The black man was lean with short cropped hair and delicate features. His dark cap had the letters CBP across the front. As Barley tucked the GPS into its holster, he felt the officer noting his every move, taking in the black eye and swollen nose. He was scarier than yesterday's traffic cop.

"I wasn't trying to sneak in," Barley gulped. "I just have to pick something up and then I'm going right back to Canada."

"Sure, you are," said the man. His nametag read *Jackson.* "And what, might I ask, are you picking up?"

"Nothing," said Barley, turning back towards Canada. *Forget the cache. Forget Phyllis. Forget Newton.* But he couldn't forget Benjamin. He changed tact. "I'm helping out with a police investigation."

"I see. You're pretty banged up. Why don't you come with me, son, and tell us all about it?" Jackson took Barley by the arm. Barley pulled away; another arsehole calling him his son.

Jackson's fingers pinched his skin. "Calm down, cowboy. I just need you to answer a coupla questions." He indicated towards the white building topped with a blue stripe.

"No." Barley tried to run back towards the fence and Stanley. He didn't want to deal with this man anymore. He only got a few strides away when another officer blocked his path. This one had his gun drawn.

"First runner of the week," said Jackson. "Said he's just here to pick up a package and then he'll be on his way."

"Fancy that," said the second officer, taking Barley by the arm and passing him off to Jackson. Jackson began dragging him towards the US Border Patrol Building.

Before Jackson yanked him inside, Barley caught a glimpse of the white concrete Peace Arch monument almost silhouetted by the five o'clock sun, "The Star-Spangled Banner" on one side. He just made out the words "Children of a Common Mother" before Jackson pulled him inside.

Who the hell is "the common mother"? he thought, as his eyes adjusted to the artificial light in the customs office. Jackson continued to push him toward a door with a sign that read *Detention Room #2.* The room was sparsely furnished with a table, chair, and bench. Barley felt cheated. Not only did he not get the cache, he hadn't locked on to the elusive 49 degrees north either.

"Keep your hands on the table. I am going to empty the contents of your pockets and place them in this bin," said Jackson.

Jackson dropped Barley's housekey and boy-scout wallet into the grey plastic receptacle. Next, he dug three vegetable-flavoured Milk-Bones from the other pocket.

Shoot, Stanley. I should never have left him, thought Barley, trying not to cry.

"Turn around and spread your legs and arms." Jackson gave Barley a pat down. Legs first. Then arms. It wasn't until he got to the torso and felt the belt with all the sheaths that he spoke.

"I am going to remove your belt."

"My pants don't stay up without it." Barley didn't know why he always had to be antagonistic.

"I am going to remove the belt," Jackson repeated in a tone that let Barley know he had no choice.

He slid the leather through the loops on Barley's pants, dropping each sheath separately into the bin as it came off in his hand.

"What have we here?" Jackson asked. "One Blackberry." He removed the machine from its pouch. "One Leatherman tool," he added, removing that as well.

Next came the GPS. "What's this?"

"It's a global positioning system."

"What's it for?"

"I use it to find caches." Barley spoke as if Jackson were hearing impaired.

"What the hell are caches?" Jackson was a typical close-minded Muggle. He looked at Barley like he thought he was psycho.

"Hidden containers. I was picking up a container outside your building when you stopped me."

"A container? What's in this container?"

"I don't know."

"You don't know?" said Jackson, looking as if he had just tasted rotten meat.

"No, but most have things like key chains and golf balls in them."

"Let me get this straight. You're telling me you snuck across an international border to pick up a container full of golf balls?" asked Jackson, picking up Barley's boy-scout wallet and rummaging through it.

"No, well, yes."

Jackson removed a driver's license for one of the three stooges. "Doesn't look like you."

"Nope."

He squinted at the text. "This here is an 1897 driver's license for Moe Howard. Could you please give me your passport?"

"I don't have it on me." Barley thought of the safety deposit box in his mother's closet where all important papers were kept.

"Surely you have some identification on you." Jackson's eyebrows curved into two inverted smiles.

"Sorry, I don't have any ID on me at all." Barley didn't feel so bold anymore.

"You mean to tell me that not only did you attempt to cross an international border without checking with a Customs and Border Protection Officer, you did so with no identification?" Jackson's expression changed from one of incredulity to that of a wolf stalking a hen.

"Honestly, I thought the cache was going to be on the Canadian side."

"Right," said Jackson, making a note in a little hardcover book, his nostrils flaring. "And I thought kittens laid eggs. How long were you intending to stay in the States?"

"I wasn't intending to stay. I was coming right back."

"What is your occupation?"

Barley shook his head. "I'm in high school."

Jackson made a note. "Do you have anything to declare?"

"No, I don't have anything to declare," Barley shouted.

"Relax, cowboy; we're going to be here for a little while…"

Barley didn't hear the end of Jackson's sentence because at that moment the late afternoon tourist train chugged by from Seattle. Barley jumped up. *Stanley! He was alone. Oh God, what have I done?*

"What's up, cowboy?"

"I left my dog tied on down by the train tracks." *What if the train hit him? I've had the dog less than forty-eight hours, and already I am going to lose him, just like Dad. Will Mom go next? Colin? Will everyone I love die?*

"This story just keeps getting better and better," drawled Jackson.

"I have to go get him!"

"You're not going anywhere," said Jackson, as the train whooshed past, its deafening horn blaring. Barley sat back on the bench in a heap. Tears threatened the corners of his eyes. *I will not cry,* he told himself. "Can I please go check on him?"

"Not quite yet. We still have some things to discuss."
Jackson held his pen over the notepad ready to write.
"Where do you live?"

"Cloverdale."

"Where's that?"

"Part of Surrey."

"What business did you have in Washington today?"

"I wanted to find the cache, and then I was going back."

"Ah, the mysterious cache again. I'm going to ask you once more: what's in this cache?"

"I told you, I don't know."

"You don't know? Or you won't say?" said Jackson.

"I don't know."

"Hmm. Well, if you don't know what's in it, then why do you want it?"

"Because it holds a clue to find a kidnapped boy."

"Hold on a minute; now you're talking about a kidnapping?"

"The boy's name is Benjamin. He's the son of some rich logging guy."

"Did you kidnap him?"

"No. I told you already. I'm trying to help the police find him."

"By sneaking across an international border?"

"No, well yes, but only to find a clue. If you don't believe me, you can call the police officer. He's with the Serious Crime Unit in Surrey."

"I wasn't aware the RCMP employs teenagers?"

"Believe me, I wasn't either."

"What's this officer's name?"

"Newton. Sergeant Fred Newton." Barley choked out the words. It was Newton's fault he was in this mess. If his mother hadn't got mixed up with him, Barley wouldn't have been dragged into the whole kidnapping thing.

Jackson made a note.

"Why did he come to you for help? Why not get one of his own men?"

"Because I'm a geocacher, and the kidnapper is using geocaches as clues."

"Back up a bit. The kidnapper is using what?" said Jackson.

"Geocaches. The hidden container I told you about." Barley resigned himself to the fact that he would have to spend his whole life explaining geocaching to people.

Jackson looked blank.

Barley continued. "The thing I was looking for when you stopped me."

"OK. You're going to have to tell me what geocaching is."

"I will if you get me my dog."

"Do you need him to interpret?"

"No, but..."

"I didn't think so. I don't think you're in a position to negotiate." Jackson got up and left the room.

Barley tried to open the door. Locked. He looked through the little window. Jackson was nowhere in sight, but the other customs officer was just outside the door. He started banging on the glass and motioning like someone possessed. The officer ignored him.

A second train whooshed by, its deafening horn blaring. *Poor Stanley.* Even though Barley only had him a couple of days, he suddenly couldn't imagine life without him. Five minutes passed. Ten. Barley held back tears.

The door opened; it was Jackson with a coffee.

"What's up, cowboy? My man says you were looking a little spooked."

"I need to get my dog." Barley felt stomach sick.

"If you can provide me with a number for your father, maybe he can come down here and get this mess sorted out."

"My father's dead." Barley avoided eye contact with Jackson and focused on a non-descript spot on the wall. If he could just have his father back, he would never get in trouble with the law again. He would never insult anyone. He would be polite and kind. But his father wasn't coming back, so what was the sense?

Barley blinked hard. "Please let me check on Stanley."

"Not quite yet. We still have some things to discuss. What you say about the kidnapping case is true," said Jackson.

"Did you think I would lie?"

Jackson smiled as if that was the most amusing thing he'd heard in his life. "Sergeant Newton is stuck in Green Lake."

"I could have told you that," Barley interrupted. "That's why he sent me here."

"They say you have some coordinates for them. They want you to call."

Jackson returned Barley's small grey Blackberry Pearl. "Put it on speaker phone," he ordered.

"Barley, what was in the cache?" Phyllis's usually chipper voice sounded worn, like a holey sock.

"I don't have it yet," he answered.

"What do you mean?"

"I got stopped at the border. You've got to get me out of here."

"You've been gone a long time, Barley." She sounded even more pissed off than last night. "It's been hours since we last spoke."

Barley tried to interrupt to explain about having to ride his bike with Stanley running alongside, but even tired, Phyllis's jet-speed voice was hard to quell. "What have you been doing? Benjamin could die..." She finally paused to take a breath.

"I was just about to get the cache when the customs officers took me in for questioning."

"Yeah, but where were you up till then, Barley?"

Barley felt the energy ebb out of him. He figured there was no sense trying to reason with Phyllis while she was so angry. "Listen, Phyllis, if Newton can get me out of here, I can have the new coordinates for you in less than ten minutes. Then I'll be able to tell you what's in the cache."

"We're already en route. We can be there in less than an hour, Barley. Your services are no longer required."

"But I can find it right now, and then you won't have to waste time here at all."

"Just a few hours ago you weren't too keen to help out. Now that you're stuck, you're all gung-ho."

"I'm worried about Benjamin." Barley knew he sounded lame, but it was the truth.

"You're worried about Benjamin? Benjamin could be dead because of you."

Stanley, too, he thought. "Listen, Phyllis. If it's true that we have less than twenty-four hours before Bush pulls the plug, we're going to have a hard time finding any other caches. So, the quicker we find this cache at the border, the quicker we can find Benjamin."

"We'll be there in no time."

"But the line-up. You should see it."

Jackson, who had remained silent to this point, spoke to Phyllis. "I'll wave you through," he said. "Just ask for Agent Jackson."

"Thank you," said Phyllis. "We'll be driving a silver Mercedes. Rot in hell, Barley Lick."

"Angry lady," said Jackson, removing the Blackberry.

Barley glared at Jackson. "Come on, you have to let me go."

"You're going to be with us for a while," said Jackson. "You're a criminal. An illegal alien."

"But…"

"Sorry, cowboy. No 'buts'. Anyway, you heard what your lady friend said. She doesn't need you anymore."

A knock came on the door, and Jackson rose to leave.

"Where are you going?" asked Barley.

"Quarter to six," he said. "I can't be late for dinner. I'll get the receptionist to come in and call your parents." Jackson made his way to the door.

Not parents. Parent. Singular, thought Barley. Hadn't he just told him his father was dead? "You can't just leave me here. What about Stanley?"

But Jackson had already gone.

Barley was talking to an empty room.

25

Benjamin

Benjamin coughs and rolls on his side. He can feel his throat closing in on itself. It's the smoke from the fire that's causing his breathing passages to contract. Every breath feels like he has to drag it through a tiny straw. He knows he won't last long without his puffers.

He wishes he knew where he was. They have moved again. Benjamin hopes he'll see his father soon. He is tired of travelling and of feeling so groggy. He closes his eyes and imagines his father's face on a screen talking to him, talking to Benjamin and only Benjamin. He is telling Benjamin to stay strong, that he'll come and get him.

Benjamin imagines himself setting out over land to find his father. But he is all alone. All alone in the woods. It is hard to find a path through the old-growth forest without a map. It would take weeks to reach his house even if he knew the way. And what about food and wild animals? What if he runs into another cougar? Maybe next time he won't be so lucky.

He's stupid to think about finding his father.

He is totally at the mercy of one person.

And that person isn't his father.

26

A Nasty Surprise

As Barley watched the seconds tick by on the white clock above the door, he formulated a plan. The next time the door opened, he would make a run for it. He'd whip out the door, hop the fence, and rescue Stanley—if Stanley was still alive for the rescuing.

What about the gun? he thought. *Maybe the receptionist won't have one. But the others will. I'll go for it anyway.What have I got to lose? A bullet to the knee couldn't be worse than being locked up in this claustrophobic room with its stale air. Who am I kidding? It's not like I'm in some sort of western? If only there were a window to the outside, at least I could keep an eye out for Newton.*

Barley couldn't believe he was actually looking forward to seeing Newton. He checked the clock again. More than an hour had passed. He started to panic. He couldn't stay in there any longer. He went to the small window in the door, about six inches square. He peeked out, only to see Newton standing at a wicket.

He started hammering on the door with his fists. Faces shifted; Newton looked almost amused.

Barley kept hammering until the knuckles of his left hand

bloodied, leaving rust-colored stains on the white paint.

Newton was talking to the lady at the counter. *That frigger. How can he leave me here?*

Barley beat harder. A guard arrived, hand on holster. He made a sign for Barley to back up.

Barley pretended to move away, but when the armed man opened the door, Barley tried to push past him. The guard was like six feet of lead. Barley couldn't budge him. "Newton," he screamed. "Get me out of here." Before he could hear Newton's reply, the guard pushed him back in the room and slammed the door with such force, the walls shook.

The guard opened the little window to talk. "Calm down," he said in a monotone. "Or you'll be with us for longer than you'd like."

"I gotta talk to that man out at the counter."

"I don't think so, buddy. And no more crazy stuff, or I'll have to subdue you."

Barley was thinking of ways to get the guy's gun off him when the door opened again. Jackson entered followed by Newton.

He looked up at the gum-chewing mountain. "You have to get me out of here."

"What did you think I was doing?" asked Newton, a hint of a grin forming around his pumping jaws.

"I don't know. Phyllis gave me the impression you were going to leave me to rot in here."

Newton shook his head. "That wouldn't go down very well with your mother now, would it?"

Barley hated him mentioning his mother, and was about to tell him as much when he was interrupted by Jackson,

"See you around, cowboy." Jackson held out the bin with Barley's belt, phone, GPS, multitool, and wallet. Even the Milk-Bones. "Next time you come visit us, be sure to bring some real ID."

Newton raised his eyes and gestured for Barley to follow him outside the building. Once past the door, Barley started booting it towards the fence and the tracks.

"Barley, you trying to get yourself arrested again?"

"I've got to get Stanley."

"Relax. He's over by the car." Stanley was lying on a grey wool blanket looking completely unfazed. In fact, he looked like he was at a doggy spa. Two Canadian customs and border protection officers were rubbing down different ends of his body. Stanley raised his head and looked up at Barley as if suggesting he should come lie down next to him and get a piece of the action.

Barley bent down to make sure he was OK. He didn't want to give him a hug with everyone looking. He had been so sure Stanley was a goner. He willed himself to hold it together. Stanley daintily brought his nose close to Barley's. Barley pulled one of the Milk-Bones from his pocket and used it to lure him towards Newton's car. There was no way Barley was going to make him run alongside the bike again.

Newton arrived and gave Stanley's head a pat. "The guys said to tell you they gave the dog some raw eggs so he shouldn't be too hungry. Said eggs will make his coat shine. Your mother's going to have both our hides when she catches wind of this." He took Barley's chin in his hand and turned it to size up the shiner. "Wow, that girl can pack a punch. I'll say that for her. How's your head?"

"Fine. How's yours?" Barley indicated towards the bandage on the back of Newton's skull.

"I'll be right as rain once the dressing comes off."

"Did Phyllis find the border bucket?"

"You can ask her yourself." Newton indicated towards his Mercedes. "I'll be over in a minute." He turned to talk to another RCMP officer.

Barley stood by the driver's door. The window was

down, and a tartan key chain dangled from the ignition. Phyllis was sitting in the passenger seat. Barley's blood felt as if it had stopped circulating.

"Hi, Barley." Phyllis averted her eyes as soon as they met his face, perhaps shocked at the damage she had inflicted. "Have a nice stay at Hotel Peace Arch?" She was holding a small log-shaped container designed to hide a house key in the garden.

"You're too funny, Phyllis. I see you got the cache. They let you across the border?"

"Yes, it wasn't far. Strange though, I thought those coordinates would be on the Canadian side, being north of 49 and all."

"Me too. So, what's in it?"

"I haven't opened it yet," she said. "I was waiting for Fred to get back."

Newton arrived and stood next to Barley. "Go on, open it up, as long as you've got gloves on. If we're lucky, it'll say, 'Last clue. X marks the spot. Come and pick up Benjamin.'"

"I hope we're lucky," Phyllis's eyes had dark rings underneath. She flipped the container over. When she pulled back the plastic sliding door, an involuntary wave racked her body, and she dropped the container to the floor. She made a noise like she was trying to scream but couldn't get it out. Newton ran around to the passenger, opened the door, and picked up the container. He recoiled. Barley ran around to see what it was. He covered his mouth with his hand and thought he might vomit.

On the carpet next to the plastic log was a severed human finger.

27
The Clock is Ticking

Things happened quickly after that. Newton called to another officer in street clothes and made arrangements for him to take the finger back to the station. Phyllis was bouncing her heels up and down on the passenger seat floor. "Come on, come on, Fred. We've got to go."

Phyllis hadn't looked at Barley since opening the container. He and Stanley had somehow ended up in the back seat with the beige stationary embossed with a tree. The next coordinates were on Grouse Mountain.

"I can go with Newton, you know." Barley pulled Stanley back from climbing up front with Phyllis. "You should go home and get some sleep."

"Why? So Super Barley can take over and save the day?"

"Frig, Phyllis, all I'm saying is you look tired."

"I'm not going home, Barley. We've only got till 2:00 tomorrow to find Benjamin."

"What? Why 2:00? I thought SA comes back at 5:00?"

"I did too. But we just found out it's 5:00 Eastern Time, not Pacific."

"But the press conference was in Oregon. They're the same time zone as us."

"It was. Listen, Barley, I don't know why they announced Eastern Time, but they did." She looked at him then, and he could see regret in her eyes. Regret for breaking his nose? Or regret for screwing things up back in October? He didn't know.

"I'm coming with you to Grouse Mountain," he said. "We just have to pass by my house to drop off Stanley and my bike and let me grab something to eat."

Phyllis put her hand in her jacket pocket and produced two PowerBars. "I don't go anywhere without these." She tried to smile. "What kind do you want? Vanilla or chocolate?"

"Vanilla." He had never eaten a PowerBar before. He was surprised at how chewy it was. Like shoe leather. Stanley was doing his best to have a lick when Newton opened the back door of the Mercedes and held out his hand for Stanley's lead. "My colleague will take your bike and the dog home. Your mother'll be spitting tacks when she hears about your adventure at the border. I'll call her to let her know what's happening."

Barley gave Stanley a rough noogie and handed over the leash.

"So, you really biked all the way here with Stanley?" Phyllis's eyes were round.

"Had no choice. Took a long time though. He's no track star."

Phyllis laughed, a small low laugh but at least she managed that. "Sorry I blamed you for taking so long. I thought you came by helicopter."

Newton arrived and installed his huge frame behind the wheel. Barley leaned forward in his seat. "Newton, you do know that whoever is setting up these clues is very familiar with geocaching, don't you?"

"I do." He looked at Barley in the rearview.

"So, have you checked all the geocaching.com profiles?"

"Investigators are in the process of working through them," he said. "So far there are no matches. The people I work with, Barley, they're experts. They work Amber Alert cases every day. They know how to profile a kidnapper."

"What have they found?"

"That's classified..."

"Information." Barley finished for him.

"What I can tell you is that you might be surprised by what they have found."

28

Grouse Mountain

N 49° 22.986, W 123° 04.724

Grouse Mountain was home to two grizzly bears named Grinder and Coola. Grinder, the smaller one, swaggered back and forth on a huge log, swiping at nothing and growling menacingly as Barley and Phyllis searched the paved path skirting the enclosure. Coola was shoulder deep in a small pond eating a whole watermelon. Newton searched the surrounding trees. Gusts of wind brought the musky pong of damp bear fur to Barley's nostrils.

They had been searching for over an hour. Tourists came and went, hanging over the handrail on the viewing platform.

"We should check underground," said Barley.

"You know you're not allowed to bury a cache, Barley. It's against the rules," said Phyllis.

"Kidnapping is against the rules too."

"True enough." Phyllis shivered in the elevated air. The temperature was dropping quickly as the wind picked up, and the surrounding trees provided little shelter. "Do you think someone found it before us?"

"No, but could you have made a mistake with the coordinates?" Barley kept his eyes down when he spoke.

"What do you take me for, Barley? Today is not the first time I picked up a GPS, you know."

"All right. Now you know how I felt when you questioned the border."

Barley's stomach grumbled, and a headache had taken over the space behind his black eye. He was also dehydrated, but thoughts of the nine-fingered kid with the unibrow pushed the hunger and thirst from his mind.

Newton reappeared. He'd examined every inch of the trees and gardens around the enclosure. "Anything hanging off the fence?" he asked.

"Nope, and I don't think the cache is in with the bears." Phyllis rubbed her forehead with her open hand.

"I wouldn't be so sure," Barley answered. "What's the clue again?"

Phyllis sighed. "There are some places boys shouldn't go."

"That sounds like it's in with the bears."

"It can't be in with the bears, Barley," said Phyllis.

"It has to be. I've searched the ground. There's nothing hidden in dead leaves. There's no freshly turned soil."

"I'm going to check the perimeter again." Newton backed away, almost hitting a young couple strolling arm in arm. The man said something, and the woman laughed.

"We've been over it a dozen times." Phyllis sounded exasperated. Her stomach was also audibly announcing the fact it was way past suppertime.

"OK, then. See anything in the trees?" Barley looked up at the darkening sky.

"Nope. No bags. No tape. No buckets," said Phyllis. "Just one of those birdhouses the park rangers put up."

"That's it," said Barley.

"What? The birdhouse?"

"Yes, the birdhouse. Show me." He perked up like a squirrel.

Phyllis pointed out a tree overhanging the bears' enclosure. The trunk was outside the enclosure on the path. Sawed off branches jutted out of the trunk.

"There are some places boys shouldn't go."

A white birdhouse with a little black hole and peaked roof dangled from a branch thirty feet up. Barley was up the tree in no time. He removed the house from the branch and started working his way back down. He was five feet from the ground when the branch he was standing on cracked. The impact of hitting the ground, back first, winded him. Grinder rose up on his hind legs sniffing the air. Coola ditched the last bites of the watermelon and ambled out of the pond towards Barley.

Barley dropped the bird house and ran, lunging at the fence. Grinder pawed at his leg, ripping the denim and slicing the skin on his calf. Luckily, the barbed wire was angled out to make it difficult to access the enclosure from the outside, but easier to navigate from inside the pen. Barley scaled the fence before the grizzlies had a chance to pull him back in. He jumped wide and cleared the barbed wire but landed hard and rolled into a rock wall. "Whoa," he groaned. He tried to get up but decided it was best to just lie there, on the ground, panting, while a crowd gathered around him. He could see the agitated bears scratching and sniffing on the other side of the chain link fence.

"Oh my God…" said one woman.

"Did you see that?" said a boy of about ten.

A man broke away from his family and ran to the building to alert staff. Three park attendants came running; a manager appeared with stun gun in hand.

Newton took charge. "It's OK, everyone. Calm down." Out of earshot of the visitors, he explained to a manager about the RCMP investigation. The manager went back inside, reappeared with a long metal pole with a hook on one end, and retrieved the bird house.

The black hole on the house was not a hole at all. Just painted on, an illusion. How could the kidnapper have got it up there without someone noticing? Could he be an employee?

Barley scanned the curious faces to see if anyone looked like a psycho. Wearing gloves, Phyllis removed the stick perch, and the roof slid off to reveal an open Swiss Army knife with a sheet of the homemade tree stationary speared to the end. The words "Where twins and redwoods meet" were written alongside the coordinates.

Barley found a bench and sat himself down while a park interpreter patched up his leg. Phyllis looked up the coordinates. Even though he was slightly dazed, Barley could tell they indicated a site in Surrey. About two degrees east of Peace Arch.

"South Surrey. Redwood Park, you know it?" Phyllis looked at Barley.

"I know it; largest stand of redwoods north of California."

Phyllis looked at Newton. "Bang him on the head and he's still amazing." She shook her head and smiled.

"He does know the lay of the land."

Barley guessed he wasn't in their bad books anymore. "Let me take a look at the knife."

Newton passed him a sealed baggy in which the knife sat, blade still out.

Barley examined the blade. Two letters were engraved in tiny font. BF.

29

The First Clue

Newton pulled into a gas station to buy sandwiches and drinks. "It's too dark to search at Redwood Park tonight," he said, biting into his ham and cheese.

"We're running out of time," said Phyllis. "When SA gets turned on at 2:00 tomorrow, it's game over. The GPS will only be able to bring us within eighty metres of the cache sites."

Barley stopped chewing and turned to Newton. "Yeah, you're going to have to tell us what you know."

"He's right," said Phyllis. "I know you're not supposed to, but we have a better chance of locating Benjamin if we know what you do."

Newton sighed, took a final bite of sandwich, and jammed the remainder in the paper bag. "Benjamin Fagan was at a week-long Outdoor Extreme Camp on Vancouver Island. The day before he's due home, his father, Phonse Fagan receives a call from the head camp counsellor saying that Benjamin hasn't come back from the orienteering exercise that morning and a search party has been organized. He doesn't tell Mr. Fagan, but he tells me later, that they fear Benjamin may have been victim of a cougar attack since a mother and her cub had been spotted in the area."

"Before Mr. Fagan flies to the island, he goes into his son's room to grab some of his clothes for a sniffer dog. That's when he notices the GPS on Benjamin's pillow. He's never known his son to own a GPS."

Barley interrupted. "Was there a note with the first coordinates?" asked Barley.

"It's classified."

"If you keep holding back stuff from us…"

"OK. OK. It said: 'Mr. Fagan, now that I have your attention, I'd like to take you on a mystery tour.'"

"That's it?"

"Yes." Newton nodded.

"On the same paper as the other clues? With the tree?"

"Yes, the note was wrapped around the GPS and secured with an elastic. So, Mr. Fagan calls the police. We send a constable to the house to size up the GPS. She turns it on and finds only one set of coordinates plugged into the machine's memory. That's when they conclude that a kidnapper has deliberately left these coordinates for Mr. Fagan to find. And that's how Phonse Fagan ended up in my office."

"Why?"

"Because kidnapping that crosses judicial boundaries is considered a serious crime."

"I know that," said Barley. "I meant, why you?"

"Because I'm the superintendent of the Serious Crime Unit."

Barley shut up then. He knew Newton worked in Serious Crimes; he didn't realize he was the head of it.

"So, if you figured that if you went to that exact spot, you'd find Benjamin, why didn't you just go to the cache site with Mr. Fagan?"

"Because we thought we'd find Benjamin, and we didn't know what kind of shape he'd be in." Newton took a swig of his coffee. "It seemed prudent to keep Mr. Fagan here."

"Why not just send the constable who went to his house?" asked Barley.

"Because she recommended we get you or Phyllis to help. She saw the interviews you did with the *Cloverdale Reporter* about the contest. I had met you, so I called M.J. for your number."

"Anything else you're not telling us?"

"Just that our handwriting analyst concluded that it may be a woman we're looking for."

"I can't picture a woman chopping off a nine-year-old's finger." Phyllis scrunched up her nose.

"I'm hoping that she won't do worse than that." Newton balled up his napkins and stuffed them in with the half-eaten sandwich.

"Also, the boy, Benjamin, is asthmatic, and his puffers were left at the camp when he disappeared. His father is worried that he may need them."

"That's not good," said Phyllis.

"No, that's not good at all." Newton nodded, and his phone sounded from his pocket.

He picked up and excused himself while he got out of the car.

Before Phyllis and Barley had a chance to talk, Newton opened the door and said: "Barley, I need you to do something for me."

"What?"

"Open the battery door on the Garmin and see if there's a number written on the inside."

"Why?"

"Just do it."

Barley twisted the attached semi-circular key to open the door. "There is."

"OK, read it out."

"It says: FC5974."

Newton's voice read the code into the phone and hung up.

"What is it?" asked Barley.

"Not sure," said Newton. "Listen, in the morning, I have to meet with my team. Go over some things. I'm going to get you two to drive to Redwood Park without me. I'll catch up with you once you find the clue."

"Sounds good," said Barley, "except, you know, I don't have a car."

"I can drive," said Phyllis. "Come to my house for 8:00 and we'll go together."

30

Thursday, Where Twins and Redwoods Meet

N 49° 02.144, W 122° 43.565

Barley dreamed he was standing in front of the stucco house on 62A Avenue, and there, sitting in the glider rocker on the wooden verandah, was his mother. He could tell by the expression on her face that she was doing one of her cryptic crossword puzzles.

She looked up, not at all surprised to see him there, and said: "There are only two kinds of people in this world, those who finish crossword puzzles and those who don't."

"What about those who don't do them at all?" he asked.

"They're not worth considering." She filled in an answer, not with a pencil but some sort of makeup wand. After she finished writing, she began applying blue eyeliner to her right eye. She stopped and looked directly at Barley; her iris had turned blue like a Siamese cat's.

Colin, who often showed up in Barley's dreams, said: "Hey M.J., you're pretty hot for a forty-five-year-old."

Barley's mother turned and licked Colin's cheek with a little pink tongue.

Barley jolted awake. Stanley was standing over him licking his face. At least it wasn't his mother licking his best friend. He pushed the dog away. The dream had seemed so real that it took Barley a few seconds to adjust to his waking state. He sniffed and smelled bacon. He could hear his mother banging around downstairs in the kitchen. What was she even doing home? It was a weekday, wasn't it?

Ever since his father died, Barley never knew quite what to expect from his mother. It was as if she wanted to change everything about her life. She renovated the house. Inside and out. She started wearing makeup. Before this year, Barley had only ever seen her wear lipstick once. Now she wore it every day. She even started putting that black goop on her eyes.

Stanley stepped off the bed, and Barley sank back into his pillow and tried to imagine his mother how other people saw her. Her hair was still its natural colour. But he thought she must do that Botox thing to her forehead, because he seemed to remember her with more wrinkles when his father was alive than she had now.

Ever since Barley had started school, she had worked as secretary to the mayor. She seemed to enjoy working in the mayor's office, but in February after her bereavement leave, Mary Jane Lick announced that she was taking a new job in marketing for the town of Cloverdale. Her duties included wheeling and dealing to get movie producers and directors to consider Cloverdale, as opposed to downtown Vancouver, for their projects.

"But why?" asked Barley, meaning why did she leave the mayor's office.

"Vancouver gets lots of movies," she said. "Cloverdale needs to fight for its piece of the pie."

He didn't bother explaining that she had misunderstood his question. Maybe she had understood but didn't know the answer herself. Death does strange things to the people it leaves behind. He went along with her.

"We've got *Smallville*." *Smallville* was Canadian TV's answer to Superman and kryptonite, and had been filming in Cloverdale for seven or eight seasons.

"We need big movies, Barley. Hollywood movies. Blockbusters."

Barley didn't know what to think of her makeover. The house looked amazing. But the new job kept his mother super busy. Her old job had been great. She could get time off almost whenever she wanted. Now she couldn't even find time to switch over the stupid ownership on the Corvette.

He lay there for a moment feeling his nose. The throbbing had subsided. And, when he got up and looked in the mirror, he saw the swelling had gone down quite a bit.

He dressed quickly, then headed to the kitchen, taking the stairs two at a time, Stanley on his heels. As long as his mother didn't have cat eyes, everything would be OK.

Barley watched the expression on his mother's face to gauge how much she knew about what had happened yesterday morning after Barley discovered Phyllis was helping Newton. If Newton had told her anything about Barley's reluctance to help, she wasn't letting on.

She took in the mangled nose and black eye. "My poor baby. Fred said you cut your leg too?"

"Surface wound." Barley yawned and rubbed under Stanley's chin while she analyzed his bandaged skin.

"How come you're not at work?" He looked at the clock. "You're usually long gone by now."

"Canada Day, I don't have to go in until 7:30. We're filming the Canada Day parade." She forced a smile. "Plus, we haven't had our breakfast special since... in a long time." Barley's mother presented him with a plate of bacon, eggs, chocolate chip pancakes, and guacamole toast. She ran her fingers through Barley's hair and kissed him on the top of the head, before sitting down to her coffee.

"Aren't you having any?"

"Already had some. Now tell me your plan for the day."

"I'm going to Phyllis's house, and then we're heading downtown where Newton is gonna meet us."

"Mr. Newton, Barley."

"Oops, *Mr.* Newton." He smiled a fake smile like in a tooth paste ad.

"I heard Phyllis was helping too. That's great. The more people working, the faster they'll locate the boy."

Barley inhaled the plate of food, making snuffling noises because he still couldn't breathe well through his nose. Stanley sat by his chair watching every forkful move from plate to waiting lips. When his mother went to rinse her cup in the sink, Barley snuck him a bit of bacon.

"Fred told me what a big help you've been, Barley. He says I should be proud."

Wow, Newton was not such a bad guy after all.

"He also said he was getting the mess with the Corvette straightened out."

Barley grunted as he ate. When he finished, he went to the fridge, got two eggs, and tossed them one by one up in the air. The first one landed perfectly in the Stanley's mouth; he swallowed it in one gulp. The second one smashed on the floor, but Stanley licked it up off the linoleum. Cracked shell and all.

"What are you doing, Barley?"

"I heard eggs are good for Great Danes. Gives them a shiny coat."

"I'll give you a shiny coat if you don't clean up that mess." She unrolled some paper towel and passed it to Barley.

Barley mopped up the remnants of the egg that Stanley had missed. "You're going to have to take the dog with you today, because I won't be able to come home and let him out." Mary Jane Lick blew him a kiss, picked up her purse, and disappeared out the door. "Love you," she called from the porch. "See you this evening."

Barley put his plate in the dishwasher, gathered what he needed for the day, and reluctantly led Stanley to the garage. "You had better behave yourself today, big guy. Phyllis and I have important stuff to take care of."

Stanley looked at Barley with a sort of pained expression on his face.

"That's right. You should feel sorry." Barley led Stanley out the garage door. Mr. Jewer was struggling to roll his huge garbage can down the slope from his garage, but Angel, his dog, kept getting in the way of the wheels.

"Here, let me get that for you, Mr. Jewer." Barley dropped the lead, and Stanley lowered his head to the cowering canine parcel and sniffed his butt. The little fluff-ball yelped and jumped away.

"That's quite the beast you have there, Barley. He yours?"

"Yeah, his name's Stanley. Mom got him for me. You know, so I won't think about Dad so much." Barley's voice cracked at the end.

Mr. Jewer nodded solemnly. He might be nosy, but Mr. Jewer had always helped Barley's father with any car troubles. He had been a mechanic back in the day. He still had sausage-sized fingers from working with his hands for decades.

Stanley lifted his back right leg and sent a shower cascading over Angel's back and head.

"Gotta go, Mr. Jewer. We're in a bit of a hurry." Barley didn't wait for Mr. Jewer to notice the urine streaming over Angel's back. Instead, he pulled Stanley down the street, and when they were out of earshot, said, "Stanley, you can't pee on other dogs."

In response, Stanley passed gas.

Barley pulled Stanley away from garbage bins and flowers, trees and fire hydrants. He tried to jog with him, but Stanley's run to the border yesterday must have put him off. Barley made a mental note to look up if running was healthy for Great Danes. The whole way to Phyllis's, Barley could hear the pipes gurgling in the dog's abdomen. Barley wondered if the guys at the border knew what they were talking about. Was it safe to feed raw eggs to a dog?

Barley and Stanley arrived at the brown brick town-house just before 8:00. The door was decorated with a welcome sign featuring the three little pigs and the big bad wolf sitting down to a picnic. Barley momentarily forgot about Stanley's gastrointestinal issues; his own stomach was in knots. He hadn't been here since last October. If someone had told him even yesterday that he'd be on this step today, he would have laughed in their face.

He took a deep breath and rang the bell.

Mrs. Henderson was a looker, olive complexioned like Phyllis, with the same high cheekbones, but she had a bee-hive of Marge Simpson hair and was constantly accom-panied by Fifi, her Chinese Crested Hairless. What was it about little dogs today?

Fifi had a wiry tail with a big poof of fur on the end and tufts of fur around her head and feet. Stanley could have eaten her in one gulp.

"Hello," Barley said, addressing both Fifi and Mrs. Hen-derson.

"Hi, darling. I didn't know you had a dog." Everyone was "darling" to Mrs. Henderson.

"He's new. How have you been, Mrs. Henderson?" Bar-ley did have manners when he chose to.

Fifi was beside herself to see Stanley's crane-like body hovering above her. She sniffed his privates, and Barley prayed Stanley would not pee.

"Every day I wake on the right side of the sod is a good one."

Barley wasn't sure how to respond to that. "Uh, is Phyllis home?"

"Oh yes, darling, she said you were coming. She told me all about yesterday." Barley hoped she wasn't going to bring up the severed finger. Instead, she said: "Darling, your face looks tender. Is it tender?"

He guessed Phyllis had not mentioned to her mother that she was the one responsible for his broken nose. Barley felt a flush moving up his neck to his cheeks. He reached down to give the mutant dog a rub to avoid answering. Fifi's skin was like leather, and it had always given him the willies to touch her.

Phyllis arrived at the door behind her mother.

"You brought Stanley?" She sounded shocked.

"Yeah, Mom had to work."

"On Canada Day?"

"Yes, they're filming the Canada Day parade in Cloverdale. They've got the main street shut down."

Phyllis spoke to Fifi. "Fifi, did you see that huge doggy? You think you'd like to play with him someday?" Phyllis kissed both her mother and Fifi good-bye. She was wearing a pair of khaki shorts and a red cotton t-shirt with Canada embroidered across the chest. A water bottle holder strapped around her waist was filled with a red liquid. A separate waist pouch, containing who knew what, dangled off her arm.

"Did Newton give you the Garmin?"

"No, but I have the coordinates. You have your GPS, don't you?"

"Yeah, I've got Dad's Magellan." He followed her to the yellow Mini.

"How are we going to get him in?" Phyllis nodded at Stanley.

"You'll see," said Barley. "He's a contortionist."

"Well, who gets the front seat? You or him?" she asked.

Barley opened the back door and got Stanley to load up. One paw at a time, the Great Dane disappeared into the back seat. No sooner was he installed in the back than he tried to push his way up front.

"Are you sure this is going to work?" Phyllis was behind the wheel pushing Stanley's massive head back towards the rear. "Barley, he's drooling on me." A long rope of slime attached itself to Phyllis's shoulder.

"It'll be OK," said Barley. He was not so sure. Stanley's big gob was floating between the two front seats like a giant bobble head. He was so tall that there was not enough room for him to straighten up.

To add to matters, Stanley's gurgling intestines were in overdrive. Barley could picture the air bubbles making their way through Stanley's long torso, all the way out his bottom. He glanced at Stanley's face. It was twisted with pain. It stayed that way for a few seconds until he shifted his back legs, his face moving a foot forward towards the radio. A less than discreet noise erupted from his behind. Stanley exhaled and sat back down. Barley pretended not to smell the foul odour. Phyllis, however, pretended nothing.

"Barley, what have you been feeding him? He smells like sulfur."

"It wasn't me. It was the border guards. Remember they gave him eggs?" Barley wasn't about to admit he had given him more.

"Whoo-wee. I can't drive like this."

"Just open the sunroof."

Phyllis's brow furrowed as she turned on the ignition and opened the roof. Stanley's torso retracted and his head burst through the hole.

Phyllis started to laugh. It was nice to hear. She put the car in gear and headed east on 64th and south on 176th. Barley hoped Stanley would hold in any other gas bombs he had brewing. He was nervous sitting with Phyllis in her car. It reminded him of last year. Back then, when they dated, Barley didn't have his license, so she always drove. She turned on the radio. Neil Diamond was singing "I Thank the Lord for the Nighttime."

Barley looked at the dial; it was tuned to 600 AM.

Phyllis started singing along.

Barley gave her a sideways look. He didn't remember her being a golden oldies type. "Where are we supposed to meet Newton?"

"He said he'd call when he finished the briefing with the other investigators. He's thinking they might find out if Benjamin owned the GPS with the first coordinates. If not, they can track down sales of Garmins in the lower mainland."

"That's crazy. A thousand Garmins could have been sold in the past month alone. I don't see how that's going to help."

Phyllis shrugged. "They're desperate."

Diana Krall began singing about dancing in the dark.

"Have the investigators found out anything at all?"

"I don't know. They're still checking reservation lists at all the hotels and B and Bs around Sun Peaks, Barkerville, and Green Lake to see if any one name keeps popping up."

"I'm sure a kidnapper would use fake names, but what about video surveillance? All those places have cameras."

"Fred says he has about ten officers working on interviewing all the people at camp, the protesters on Vancouver Island, and Benjamin's friends and neighbours. They're examining security tapes with Mr. Fagan to see if any of the cameras might have picked up Benjamin. They're also checking to see if one person shows up on tapes at different sites."

"Have they had any luck?" asked Barley.

"No luck with the camera in Green Lake, but they haven't got to the Barkerville tapes yet. The gift shop sent all their tapes from Sunday to Tuesday. Mr. Fagan thinks he may have spotted someone he knows walking into the gift shop, but there was no sign of Benjamin. He still has to watch the footage from Grouse Mountain."

"Newton shared all this with you?

"I overheard most of it."

"Phyllis, who do you think would cut off a boy's finger?" Barley didn't want to think about the gruesome grey digit, but they couldn't just ignore the fact they were dealing with dangerous people.

"Not sure, someone who has a big vendetta." Phyllis made a left turn, and Stanley's chest banged into Barley's shoulder.

"What about Mrs. Fagan?" Barley stabilized the dog.

"Which one?" asked Phyllis.

"Benjamin's mother."

"She's on her way home from Europe. She was apparently vacationing in Portugal. There's an air traffic controllers' strike on so she'd had to travel to France to get a flight there. But, yeah, she must have been pissed when her husband ran off with a twenty-something year old. I think I'd shoot my husband if he traded me in for a newer model."

"So, she could be a suspect?" Barley wiped drool from his shirt.

"God, I hope it wasn't her. Why would she do that?"

"I dunno," said Barley. "To punish her ex?"

Phyllis shivered. "Can you imagine cutting off your own son's finger?"

"Definitely not. We are dealing with a very sick person."

"I heard she's a complete mess," said Phyllis. "According to my mother, she's popping tranquilizers like jellybeans; can't talk without bursting into tears. But who knows, she was probably like that before her son went missing."

"Has Newton told her or Mr. Fagan about Selective Availability?"

"No, he said they might freak out even more than they already are." Stanley brought his head back inside, and Phyllis pushed his nose away from her cheek. "Stanley, I am not your personal facecloth."

"Do you think Newton understands what we're up against?" Barley pulled the dog's head more towards his side of the car.

"I think he understands that if we don't find Benjamin before 2:00, we're done."

"Do you think there's any other way to get information from the satellites?" Barley had read magazine articles about how the US had two kinds of satellites and could block the data coming from some and not others.

"The Russians and Europeans are working on their own systems."

"Yeah, but they're a long way off." Barley sighed.

"True. What about Loran-C for ship navigation?" Phyllis took a sharp turn, and Stanley swayed first one way, then the other.

"I don't know much about it. I think it only works on the ocean."

"I don't know much either." Phyllis turned south onto a wooded drive and pulled into a space in the small lot at Redwood Park. It was a truly beautiful day. Song sparrows and robin red breasts sang in the trees. Flowers were in their full glory. It looked like paradise.

Barley helped Stanley out of his cramped position in the back seat. "I can't believe we're down to less than six hours and have no idea how many caches are left."

"I know. But c'mon, let's not think about it." Phyllis closed the sunroof before getting out.

Barley attached Stanley's lead to his collar and let him pee on a gnarled redwood. The dawn redwoods were brought to Vancouver from China. They have cones like evergreens but shed their needles in autumn. Twin brothers received the property that was now Redwood Park from their father as a twenty-first birthday present in 1893, and began the arboretum, adding Norway spruce, Scots pine, and Chinese chestnuts.

Stanley wanted to sniff every little twig along the way; Barley had to pull on his choker until he gagged.

"It's like he's in antenna mode," said Phyllis. The black tips of his ears almost touched above the centre of his massive head.

"I know, you can hardly notice that one ear droops when they stand straight up like that. I think he's trying to find out what other dogs have come this way and if he's met them before." Stanley strained to make his way over to a toy poodle with a pink bow on either ear. The entire poodle, which was smaller than Stanley's head, was shaking visibly. Barley had to wrap the lead around his hand a couple of times and tug. Stanley gave a dry heave as he was dragged past a corrugated iron picnic shelter and down a narrow tree-lined trail. Barley gave the lead to Phyllis while he checked the coordinates.

"I can't believe how many people are out walking their dogs this morning." She was patient and let Stanley, who seemed keen to socialize, make his way over to some sort of doodle. They smushed noses.

Barley took the lead back from Phyllis and pulled Stanley away from his new friend. "We're running out of time," he said.

Following the GPS, they left the open area of the park and entered a forest of trees with green, moss-covered branches that seemed to want to reach out and consume them.

"They look like horror-movie spiders," said Phyllis.

From hiking with his father, Barley could identify the red cedars and Douglas firs. But there were a bunch of species he didn't recognize. He wished he had listened more carefully. It was considerably darker off trail than on the path, and the tree cover prevented the Garmin from getting a good reading. Barley had to keep ducking out to find an open space so the GPS could get a view of the satellites.

"Hey, we're as close as we're going to get with the GPS."
Heart thudding, Barley tried to drag the dog over a log.
He hoped they wouldn't find another finger. "Come on,
Stanley."

"What's wrong?" Phyllis, who was in the lead, turned back.

"I don't know. He looks like a show horse, but he's afraid
to jump over anything." Barley felt guilty, but he wished
he had left Stanley home.

"Why don't you take off his leash?"

"No, he'll go off hunting for the doodle. Plus, I'm pretty
sure we're as close as we're going to get to the coordinates."

Phyllis crouched down and spread the ferns with her
fingers. "You see anything?"

"Not yet."

"Wait, I do. Come over here." Phyllis was down on
all fours.

"What is it?" Barley dragged Stanley closer.

"It's like a little elf door built into the trunk of this tree."

Barley looked at the tree; it was a western white pine.
Down at the bottom was a door about six inches tall with
a little frame and doorknob. "Can it open?"

"No."

"Anything else there?"

"Nope." Phyllis patted around the trunk.

"Then I don't think it's what we're looking for."

A flock of black-capped chickadees surfaced and took
flight. A brown squirrel with an unusually bushy tail took
one look at Stanley and fled, clicking distress signals from
a neighbouring tree.

Phyllis turned her attention to the inside of a rotten log.
Barley dragged Stanley through a maze of bracken fern.
Suddenly the screen on the GPS went blank.

"Oh my God, I think the SA satellites just got scrambled."

"It's not 2:00." Phyllis popped her head out of a two-
foot log.

"I know, but the screen just went completely blank."

"That just means the batteries are dead."

"Oh yeah, of course." Barley laughed to cover his embarrassment. He hit the ON button again. Nothing.

"Shoot! I don't have extras. I'll keep looking while you run to that service station we passed and get some new ones."

"What service station?"

"The Arco on the corner of 176 Street and 8th Avenue." She threw him the keys. "I saw you driving in Hope, so I assume you've got your license now."

Yeah, just no insurance and no registered car. Barley dragged Stanley back the way they had come, around the fallen trees, through the spidery limbs, past a dozen dogs, and back to the Mini.

He pushed Stanley's head into the car. The dog seemed happy to have the front seat, but sad to leave the park. The Mini roared out of the parking lot and onto 20th. They had less than six hours left.

Whipping up to 20th, Barley took a left on 176th. Stanley spotted some llamas in a yard grazing, and Barley hoped he wouldn't attempt to get out of the vehicle. He parked and swooped into the store. No Double As.

He asked someone in the parking lot where to find another store. They directed him farther south to a corner grocery on 184th and 16th. He was at the cash when his phone rang.

"Barley, where are you? I found it."

"I'll be back in a minute. Open it up and see what it says."

"I'm scared."

"OK, wait till I get there."

Barley raced back to Redwood Park, but memories of Demon Cop made him careful to not go over the limit. Stanley was excited to see a well-groomed cocker spaniel named Charlie. Barley forcibly pulled him away. Stanley gagged and urged. "Stanley, I do not have time for this."

He handed Stanley's lead to the cocker spaniel's owner. "Here, take him."

Charlie's owner, a woman in her sixties, looked incredulous.

"I won't be gone long." Barley sprinted over logs and through trees, limbs whipping him in the face.

"What took you so long?"

"I had to go to two stores." Barley caught his breath.

"Where's Stanley?"

"Left him with someone out on the path."

"I found this as soon as you left. It was shoved in under the steps of that treehouse over there." She indicated to the wooden structure where the brothers who planted the trees had lived for decades.

She held up a silver, stainless steel container. About two inches wide and four inches high.

"I found something like that already. Is it a cigarette case?"

"Card case," she said. She tossed Barley a pair of blue gloves like the ones she was wearing and flipped over the top card, which was decorated with a Douglas fir. The letter K was scrawled on the top corner in black Sharpie. She flipped over the second card. E was written on the corner with a picture of a vine maple. Barley wouldn't have known the name of the tree, but it was written below the picture.

"Wait a minute," Barley dug in his pocket for his notebook and pencil. He transcribed letters as Phyllis flipped the cards. The letters E and P were next.

After a minute or two he had written: "Keep these in order if you want to find your..."

Phyllis dropped the deck. She muttered expletives as she picked up the cards. "Here—you take them, and I'll transcribe." She waited for Barley to put on the gloves and passed over the cards.

"S-O-N," Barley read the next cards. Then "N 53°

52.053." Then he dropped the stack.

"I can't believe I did that. It's the gloves; they make it hard to handle things."

Most of the cards had stayed together, but Barley and Phyllis watched the last two flutter to the ground. One with a western yew landed face up.

"Sorry." Barley's hands were shaking.

"It's OK, Barley. I dropped them too, remember. Just read me what you've got."

"W 100° 053. Then it's either 682 or 628. I can't be sure." He shrugged his shoulders.

"We'll go to both," said Phyllis. "Until we find something."

"Shoot. I forgot about Stanley." Barley laid the notebook and the card case on the moss-covered ground at Phyllis's feet and bounded out to the path where the shocked owner of the cocker spaniel still stood watching Charlie and Stanley take turns sniffing each other.

"Thanks a lot," Barley grabbed the lead.

Phyllis was out of the woods with the cards safely back in the case.

"The coordinates are in Vancouver," she said. "I can't tell exactly where. Look them up, would you?" Barley took the notebook from Phyllis and plugged the playing card coordinates into the GPS. Stanley was trying to follow the retreating cocker spaniel. The owner had met up with a friend and was shaking her head, pointing back at Barley and the Great Dane. Twice Barley had to re-enter numbers because Stanley yanked his hand away from the mouse.

"Maybe it wasn't such a good idea to bring the dog." Phyllis took the lead.

"Too late now. No time to drop him off." Barley had the map on the screen. He didn't know Vancouver as well as Surrey, but he had done some mega-caches there. "It's downtown. It's either right near Canada Place where the cruise ships dock or… at the corner of Hastings and Main."

Phyllis looked at her watch. "It's almost 9:00. Fred said he'd call about 9:30 after the briefing. We'll tell him to meet us downtown. We gotta hurry."

"Traffic shouldn't be too bad mid-morning on a weekday," said Barley.

"Barley, it's Canada Day. They do the citizenship ceremony right at Canada Place, and some Brazilian gymnastic group is performing there as well. There are live bands playing all day on Granville Island for free. On top of all that, there's a ten-kilometre road race along Water Street and the sea wall that'll have streets closed for hours. Downtown is going to be a circus."

31

Canada Day

Phyllis ripped down Highway 99. "Man, Phyllis, you got a bit of lead in your feet today."

"You're one to talk."

"Whaddya mean?" With the sunroof open to deal with Stanley's flatulence, Barley's eyes watered so much he could hardly see.

"I heard about your trip home from Hope."

"Yeah, well, I was in a hurry."

"We're in a hurry now." Phyllis's long hair was blowing around like she was stuck in a whirlwind. Stanley, however, seemed to be enjoying the wind in his face. It made him smile.

As they approached the George Massey tunnel, linking downtown Vancouver with the Lower Mainland, Phyllis geared down. "It's as bad as a Friday rush hour."

Barley didn't like driving through the tunnel. When his father had his heart attack, they had to shut down traffic while the police completed their investigation. Barley remembers the call from his mother, telling him to stay home, she'd be there soon. He had waited a long time. Barley gripped the door.

"You all right?" Phyllis looked over.

There was no way Barley was discussing his father's death right now. "You ever think about the fact that we're driving under the Fraser River?"

"Yes, but there's ground between the roof of the tunnel and the water. It's perfectly safe."

"I know, but it gives me the creeps all the same."

Phyllis let out the clutch and rolled into the tunnel. The dash lights came on, and noxious fumes poured in through the roof. Phyllis covered her mouth and nose with her bandana. Stanley lowered himself down through the sunroof and lay across the back seat as if he were a sphinx guarding an Egyptian tomb. Phyllis closed the sunroof. In response, Stanley let go a bomb.

"I'm not sure which is worse—exhaust fumes or Barley's egg farts."

After three or four minutes, daylight came into view on the other end. They were just about to exit on the north side of the Fraser River when a fast-moving truck marked Filaney's Building Supplies lurched over into their lane. Phyllis leaned on the horn. Barley had no time to brace himself. It was too late. The truck driver rammed into the Mini's front bumper. The impact whiplashed Barley's head and neck backwards. Stanley elongated body almost catapulted into the front. Horns started honking. Not friendly honks; they were get-the-hell-out-of-the-way honks.

"You OK, Barley?"

Barley was definitely not OK. He saw his life flash before his eyes. How could they possibly have an accident here of all places? He thought of his mother losing not only her husband, but also her only child. On top of that, nerves were zinging down from his neck through his bicep and elbow right down to the tips of his fingers, and he thought he might throw up. He swallowed. "I'm OK. You?"

"Yeah, I just have to get the car out of the traffic."

Phyllis guided the car out of the tunnel and pulled over. The truck pulled in ahead of the Mini, and the driver appeared at the passenger window.

"Everyone all right?" he asked. "I hit a puddle of oil."

Phyllis looked questioningly at Barley. "I think so." She turned back to the man. "How about you?"

"Nothing a few Band-Aids and a beer can't fix." The truck driver nodded. A tattoo of a spider web covered his left elbow. "I'd better get your insurance info."

Phyllis took her registration and a notebook out of the glovebox and wrote down her information.

Stanley stood up and when his head hit the roof, he tried to manoeuvre around Phyllis's to sniff the truck driver. A thick string of saliva drooled down and once again connected Stanley's mouth to Phyllis's shoulder.

The guy took his arm off the window frame. "Whoa, he's like Spiderman."

"Yep," said Phyllis. "A regular web-making machine." She used her bandana to wipe away the drool.

He gave Phyllis his information and headed back to his truck. As he drove away, Phyllis got out of the car to size up the damage. "It's not too bad. But I have a thousand dollars deductible."

"Maybe Newton can help." It took effort for Barley to speak.

Phyllis put the Mini in gear and opened the sunroof again. They drove past the Steveston Highway and over the Oak Street Bridge. It was slow going.

"Are we ever going to make it downtown?" She turned east on 6th.

Barley was relieved she was driving. He did not feel well at all. He didn't want to let on, however, so tried to keep the conversation going. "How do you know your way around downtown so well? I still have to consult the map book."

"Got a good memory."

Phyllis's phone rang. She passed it around Stanley to Barley. Stanley had just spied a German Shepherd on the sidewalk and was wiggling around the gear shifter. "Put it on speaker, will you?" She pushed Stanley back so she could shift.

Barley hit the speaker phone. "Hello, do you have any news?"

"Not that I can share." Newton's voice came from the tinny speaker. "Where are you?"

"We're on our way to Gastown," answered Phyllis, gearing down for runners.

"What about Redwood Park?"

"We found the cache. It was a deck of playing cards. The clue said: 'Keep these in order if you want to find your son.' Then a bunch of cards had coordinates on them."

"Excellent work."

"Yeah, but traffic's bad; we hit a bottleneck near Granville Island."

"We'll leave now to meet you."

"Who's we?" asked Phyllis.

"My colleague and me."

"You can try, but it's crazy with all the crowds. The Canada Day race has a bunch of streets closed to traffic."

"OK, we'll take the bridge. Stay safe and check in when you find the next clue."

Barley clicked off the phone. It was good to have Phyllis as a buffer between him and Newton.

Phyllis glanced over. "Humidity getting to you?"

He knew it wasn't the humidity. "It feels like it's above 30." Plump beads of sweat navigated their way from Barley's scalp and inched their way down his face.

"Barley, are you going to be all right?"

"You think I have a low tolerance for heat or something? Just because you competed in the Death Valley

Marathon in February..." His light tone had the effect he hoped for.

Phyllis laughed. "So, you do keep tabs on me."

"No..."

She laughed again. "Seriously though, you're looking flushed." She crawled up to Beatty Street and sat drumming her fingers on the steering wheel at the red light.

"I'm fine." Barley was determined to sound more animated than he felt.

"Good, 'cause I'm going to hop out here and run the rest of the way."

"What? You can't."

"I have to, Barley. With the Canada Day 10k on the go, it'll be much faster if I go on foot. You find a place to park and call me when you get to the steam clock. I'll tell Fred to meet us there too." She dropped a business card into one of the drink holders between the two front seats. "My cell number is on this card."

He already had her number. "You're nuts."

"Listen, Barley, you've only got one more bridge to cross." They had come to a dead stop. Phyllis tightened the laces on her left sneaker. "Make sure you take Cambie because of the bands on Granville Island. "I'm taking your GPS. Remember, call when you get to the steam clock."

"We should stick together." Before Barley had all the words out, Phyllis had slammed the driver's door and was bounding past the thousands of runners climbing the Cambie Street Bridge. Traffic was reduced to one lane in either direction. Phyllis disappeared from sight behind an ambulance that had stopped to pick up an older runner lying on the road. A car honked behind them. Barley gulped and slid over the gear shifter into the driver's seat. He inhaled and said aloud: "You can do this." Stanley nudged the back of his head, before climbing through the centre and reclaiming his spot up front.

"How the heck am I going to find the steam clock?" Barley said.

Stanley didn't answer, just lifted his rear end and passed gas.

32

Gastown

N 49° 17.068, W 123° 06.533

Gastown was Vancouver's oldest neighbourhood. It took its name from a gold panner named John Deighton who opened a tavern there in 1867. Deighton, or Gassy Jack as he was called, was well known for extrapolating on any number of topics. A bronze statue on Water Street depicted him standing on a barrel in his vest and long coat, delivering one of the speeches that made him famous.

Barley was relieved to reach Gastown without incident. He found a shady spot in a pay lot near the Delta Hotel, the only real landmark he knew in this area of downtown. He had once come here with his parents, and generally, if he had been somewhere before, he could find his way back. He knew, for example, that if he went north towards the water, he'd come across the steam clock.

Stanley was ecstatic to get out of the car. He stretched and peed while Barley filled a plastic bowl with bottled water and held it up for him to drink. Stanley lapped loudly and drooled long strings of saliva before lying down on the cool pavement in the shadow of a red maple. Barley gave his tummy a rub for a couple of seconds and fed him a couple of pinkish biscuits.

"Sorry big guy, but you're going to have to get back in the car."

Stanley was not at all pleased with this news and gave Barley a do-I-have-to? look.

"You'll be more comfortable here in the shade than being dragged around in this heat." Barley got him on his feet and brought him back to the Mini. He left the sunroof open for Stanley to get air, grabbed a bottle of water for himself, and started running east down Water Street. If he remembered correctly, the steam clock wasn't far. He felt bad about leaving Stanley alone, but knew he wouldn't be long.

He reached Cambie Street just as the four-faced clock was chiming eleven. Dum. Dum. Dum. Dum. Small clouds of steam puffed out the top as the final chime faded. Phyllis was nowhere in sight.

Only three hours left, thought Barley. *Maybe the kid is here in Gastown somewhere. Tied up in a back room. Blood oozing where his finger had been. If we only knew how many clues are left, maybe we could relax a bit. How did the kidnapper even have time to set up the clues?*

He called Phyllis's cell and prayed she'd pick up. Even if he had the coordinates, Phyllis had the GPS.

"Keep coming east," she said. "I'm down at Main and Hastings."

Although great efforts were made to clean it up, Main and Hastings was Vancouver's most notorious neighbourhood for the down and out. Just on the border of Chinatown, it was a place for prostitutes, druggies, and homeless people to gather with their shopping carts. It was also the site of the city police station.

Barley started running along Water Street until it turned into Powell. He made a right turn onto Main. Still no sign of Phyllis, but the usual suspects were shuffling along the sidewalk. Worn clothes. Greasy hair framing sunken faces. Dead eyes. A couple, not much older than Barley, was engaged in an animated conversation in an alleyway. Behind them three or four middle-aged junkies were shooting up. Barley's heart skipped a beat. Where was Phyllis? He didn't know what he'd do if someone spoke to him. The last time he was down here with his parents, his mother had told him not to judge, that until you knew someone's story, you had no idea what had brought them here. "Addiction is a disease," she said. "Like cancer or diabetes."

Still Barley couldn't bring himself to make eye contact, even when a legless man in a wheelchair asked for loose change. He tried not to be prejudiced, but at the same time hoped no one would try to steal the GPS. He was relieved to see Phyllis on the corner of Pender and Main. Barley saw Phyllis before she saw him. Her red Canada Day shirt was soaking wet; huge dark patches of sweat showed through the front and back. Looking at her like this, her skin glistening, he forgot to be mad at her, forgot to hate her for humiliating him back in October.

She was talking to a man with a shopping cart piled high with green garbage bags, a four-foot plastic Jesus, and what looked like a Mickey Mouse lawn chair. Phyllis was digging in her pocket. Barley caught up with her just as she deposited a toonie into the man's filthy palm. She also pulled an apple from her waist pouch and offered it to him.

"God bless you, but I got no teeth." He bared his black gums.

"Uh, Phyllis?" said Barley.

"Oh good, you're here." She waved as the man moved on.

"Did you find anything?" asked Barley.

"Not yet, but it should be right around here. I've sized up everything but the ground."

"Let me see the GPS."

Phyllis passed it over. Barley put his face down to the machine. He searched the street, the buildings. Nothing.

"I don't think it's here, Phyllis. I think we'd better try the coordinates from the second configuration of playing cards." He plugged them into the machine. "It says Ground Zero is to the west on Water Street."

Phyllis grabbed the GPS and took off, the muscles in her calves flexing with every spring-loaded stride. Barley picked up his pace until he felt like he was going to throw up. Now it really was the heat and humidity getting to him.

He caught up to her in front of Gassy Jack wearing his gold panner's hat. She was crouched at the base of the bronze statue, which was green with oxidization and stood a good twelve feet above the street. Black cast-iron chain links separated the brick sidewalk and statue from the traffic. "You think this is it?"

"Pretty close," she answered.

Behind the statue sat a concrete store called the Boot Corral; it had a giant red cowboy boot sticking out the front. Barley walked over near the store to study the statue from back on. The pedestal was like a skirt of red brick that got wider near the bottom. He began to move systematically from the storefront studying the brick sidewalk at his feet. When he reached the base of the statue, he still hadn't found anything. "Can I see the GPS?"

He checked the coordinates against what he had recorded from the playing cards. "I think it's over there more." He pointed across the street where a six-storey wedge-shaped brick building with an overhanging collar was squat between two blocks. The Flatiron Building was famous in Vancouver; it was featured on every postcard rack in every tourist boutique.

They crossed the red brick road.

"Barley, look." Phyllis pointed to a brass plaque mounted

next to the front door.

"Fagan Contracting," he read.

"That is *not* a coincidence," she said.

Barley swallowed. "No."

Phyllis looked in a window. "Should we go in?"

"No, but look; I see something on a brick." He got down on his knees. The letter N was written in thick black ink on the edge of a brick. If you weren't looking, you'd never see it. On the next brick the number 49 was also written in black ink.

"Phyllis, come look." She turned from where she was standing, trying to see in a ground-floor window.

"Barley, you've got it." She began jumping up and down. Then she leaned over a gave Barley a kiss on the cheek. Not a boyfriend-girlfriend kiss, more like a kiss from an elderly aunt.

Barley flushed. On the next brick, the number 18 was written and below that the number 424. Phyllis got out her notebook to record the latitude.

"It's not far from here," she started hopping up and down again.

"Don't be so sure," said Barley. "Until we get the longitude, we have no idea. It could be in Timbuktu." He crouched again and inched backwards like a porcupine until he located more Sharpie marks.

"Timbuktu is only 16 degrees north, Barley." Phyllis shook her head. "And you call yourself a geography expert."

"Give me a break, will you?" he said. "Here it is. I've got the rest."

This time the W was on the lowest brick and the numbers 123 09 199 were written on each brick up from the bottom until they reached the road. On the final brick, a picture of what looked like a tree was drawn in the same black ink.

Phyllis crouched with Barley on the sidewalk. Hundreds of people walked around them paying no attention. She wrote down the rest of the numbers and sketched the drawing into her notebook. Then she leaned into Barley, so close he could feel her breath. He swallowed.

"That first one was from the Fagans," she said. "And this one is from me."

She kissed him again, this time on the lips.

33

Stanley Park Hollow Tree

N 49° 18.424, W 123° 09.199

Barley could feel his cheeks burning from the kiss. He found it impossible to be angry at Phyllis when her lips were on his.

Phyllis pulled away and smiled. "There could be more where that came from."

Barley didn't trust himself to speak. Instead, he double-checked the numbers in the notebook. "It's in Stanley Park. That's only a ten-minute drive."

"Not with the roads closed for the race, it's not. A car won't be able to get near Stanley Park until this time tomorrow, not even to cross Lion's Gate." Phyllis looked up to the left and tapped her bottom lip with her index finger.

"I know, we can rent bikes," she said.

"That's a good idea. I've always wanted to bike around Stanley Park."

"Well, I don't think it'll be leisurely ride." Phyllis stopped and turned her head suddenly towards Barley. "Speaking of Stanley Park, where's your dog?"

"I left him in the Mini."

"He'll suffocate in this heat."

"Relax, I left him water. And the sunroof is still open."

"What about if he gets out?"

"What do you think he's going to do, climb through the sunroof?"

Phyllis looked sceptical. "Your dog better not pee in my Mini, Barley Lick."

"Or what?"

Phyllis took a sip from her plastic bottle. "Or I'll make you scrub every inch of the interior with a toothbrush. Gatorade?"

Barley couldn't help but smile. "No thanks. I've got water." He drained the bottle and stuffed it in a recycling bin on the sidewalk.

"Listen, I'll probably get to the bike shops before you," she said matter-of-factly. "Look for me at one of the two rental places on Denman and Georgia." And then she was gone. She made running in thirty-degree heat look effortless.

Barley began jogging along West Hastings towards the two competing bike rental shops. His tongue felt like sandpaper. A water station was set up for the race. Barley stopped and chugged five small cups of water and resumed running.

One ankle started to chafe. He was wearing good sneakers, but no socks. What had he been thinking? That he'd impress Phyllis?

The friction of the sneakers on skin was soon creating big blisters on both ankles. The right one popped and the exposed flesh throbbed. After limping another three blocks, he got a cramp. He held his side and slowed his pace. By the time he reached the bike shops, Phyllis was ten people back in a long lineup at Spokes. She smiled when she saw his dripping face.

"We'll make a distance runner out of you yet."

"I don't think so. At least not in the summer. My feet feel like they've been through a grinder." Barley scanned the customers ahead of Phyllis.

"Eww," said Phyllis. "Why didn't you wear socks?"

Barley shrugged.

"They say it's extra busy today; people are renting bikes to go in the park since they can't take their cars."

"Any word from Newton?" Barley took off a sneaker to survey the damage to his heel. Blood had coagulated around the popped blister. He examined the other foot. It was much the same.

"Yes, he and his coworker are stuck in traffic." She shrugged. "He said we should keep going, but be careful looking for the caches on our own. And he said thanks."

That was fine with Barley. The less he saw of the Big Fig the better.

"Oh, he also said Mr. Fagan should never have gone to the media."

"Why not? It seems the more people he tells, the quicker he'll get his son back."

"Not necessarily," said Phyllis.

"How's that?"

"He said if the police aren't in control of the negotiations, you never know what can happen. If you leave the negotiating in the hands of the parents, they might let some crucial piece of information slip."

"Like what? Like where that GPS came from with the first set of coordinates."

"I don't know if they found out if it's Benjamin's, but I'm thinking more like if there's a SWAT team. Or the fact the police might know where the boy is being held," she said.

"Do they?"

"I don't think so, otherwise why would we still be searching for clues? But even if they did, they wouldn't tell anyone."

"That doesn't make sense. They could just barge in and get him back."

"No. If the kidnappers knew the police were coming, they might kill the boy." Phyllis was getting closer to the bike rental counter. "Phonse Fagan is one of the richest people in the province. I can think of at least a dozen groups who might want to kidnap his son for ransom."

"But there's been no ransom," Barley scratched his chin.

"Really? Who told you that?

"They said it on the news."

"That makes things even weirder."

Phyllis handed over a credit card and accepted two helmets. Barley was impressed. Phyllis was only six months older than him, but she had her own credit card. She snapped on her helmet and passed the other to Barley.

"I'll pay you back," he said. "I'm happy we'll be on bikes. There is no way I could run much farther with these blisters." Barley stopped to watch the shop attendant roll out a bright red bicycle built for two and pass it to Phyllis. She rolled it over to Barley.

His eyes widened. "You have to be joking."

"It's all they had left," she said with a shrug. "Except for kids' bikes."

"I've never ridden a tandem before."

"What kind of sheltered life have you led, Barley Lick?" She climbed on the front saddle and offered another swig of Gatorade.

"No thanks, my stomach tells me it's probably not the best thing right now." He mounted, and Phyllis started peddling furiously down the road marked Aquarium. Barley looked around and gasped. "Phyllis, we're heading straight for that tree."

"We're not."

"I've never felt so out of control in all my life."

"Just shut up and pedal." She laughed maniacally. "I know what I'm doing."

They entered Stanley Park. Even though he tried to

resist, Barley couldn't help but try to look around Phyllis's shoulder. When they reached the Lost Lagoon, she slowed. "Barley, can you check the GPS?"

"It's showing Ground Zero west towards the water."

Phyllis veered left until they were at Second Beach, then turned them north and started following the road in the wrong direction on a one-way street.

"Phyllis, you're freaking me out."

"Sorry, I thought there'd be no cars. I guess they can still enter from North Van. Check the coordinates again, would you?"

"We're getting real close." Barley indicated a small parking lot on the right. "I think it's in here."

"The Hollow Tree?"

"I guess so. Take a look." Barley held out the screen.

"Naw, I trust you." She looked at him.

Barley was breathing hard through his nose. "You sound like a pit bull."

"I wonder why?" He rubbed his nose.

Phyllis looked sheepish. "Let's leave the bike where we can see it. I'll go in the tree, and you look outside."

The hollow tree was wide enough to allow a small car inside the crack in its base. A man was taking a picture of his wife standing inside. Phyllis waited for them to finish. But just as the lady came out, a Japanese family of four piled into the tree. Gesturing, they asked Phyllis to take their picture.

"Say no." Barley was losing patience.

"Keep your lid on, Barley." Phyllis snapped the picture.

"Arigato," said the father, bowing his head in her direction.

Fearing she might play photographer all day, Barley pushed his way past her and inside the tree. Side by side they examined the interior. Barley inhaled her strawberry shampoo.

The sound of airbrakes made Phyllis turn her head. "What's that?"

"Shoot, it's a tour bus."

About fifty tourists began clambering to get their picture taken inside the tree.

"I am not moving until I find the next clue. Time is running out. They'll just have to take their pictures with me in here." Barley's stomach growled and he checked his watch. His stomach always let him know when it was past noon. "We're down to less than two hours. What if we don't find the kid before SA starts up again?"

"I don't know. Don't think about it." Phyllis's stomach growled in response to Barley's. She went outside around to the back of the tree and began scouring every square inch of the bark. "Barley, I've got something. It's the same notepaper, but I can't reach it."

Barley ran out and spied a piece of paper tacked to the tree high enough that a normal human would need a stepladder. "Whoever put it up there had something to stand on. Maybe I can hold the bike, and you can climb up on the seat."

"I've got a better idea—hoist me on your back."

Fine for you, thought Barley. *You're not the one boosting 150 pounds of muscle.* He grunted as she climbed up on his shoulders. He could feel the treads of her sneakers digging into his collarbone.

"I've almost got it, Barley. I've just got to get a little higher." She placed her left foot on his head.

"Good thing I'm wearing a helmet."

Phyllis teetered precariously. The tourists snapped pictures. Barley turned his face so his blackened eye wouldn't become a screen saver. Phyllis wobbled, and her foot slid off Barley's head. She landed on his shoulders with a thud; one leg draped over each side of his chest like a five-year-old on a parent's shoulders. "What are you doing, Barley? Trying to kill me?"

"I think it's the other way around, Phyllis." He grimaced. "Did you get it?"

"Yeah, let me down so we can look." She slid off Barley's shoulders and unfolded the sheet. "Oh my God, it looks like someone dipped their hand in blood."

"Let me see that," said Barley. "Oh yeah, it looks like those cards kids make for their parents for Mother's Day or Father's Day, only it's only got four fingers."

"Gross, that's really creepy, Barley. Is there a clue?"

"Yeah, it says: 'Are you listening?'"

"Do you see any coordinates?"

"No." Barley looked back up the tree. "But there's a metal tag up there." He pointed at the spot where Phyllis had taken the paper.

"OK, let me climb back up. Brace yourself." Phyllis got back on Barley's shoulders. He managed to stand up. She also stood and read out the words on the tag. "It's North 49° 19 805." She pulled paper and pencil from her pocket to record the coordinates.

"Uh, Phyllis, why don't you just take the tag?"

"It won't come off. Just let me write the latitude. Then I'll get the longitude."

"Whatever you say." Barley teetered under the weight.

Phyllis wiggled and scribbled. More tourists arrived on foot and waited until the busload snapped final pictures of the ancient tree trunk as well as of Barley and Phyllis.

Phyllis's sneaker settled once again on Barley's head. "Longitude is W 122° 27 838." Satisfied she had correctly recorded the numbers, she slid back down to his shoulders. "OK, you can lower me down now."

Phyllis stood up; Barley passed her the GPS and she plugged them in.

"It's in Maple Ridge." She returned the GPS.

"How are we ever going to find a cache out there before 2:00? It's already 12:30."

"Don't be so pessimistic, Barley." Phyllis had already mounted the tandem.

Cameras continued to snap photos as the strange young couple on the bicycle built for two peddled away.

34

Benjamin

Benjamin crawls out of the tent and cranes his neck skyward. It is early morning, and he is deep in the woods; the only sound is of birds chirping. No cars, no radios, no police sirens. He'd like to sneak off and find a phone to call his father's cell. But he has no idea how close the nearest town is.

The sun is just peeking over the treetops. It is dizzying to watch the sunlight sneak through from such a height. Benjamin wishes he knew where his orienteering compass was. With it, he'd be able to tell which way is which. He can usually tell by looking at the sun, but even though he didn't swallow the last pill, his mind is still muddled.

In the backpack on the ground next to him, he spots a folded topo map. He swallows and looks around to make sure he is alone. He pulls the map from the mesh pocket and removes it from the plastic bag, flattening it on the pine needles and dirt. He has no idea where he is on the map or if it is even a map for this area. He searches for the mountain range he can see to the northwest. At least he thinks it's northwest, but he can't be sure. He has to get his directions straight if he's going to escape. To find his way out of this maze of trees and trails.

The map is 1:50,000 and covered with faint orange topo lines. He knows he can't go anywhere with more than five topo lines of elevation. It would be a waste of time and energy climbing mountains or descending into valleys. He would need to find the easiest way out. With the least number of obstructions. But this map doesn't show any manmade landmarks. No settlements or large buildings, no highways or shopping centres. Just lakes and lots and lots of green.

Wait, there's a road. He can see it now. He just has to figure out what side of the lake he is on and maybe he can get there.

"Benjamin."

The dreaded voice. He quickly folds the map and reinserts it in the bag.

There's no way he's going to escape.

35

The End is Near

Even before he had a full view of the Mini, Barley knew there was no dog inside it. There was no Great Dane head sticking out the sunroof. He picked up speed, and for once Phyllis couldn't keep up with him.

"He's gone." Barley slumped against the window, completely drained.

Phyllis peered inside the Mini as if a 200-pound dog could be hiding under a blanket. "Maybe someone noticed him alone in this heat and called the SPCA," she said. "But how did they get him out through the roof without scratching up the car?" Phyllis went around to the other side. The passenger door was unlocked. "Oh, I see, they must have gone in through the roof and somehow unlocked the door."

Barley groaned and slid down to sit with his back against the wheel well.

Phyllis crouched down next to him. "Does Stanley wear a dog tag?"

"I don't know."

"How can you not know?"

"We just got him."

"I'll call the SPCA and see if they have him." Phyllis stood up and continued to examine the car for scratches as she dialled 411 for the number. Barley was vaguely aware of her conversation with the operator.

"Damn, they're not open because of the holiday," she said. "See if you can get an address for the Vancouver Pound off your Black..." She stopped mid-word and reached for a sheet of beige homemade paper tucked under the windshield wiper. As soon as she unfolded it, they both saw the tree embossed at the top. The same tree on the kidnapper's stationary.

"I feel like I'm gonna barf." Barley held both hands to his stomach.

Phyllis read the note. "'The end is near. Miss Henderson should take care.' Oh my God, how do the kidnappers know my name?"

"They must be monitoring the caches," said Barley. "They must have known we were the ones searching."

"But my name, Barley. Why is my name on this creepy paper?' Phyllis looked like she might cry.

"Not sure, maybe they looked in the glove box. Or your business card, you left it for me, remember?"

"You didn't take it?"

"Didn't need it. Your number is still in my phone."

"Oh." Phyllis slid down beside Barley. He put his arm around her.

"We'll be OK, Phyllis." He swallowed. "But poor Stanley. I know he's only a dog, but I feel like I know how the Fagans feel." Barley's voice faded away, as if sucked down a drain.

"I'm calling Fred again," said Phyllis, jumping up. "I have to let him know about the hand print and that whoever has Benjamin is watching us."

Barley hardly registered what she was saying. He stayed slumped on the ground. A dream he had the night Phyllis hit him teased the outer edges of his consciousness. In the dream, Barley was searching for his father. He had been following his father through the woods but he had vanished into the mist. If he could just find him…

"Barley, are you in there?" Phyllis was standing over him. "Fred says he'll meet us in Maple Ridge." With an extended hand, Phyllis pulled Barley to his feet. "Come on, we have to hurry."

"I can't leave. Stanley might come back here."

"Fred says the police will search for him."

"I know I haven't had him long, but I…"

"I know," Phyllis said. "I'd be the same if someone took Fifi. But I think the best thing to do now is to keep searching for Benjamin. If we can find him, we might find Stanley."

36

Golden Ears

N 49° 19.805, W 122° 27.838

Barley did his best to pull himself together when they got out of Vancouver. Phyllis kept taking sideways glances at him, and once she patted his knee.

When they got to Port Coquitlam, she turned off the Lougheed Highway and pulled into a coffee shop.

Barley raised his head to read the sign. "What are you doing?"

"We need to eat."

"But it's 1:40. What about Selective Availability?"

"I can't think straight without food."

At least you're human, thought Barley.

Phyllis left him in the car and returned with two burritos. "Barley, have you thought about how they're going to do it?" She passed him the steaming food.

"Do what?" The foil wrapper crackled as Barley opened it.

"Selective Availability. Do you think that satellite signals will be scrambled at 2:00 on the dot? You know, just bang and it's lights out?"

"Who knows? We'll find out soon enough." Barley was gutted. The sweet smell of paprika and chili powder with a hint of garlic filled the car. He knew he had to eat, but all he could think about was Stanley. He wished he had left him home.

Phyllis attacked her burrito and started the engine. One day last fall—that seemed like years ago now—Colin was out with Barley and Phyllis, and they stopped to pick up burgers. Phyllis had ordered two stacked double-pattied towers. "She eats like a 300-pound wrestler," Colin had said.

He wasn't far off. Right now, she was like a lion ripping into its prey. Bits of sauce dripped onto a napkin on her lap as she shifted gears with the burrito hand and pulled out of the parking lot.

Barley picked at his burrito and fiddled with the GPS as they watched the numbers on the dashboard clock tick away.

"1:59." Phyllis stopped eating and stared at the clock.

Barley held his breath. He wished Phyllis would pay better attention to the road.

The clock changed to 2:00.

"Anything?" asked Phyllis glancing at the Magellan's colour screen.

Barley laid down his half-eaten burrito. "It doesn't look any different."

"So, that's it," says Phyllis. "No huge lightning flash. No fireworks."

"That's it," he repeated, still staring at the screen. "I guess we won't really know if things are different until we get close to the next coordinates."

Phyllis put her hand on his. "I hope we don't find any body parts."

"Me too," he answered, squeezing her hand. "Let me check out exactly where we're going."

He brought up the map on the tiny screen. "Phyllis, the next cache is not in Maple Ridge, the town. It's in Golden Ears Provincial Park."

"How could we have missed that?" she asked. "You'd

better call Fred again."

Barley did not want to talk to Newton. But he pulled out the Blackberry and dialed.

"No answer. Where can that moron be?"

"He's not a moron, Barley."

"Only a moron would abandon two teenagers and expect them to find a deranged kidnapper. What can he be doing?"

"I don't know where he is or what he's doing, but I do know it's going to be hard to find something in the forest with scrambled satellite signals."

"I'm not sure that Newton really understands how hard it will be to get to Ground Zero." What Barley really wanted to say was: what would happen to Benjamin if they couldn't find the rest of the clues. "Phyllis, who do you think took Benjamin?"

"I think it's the CEO of this company called Mother-Lode."

"Why?" asked Barley.

"I read in the *Province* that they're taking Fagan Contracting to court because of a hostile takeover."

"You read the *Province*?" Barley thought he was the only teenage who read the paper.

"Yeah, Mom gets it. Why?"

"No reason. Anyway, I still think it's one of the wingnut tree huggers on Vancouver Island. They just applied for a court injunction to stop the clearcutting."

"Do you really think pacifist environmentalists would cut off a boy's finger?" Phyllis's eyes widened.

"You think they're pacifists? Before they hit Newton upside the head, we watched them smash up a truck. And think about it; every cache has been hidden in a conservation area of some sort, with the exception of Gastown and that was Fagan Contracting's head office."

"Hey, I never thought of that. What about the border

crossing?" Phyllis put her hand on the back of her neck and rubbed out a kink. "That's not a conservation area."

"That's true. But think about the others; we've found clues in Cathedral Grove, Sun Peaks, Barkerville, Green Lake, Greenwood Park, Stanley Park, and now we're going to Golden Ears. Do you think Fagan Contracting has logged in all those places?"

"Not sure, but the RCMP should be able to find out quickly. Why don't you give Fred another call?"

Barley reluctantly picked up the phone. He felt weary; it took energy to raise his arm.

Phyllis read his mind. "It's OK, Barley; I know Fred is dating your mother. He seems like a good guy." She took her hand off the gear shifter and rubbed his arm.

Newton picked up. "Sorry about the dog, Barley. I've got a team doing everything they can to track him down."

Barley gulped. "I'm going to put you on speaker phone so Phyllis can talk."

"One of the last clues was right in front of the Fagan Contracting Building in Gastown," Phyllis said.

She told Newton where they were headed and finished up by explaining Barley's environmental angle, reminding him how many people were upset by deforestation.

Newton listened without interruption, and when it was clear she had finished, he said: "Our team has been working on the environmental lead, but I hadn't thought about how almost all the cache sites were in sensitive areas. Good thinking, Barley. I'll bring the team up to speed and meet you at Golden Ears."

*

It was 3:45 by the time they turned onto Fern Crescent and entered Golden Ears proper. The GPS directed them north for about twenty minutes until they passed

Alouette Lake on the right. It started motioning to the west, so Phyllis veered left off the main road and then left again into the West Canyon parking lot.

Barley called Newton to say they had arrived. Phyllis threw Barley her car keys while he was still on the phone and ran into the woods. "I'll do some recon down the main trail," she called over her shoulder and disappeared.

Barley caught the keys and clicked the lock button.

On the phone, Newton seemed to be chewing his gum as if his life depended on it. "We're almost through Maple Ridge," he said, through chaws. "You were right about Gastown, Barley. The Flat Iron Building was the original head office of Fagan Contracting before they built the Fagan Tower in Surrey. And all the other caches, except the one at the border, were left at sites Fagan Contracting has clear cut."

Barley watched as two chipmunks tumbled around the parking lot. "So now we just have to figure out why the kidnappers chose to put a cache at the border."

"Fagan Contracting just expanded into the States this spring. I remember there was a big protest at Peace Arch when your mother and I went to a SuperSonics game. Remember that time Steve Nash was playing?"

Barley did remember his mother going to see Nash play. He had always thought it was with a female friend. He tried in vain not to dredge up thoughts of Newton and his mother.

"Barley, the needle is flickering." Phyllis's voice came out of the woods. "It can't settle on a number."

"I gotta go," said Barley. "Call us when you get here."

Barley jammed the phone into its sheath and ran into the woods. Phyllis was reversing to the last point where she could check the direction and distance to the cache. "It says it's eighty-five metres up this trail."

"We'll never find it from eight-five metres out. Damn the US and Selective Availability."

"Come on. The GPS was not going to do us much good in these woods anyway." Phyllis looked up at the thick canopy.

"OK, give me a minute to size this up." Barley examined a map of the area on a bulletin board sheltered by Plexiglas.

"The cache can't be in as far as the campground," he said, pointing. "That's five kilometres from here. But it might be on one of the side trails."

They crossed a wooden bridge over a dry stream bed; about thirty paces after the bridge, a trail branched off to the left. A one-inch square orange tag tacked to the trunk of the tree had the word Geocache and a black painted arrow. Under the arrow was a crude drawing of two spiders and what looked like a stump.

"It can't be that easy," Barley said.

"We're still in the game." Phyllis barrelled ahead up a minor incline past a hobbitland of undergrowth and then a forest of green fallen logs. Barley followed, but the trail was overgrown, and Phyllis quickly disappeared from sight.

Barley took a breath. He was fatigued. His mother's big breakfast was long gone; a half burrito and some water weren't enough to keep him going. A gust of wind swept through the forest bringing with it a sudden stench unlike anything Barley had ever encountered.

"Phyllis, do you smell that?" he called out. "It smells like someone died." The wind dropped as quickly as it had come up, and the smell became less pungent.

Barley shivered. He had a feeling of being watched.

"Phyllis?"

No answer. He looked for other hikers. No one. He scanned the underbrush, all the while inching forward. Nothing but brambles. He forded a rivulet, its source obscured by a dense tangle of vegetation. Something moved and Barley jumped. A flying squirrel sailed overhead and landed on a burl about twenty feet up an ancient moss-covered trunk.

Another gust of wind blasted through the branches; the nasty odour became overpowering. Barley covered his nose with his shirt and continued bushwhacking. About a metre farther in, he stumbled upon its source, a scavenged mule deer carcass. Its donkey-like ears were still sticking up off its head, but its face and guts were no longer there.

He spied movement again. Was it the flying squirrel switching trees?

No, the squirrel was still on the burl.

He backed up. Maybe he had stumbled upon a predator with a fresh kill.

This was not good. He had to alert Phyllis. He had seen a warning back on the billboard in the parking lot about a cougar sighting. But cougars rarely attacked anything bigger than themselves.

That's when Barley caught his first glimpse of the black bear standing on his hind legs about ten feet behind the mule deer carcass. His black shiny nose was sniffing the air, sniffing Barley.

I hope he knows that humans are bad news and backs off, thought Barley.

He heard a low deep growl as the bear dropped onto all fours and made his way towards him.

Barley knew it was rare for black bears to attack humans. Unless they were protecting something. Their young or a food source. He swallowed; this bear could attack at any moment. Barley heard his father's voice in his head. 'Stay calm and increase the distance between you and the bear.'

Barley stood up straighter to make himself look tall. He began to talk in a calm but authoritative voice. He had no idea what he was saying. He just wanted the bear to recognize him as human and stay away. It didn't work. The bear kept coming. He felt on his hip for the bear spray he carried whenever he planned to be in the woods. It wasn't there. When they headed out this morning, he'd had no idea he'd end up in the forest.

Barley estimated the bear's weight at well over four hundred pounds. Every time Barley took a step back, the bear advanced.

Barley replayed the conversation with his father in his head. "If you sense an attack, whatever you do, don't run. Lie on your front with your arms covering the back of your head and your legs sprawled so he can't easily turn you over. Play dead and he should go away."

"And if he doesn't?" Barley had asked.

"Then he thinks of you as food. That's when you start fighting back."

"How?"

"Any way you can. Tweak his nose. Punch him in the face. Bite his ear. Just don't startle him if he hasn't attacked."

That's what Barley was determined to do. Get the heck out of there without startling the approaching bear. He reversed another few steps. It was working, the bear had stopped advancing.

Until Barley saw Phyllis's form running back up the path behind the bear.

"Shh, Shh." Barley put his finger to his lips. It was too late.

"I can't see anything, Barley," she called. "We're going to need better..."

Barley didn't hear the rest of her words, for at that instant the bear turned 180 degrees and exploded from the dirt. In less than three strides his powerful leg muscles had brought his dark bulk on top of Phyllis and his powerful jaws were clamping down on her left shoulder.

"No," Barley screamed, jumping over fallen trees and dense bushes to reach Phyllis. He hit the animal wherever he could. He could smell the bear's stinking body.

He heard slurping and grunting. The bear sounded like a contented dog who'd been given a ham bone, and he was swinging Phyllis back and forth like a puppet. If Barley didn't do something fast, she'd be a goner. The bear had her on such an angle that Barley couldn't get his feet around to kick him.

My God, he's going to kill Phyllis. The taste of fear rose in his throat. A thick bile. All he could think of was that he'd do anything if Phyllis could just get away. He'd stop being mad at her. He'd give up geocaching. He'd welcome Newton into his life.

"Hang on, Phyllis." He looked around and found a fallen tree limb. He struck the bear with renewed energy. It had the desired effect. The bear backed off for a second, his flat black nose snuffling, but then he attacked again, this time latching onto Phyllis's thigh.

Barley beat on the bear's nose with the heavy limb. For a split second the bear's beady eyes met Barley's. But then he was back to business ripping apart Phyllis's leg, her perfect runner's leg.

Barley remembered her powering away from the car after the accident in the tunnel. Effortlessly running in the intense heat and humidity to rent the bikes.

Barley hit harder. No matter how hard he pounded, he couldn't get the bear to release his grip on Phyllis's leg. "Barley, help." She was crying now. Thick blubbery sobs.

He charged the bear and tried to pry him off of her. But it was like a fly trying to budge an elephant. His efforts made no difference whatsoever. He charged again.

"Leave her alone," he cried.

That seemed to work. The bear dropped Phyllis and turned on Barley, latching on to his ankle. Barley screamed and beat on the bear's back and shoulders.

Then, out of nowhere, came Newton. "Close your eyes," he hollered. And something began to rain down over them.

Although Barley couldn't really make out what was happening, he felt the bear relax his grip and drop his leg. The bear roared and tore off into the sea of ferns. Barley fell back on the ground next to Phyllis, his eyes and mouth burning. He felt for her hand and gripped it. He could hear her crying. Tears ran freely down his own cheeks.

"Is it gone?" she moaned.

"Yes," he gasped, "...Newton."

"Newton?"

"Yes, it's Fred. I'm here," said Newton. He knelt down in the undergrowth.

Phyllis brought her fingers up to her eyes and then down to her thigh where several inches of skin had been torn away.

"Don't touch it." Newton pulled her hand away.

"I'm cold," she said.

Barley could see through his burning eyes that blood flowed freely from her thigh.

"Shh, don't talk," said Newton. He was busy wrapping something around Phyllis's leg.

Barley could only see blurry outlines. He could see enough, however, to recognize that a second police officer was standing guard with a gun.

"Mullins, keep an eye to make sure he doesn't come back," said Newton. "Barley and I are going to get Phyllis to the vehicle." He turned to Barley. "Barley, we've got to get her out of here. Can you see enough to help me?" He crossed his arms with his palms out in front of him. "Just do what I'm doing."

Barley stood up; his ankle throbbed but it could take his weight. He crossed his arms and Newton took his hands. Together they got behind Phyllis and lifted her to a sitting position. She tried to stand on her good leg but yelped in pain. "It hurts," she said, looking at her chewed thigh. "It hurts too much to move."

"Phyllis, listen to me, we're going to lift you now. We've got to get you to the vehicle." Newton spoke calmly but forcefully. "Try and rest your weight on our arms, and we'll do the work."

Newton looked into Barley's stinging eyes. "One, two, three."

They lifted her. She whimpered.

"Come on, Phyllis. You can do it." Barley tried to sound upbeat.

"Owwww," she moaned. "It hurts."

"I know." Barley's eyes hurt, too, but not like Phyllis's leg. "Phyllis, you gotta help us here. We're going to get you to the car."

"I should never have let them go on their own," Newton said to Mullins.

"What choice did you have, Sir?"

They managed to get Phyllis about fifty feet out the trail before taking a break. They were both breathing hard. Phyllis lay in the fetal position mumbling through her tears.

"I'm going to get a blanket from the car." Newton was already in motion. "Mullins, keep them covered." He meant the gun. Minutes later Newton returned with a grey wool blanket. He spread it out and together they moved Phyllis on it. Newton took two ends and Barley and the other officer, one eye on the lookout for the bear, each took one corner each and lifted Phyllis all the way to the parking lot. They laid the blanket with her on it on the crushed stone. The blood had already soaked through, turning the grey wool black, and Barley could feel something seeping through his shirt. Phyllis's blood was so warm.

Phyllis had begun to shake uncontrollably. They wrapped her up like wiener in the blanket.

"Barley, you get in there first." Barley's eyes still burned from the bear spray, and his vision was blurred. He could see that Newton had the back door of the ghost car open though, so he climbed in. Newton ran to the trunk and got a big red bag. He thrust a wad of thick cotton batting into Barley's hands. "Once we get Phyllis in, keep pressure on her leg to stop the bleeding."

"Shouldn't we call an ambulance?"

"Take too long for them to get here. Quicker if we drive her ourselves," said Newton. He turned to the other officer. "Mullins, the nearest hospital is here in Maple Ridge, correct?"

"Yes." Mullins was consulting a screen on the dash. "Ridge Meadows—116 and Laity Street, near the Lougheed Highway. I've got it plugged in for you."

"Thank you. Alert the hospital through dispatch. Tell them we'll be there in twenty-five or less and to have milk ready. Then drive the Mini back to the station and put in a call to Wildlife to track that bear."

"Will do, boss."

"Barley, where are Phyllis's keys?"

"I got 'em." Barley passed the keys to Constable Mullins.

"OK, give me a hand getting her in."

The police officers loaded Phyllis in on top of Barley so that her head rested on a folded jacket and her legs lay on Barley's lap. Newton opened the blanket and placed the cotton on the wound. He positioned Barley's hands. "Keep her knees bent and don't let her bleed out."

He ran around to the driver's seat. "Hang on, Phyllis, we're taking you to a hospital. Keep talking to her, Barley."

God, what was he supposed to say? Is this what it was like in the ambulance when his mother accompanied his father? Barley took a breath. "Phyllis, if you can hear me, say something. Anything. Just let me know you can hear me."

Nothing.

"Phyllis. Phyllis? Look at me." Barley looked down at her through blurred eyes. The bear spray was dissipating, and he was relieved to see Phyllis's face undamaged.

Still no answer.

"Come on, Phyllis, talk to me." Barley looked at the blood seeping through the white cotton and staining his hands.

"Phyllis, honey. We're almost there. Hang on." Newton hit the siren and swerved around an 18-wheeler. Other cars pulled over to the right as they flew past.

That was when Barley felt something on his arm. Maybe it was just the jostling of being in the back seat of a car moving at high speed with a body lying on top of him. But no, he felt it again, a faint squeeze on his arm. He looked down. She had removed her hand from the blanket. Phyllis's eyes remained closed. He heard a faint voice and lowered himself to listen. "Tyler," she whispered.

Am I hearing her right? Is she calling me Tyler?

"Tyler Kurasawa," she said. "My cousin. We had to go to a funeral the day of your party. Sorry I was late."

Then she blacked out.

37

Flashback, Phyllis at Bear Creek

N 49° 09.466, W 122° 50.226

Last July, after that first kiss in Lynn Valley, Barley was twitterpated. He had never felt anything like it. At home he was useless. He couldn't concentrate on anything. His parents would be blabbing on about whatever, and he'd be in the room with them, but he wasn't really there—in his mind he was with Phyllis in the ferns.

"What happened on Saturday, Barley?" asked Colin. "It's like you're stunned ever since."

Colin found out soon enough what was on Barley's mind, because Barley and Phyllis started spending all their free time together, and not wanting to be the third wheel, Colin pulled back.

One Saturday in early August, Barley and Phyllis went for a hike in Bear Creek Park; Phyllis wanted to check out a cache there. The relationship was fresh enough that Barley still got giddy when they went out. He couldn't believe his good luck. He couldn't believe he not only had a girlfriend, but he had caught the attention of the hot older girl he had admired on the track.

Phyllis had trouble believing he had only started geocaching the year before and still eyed him suspiciously whenever he picked up his GPS. "I don't believe you only learned how to geocache last summer."

"It's true."

"How are you so good? I've never met anyone else with the gift." The gift, that was actually what she called it.

They were becoming an item, and sometimes Barley wasn't quite sure if she was attracted to him or just his ability to navigate.

"I like your confidence," she said. "I like being challenged."

Barley's parents seemed to like Phyllis too. She was good at talking to adults. She came across as mature and knew where she was headed in life—she was going to be a sports injury doctor. Barley had met her mother as well. She was a pediatrician, and they lived together in a townhouse with her little sister and a Chinese Crested Hairless abomination of a dog named Fifi, by far the ugliest dog Barley had ever seen.

They drove up to Bear Creek in Phyllis's Mini. It was new then. Barley didn't even have his learner's permit yet. He couldn't get it until he turned sixteen later in August. Phyllis already had her full license, six months before her seventeenth birthday. Barley hadn't even known that was an option.

"It is if you go to driving school," she said, opening the sunroof. A gentle wind cooled them all the way up the highway and across the Second Narrows Bridge.

When they got into the woods, Phyllis tackled Barley and knocked him into the grass. She wrapped her legs around him and pinned his hands over his head.

"Did you miss me?" she said.

"Phyllis, I saw you yesterday." She brought her face so close to Barley's as he spoke, their lips touched.

How could people walk around all day going to work or school or whatever when they could be kissing, Barley had thought. Kissing Phyllis was better than eating or sleeping or even watching live hockey.

Barley lay there with a stupid grin on his face unable to process thought. After a few more minutes of bliss, Phyllis pulled away and spoke. "You know that to go out with me, you have to love trees. Do you love trees, Barley?"

"Yes." What else would any sane person say.

"I mean really love them. You have to care for them deeply to be my boyfriend. Do you care for them deeply?"

"As deep as Marianas Trench," answered Barley, wondering if she would accept an ocean reference when discussing trees. That seemed to satisfy her because she pulled him to his feet and uncrumpled a computer printout she pulled from her pocket. "It's All Greek to Me," it read.

"The hint says the cache is in an olive tin," she said.

"Intriguing. I've never found one of those before."

The GPS led them deep into the underbrush. You wouldn't think Bear Creek Park would have such deep woods, but where the olive tin was hidden could have been the jungles of Vietnam.

This particular cache had encrypted clues. Like his mother had taught him and Colin the previous year, all they had to do was switch the letter on top for the one below it.

"I thought encrypted clues are supposed to be kept short?" said Barley.

"They are." Phyllis sat on a rotten log, intermittently swatting mosquitoes and transposing letters. "But I guess whoever set up this cache didn't get the memo."

The encrypted clue was so long, that it took Barley and Phyllis ten minutes to figure it out.

"When you find three stumps together you will be close to..." Only one word to go. Barley was so accustomed by then to transposing letters that he immediately saw that the final word had two ee's in the middle and another at the end.

"Greece," he said. "When you find three stumps together, you will be close to Greece."

"What a useless clue," Phyllis said. Everywhere they looked, there were three stumps in close proximity. "Listen, if you can find this one before me," she said. "I'll really give you something to write in the logbook. And if you don't..."

"If I don't, then what?"

"You have to rub my feet." Phyllis's feet were the only part of her that Barley did not find attractive. She had lost two nails through distance running, and they had grown back in thick and fungus-y. She hardly ever wore socks, and the first time she took off her sneakers when Barley was there, he was in shock when he saw her thickened nails.

"There's no way I'm touching those things; they should be part of a science experi..."

Barley hadn't finished when Phyllis pushed him off the stump. He fell into fanlike yellow leaves, damp and stinky.

"Phyllis!" He catapulted back up like a jack-in-the-box; by the time he got free of the skunk cabbage, Phyllis was already ten paces away, down a side trail.

The needle on Barley's GPS had gone wonky. He wished he could get a better reading so he could find the cache before Phyllis. His heart was beating out of control, and he had started to sweat.

Phyllis's laugh came through the trees. She was clearly enjoying the turmoil she was putting him through. He had to retrace his steps back to the path to get a reading. The cache was definitely very close. He moved slowly back towards the log they had been sitting on and spied the three stumps. They stood out when he came at them from a different angle, rotten and hollowed out. He dug around in each one until in the third he caught a hint of dull silver—like pewter—covered with dead leaves.

Barley held the olive tin over his head like the Stanley

Cup. "Bring it on," he said.

And bring it on, she did. She did things to him he'd never had done before. The cedar carpet felt soft, and they rolled around not caring if they got wet or not.

Their clothes stayed on, but they may as well have been off. Barley felt like he had died and crossed over to a place he didn't know existed. He was sweaty and weak and energized all at the same time. First Phyllis was on top. Next, she was underneath. She was an acrobat, giving him a private show of all her tricks. Once she was done with him, Barley just lay there to catch his breath. He watched her pick up the olive tin. After what appeared to be a smell test, she opened it and let out a little puff of air. In her hand lay a small bust of Colonel Saunders attached to a traveller key tag.

"I've heard of this one, but never seen it," she said.

"I have," Barley said. "My father and I found this in Boswell just before I met you."

"No way, no one ever finds the same traveller twice."

"It's true." He laughed. "The owner wants it to go into space."

"That's amazing. Come on, let's take it to KFC and get our picture taken with it before we drop it in another geocache and it goes into orbit." She signed the logbook with both their geocaching names—Billy G for Barley and Ent-Woman for her.

"What the heck does that mean?" said Barley.

"You know, like the Ents in *The Lord of the Rings*." Phyllis dropped in her trademark, a white bouncy ball with an eyeball on it.

"Why did you choose that name?" Barley dug a goat out of his pocket and gave it to Phyllis to put in the olive tin before she secured the lid.

"Because like the Ents, I am wise and a defender of the forests."

September came, and they went back to school; Phyllis in Grade 12 with plans to apply to UBC and Barley in Grade 11. Colin and Barley were in the same homeroom, but Colin was fed up with Barley, who was so obsessed with Phyllis that he floated through the school day. Phyllis wasn't in any of Barley's classes, but they met at her locker between classes and after school, and hung out on weekends.

"Barley, you got it bad," said Colin one day at lunch, when he was trying to tell him about the latest NHL trades.

"What?" said Barley.

"Nothing," said Colin, shaking his head.

For three and a half months, Barley and Phyllis were inseparable.

Then, at the end of October, things fell apart.

Barley asked his parents if he could host a geocaching party the last Saturday before Hallowe'en. They were going to their own masquerade party and said they didn't mind as long as there was no alcohol.

That was OK. Barley planned to invite the people he had met at the White Rock Geocaching club. They weren't really the drinking type. They preferred trivia nights to sneaking into dance bars. Barley wanted to show them an old Michael J. Fox movie called *Midnight Madness* about a guy who anonymously sends out party invitations to college students who stay up all night following clues to an unknown destination.

Barley put out a notice on geocaching.com to all the cachers in the area. The invitation had no name, no address, no telephone number. Only the words "Urban Grizzly" and coordinates of Hope, the six-foot wooden grizzly bear carving on Barley's lawn in Cloverdale. Below the coordinates, a note explained to show up at 6 p.m., dressed like a foreign country, snacks would be provided. Although no one who had been invited, except Colin and

Phyllis, had ever been to Barley's house before, about ten people showed up.

"This the geocaching house?" Larry Lobez smiled. He was dressed like Italy with a green, white, and red t-shirt, a hat made from a pizza box, and a moustache drawn on with black marker. He clapped Barley on the back when he saw him. "Barley, nice bear. I had no idea whose house we were coming to. I thought maybe it was Chase's."

Chase, the boy from Burnaby, arrived then. He and three others were dressed like a herd of Australian sheep. They ran around Hope and head butted him a few times before coming up the steps. "Baaa," said the sheep.

Barley had never heard Chase say more than three words, but when he passed Barley in the porch, he shouted: "G'day, mate." Trailing behind the herd was Marcie Redding, dressed like Little Bo Peep.

Colin showed up wearing plastic fangs and carting a laboratory skeleton he called Mr. Bones. Everyone tried to guess what country he was supposed to be.

"Transylvania," he said. "Isn't it obvious?"

"That doesn't exist," said Marcie.

"Sure, it does, it's in the middle of Romania, in the Carpathian Mountain Range," said Maddison Coish, an older geocacher who was wearing one of those Peruvian sweaters with all the little llamas and dolls rising up off it like they were going to get up and dance.

"My uncle has been there," said a guy, whose name Barley could never retain. Joe or Jim—something old-fashioned. He was wearing a Santa suit with a sign that said North Pole or Bust, and coordinates written underneath.

Maddison gave him a scathing look. "You do know the coordinates for the North Pole are not constant, don't you?"

"Of course," said Joe or Jim, looking offended. "What do you think I am? An idiot?"

Susan Flanagan

"What country are you supposed to be, Barley?" Marcie asked.

"I can't tell you until Phyllis gets here. You'll know when you see us together." Barley was dressed from head to toe in green and Phyllis was going to come dressed like a mermaid. Together they would make Denmark and Greenland. But where was she?

"Let's get a picture of everyone before we watch the movie," said Marcie.

"Let's wait till after," said Barley. He was getting more and more out of sorts every minute. Phyllis was late. She was never late. She was the most punctual person he had ever met. What could she be doing to make her late for his party? He hadn't spoken to her since Thursday night. She wasn't at their usual meeting place Friday lunchtime. When he tried to call her, he got her voicemail. Where was she?

"I thought she'd be one of the first ones here," said Colin, low so only Barley could hear. "I'm sure she's got a good reason." Colin always sensed when Barley was not himself. It was always like that. Like telepathy, they knew each other so well. And even though Barley had scarcely hung out with him in the past three months, Colin hadn't given up on their friendship. "Come on everyone," Colin said. "Movie starts in five. Fill up your popcorn bags and find a seat."

Barley's father had borrowed a projector from Colin's father and helped Barley set it up to play the movie on the biggest living room wall. Before he went out, he had taken down the two framed prints and tested the sound and video. All Barley had to do was press a couple of buttons and it was ready to go.

"Great party," said Larry Lobez; he passed Barley on his way into the living room with a big glass of ginger ale and a bag of popcorn. "Is Phyllis not coming?" Larry always asked questions like that. In the negative.

284

Barley shrugged. He didn't trust his voice.

"You guys didn't break up, did you? I saw her with Tyler Kurasawa yesterday lunchtime." Tyler Kurasawa was a football jock. Big and loud and popular.

"Where?" Barley swallowed. The prickly heat of jealousy made it hard to breathe.

"Saw her getting into his Jeep."

That explained it. Phyllis had ditched Barley for some jock with a name he couldn't even spell. The thing that upset him most was she didn't have the guts to tell him first.

"Sorry to be the one to break the news." Larry sat down on the floor next to Chase and the sheep.

Colin was by Barley's side. "What's up?" he said. "You look like you've seen a ghost."

"Larry said Phyllis is hanging out with Tyler Kurasawa."

"Hanging out, hanging out?"

"Yep."

"No," said Colin. "I don't believe it. She's into you."

"He saw her getting into Tyler's Jeep."

"It probably wasn't even him."

"Colin, who else drives a bright orange Jeep at Cloverdale High?"

"No one, but I can't believe Phyllis would go out with Tyler."

"Where is she then? She hasn't answered any of my calls or emails since yesterday morning. Larry said she and Tyler left school together at lunchtime yesterday."

"OK, hold yourself together. I'll start the movie. I'm sure she'll be here soon."

Barley fumed through the whole movie. While the others laughed and speculated over which team would come first, Barley went through a thousand scenarios in his mind concerning Phyllis and Tyler. She didn't give him any indication of dumping him when he spoke to her

Thursday night. But he didn't have much experience with girls. Maybe they were fickle.

As the closing credits began to roll, the doorbell rang. Barley opened it to Phyllis. She wasn't alone. Tyler Kurasawa stood behind her. "Barley, you know Tyler?"

Barley couldn't speak. Phyllis wasn't even in her mermaid costume. She and Tyler were both dressed nice, like they had been to a fancy restaurant. Barley felt like he had been kicked in the guts. He could feel his heart thumping in his ears.

Colin came out of the living room. "Hey, what's up? Oh..."

"Colin, have you met Tyler?"

For a moment Barley stood motionless, anger and humiliation bubbling up inside him. How dare she show up here with some other guy?

"Sorry, we're late," said Phyllis. "We just came from Moxie's."

Phyllis's words snapped Barley out of his trance. The others had come out of the living room in their costumes. Barley began to speak. He could hear his own voice, but it sounded like it was coming from somewhere else. "Moxie's huh, well why don't you and Tyler go back there?"

"Why?" asked Phyllis, genuinely confused.

"Because I don't want to see you anymore, Syphilis." The last word just popped out. Barley didn't even know it was part of his vocabulary.

Colin gulped. Barley could see his Adam's apple go up and down in his throat. Tyler clenched his fists and went at Barley. Colin grabbed his arms from behind and Larry had to help hold him back.

"How dare you?" Tyler was red faced with rage.

Phyllis looked more sad than mad. "Don't you ever call me that again, Barley Lick."

"Or what?"

Marcie laid her popcorn bowl on the floor and crept around everyone. "Uh, gotta go," she said, and disappeared. Chase and the sheep were followed by Santa and Maddison in her llama sweater.

Although he looked like he wanted to stick around to see the action, once he let go of Tyler, Larry got his jacket. "See you next week," he said, and skedaddled.

It was just Barley, Colin, Phyllis, and Tyler left looking at each other.

"Come on, guys. I'm sure this is just…" said Colin.

"Get out," Barley yelled.

"Let's go," Phyllis said to Tyler.

"You better watch your back, man." Tyler opened the door and held it for Phyllis, who glanced back and looked at Barley, before stepping out onto the porch.

Barley didn't move until he heard the click of the front door.

"Jeepers, Barley, that was a bit intense."

"How dare she bring him here!"

"There must be a logical explanation."

"Yeah, she's a two-timing bitch."

"Calm down, Barley. I'm sure she'll call in the morning."

Phyllis did call the next morning. She called later that night too. Barley refused to pick up. He deleted all her messages without listening. It was too late to apologize. She had humiliated him in front of his geocaching friends. If she thought he was willing to stand by while she went out with other guys, she had another thing coming.

All that week, he avoided her at school. If they did cross paths, he refused to speak to her. After a week, she gave up. She still said hi in the halls, but she stopped calling. She stopped trying to find him in the cafeteria. He saw her in the stands at hockey games, but she no longer cheered when he scored. That hurt the most. For the first five weeks of the season, he had been scoring goals for her. After she stopped cheering, he stopped getting points. Not even on the powerplay. He couldn't even stop goals on his own net. Cloverdale High's Wild Horses team sank in the standings.

But by the time the new year began, Barley had bigger worries. His father was gone, his mother was renovating her way through her grief, and Barley was shuffling through weeks and months in a daze. His grades dipped, and he hardly saw anyone but Colin.

At the end of February, Mr. Franklyn called to offer him the Big Bite job—two shifts a week until summer vacation. Barley found that working at the pizza place took his mind off everything and dulled the pain.

In May, Colin heard Phyllis had been accepted into bio-chem at UBC. She brought Tyler to the prom. Barley wasn't there because he wouldn't graduate until next year. Good thing; he wouldn't have survived the humiliation.

Once school finished in June, Barley thought he might run into Phyllis at the first geocaching event of the summer down at the club in White Rock. She didn't show up. Although she kept her distance, he knew she was still geocaching. He kept track of her finds online. He also knew that she would be one of the fifteen GeoFind competitors.

GeoFind, that seemed like a lifetime ago.

38

Benjamin

Benjamin examines his mangled left hand. He knows the dressing needs changing. If only he could get some of that antibiotic cream his mother used to rub on cuts. If only he could get out of this basement. He pulls on the metal cuffs, but it only makes things worse.

Benjamin's mind is less hazy now that he has discovered how to store the pills in his cheek. He knows his mother must be worried about him. She goes ballistic if Benjamin isn't home at precisely the minute he says he'll be. If he's ten minutes late for supper, he may as well call the police himself. His mother would be pacing the floor in front of the living room window. Cell phone in hand waiting to dial 911. She'd give Jeno, the housekeeper, grief, telling her she had to get Benjamin to write down exactly where he is going and who with.

He remembers a day about two months ago, he came home from his friend's house one street over. They'd been playing a game of pick-up hockey. He had his stick flung over one shoulder as he walked up the driveway of the house he grew up in, the house his mother still lived in. The house he visited every second week. He doesn't feel like he has a home anymore, just houses he visits. Back and forth, back and forth, like a yoyo.

He didn't even know he was late until his mother comes tearing out the door screaming so loud some of the neighbours come out to see what's happening. "Do you know how worried I have been, Benjamin?" she says, her face red. "You have just taken ten years off my life."

"I was just over at Jeremy's house," he said.

"For all I knew, someone could have taken you away."

Could his mother have suspected that someone was coming for him?

Does his mother even know he has been taken?

She's off on her annual girls' trip to Portugal for two weeks. That's why his father shipped him off to a camp he didn't want to go to.

He wished his father had listened to him. He just wanted to stay home and hang out with his friends. If he hadn't gone to that camp, he wouldn't be in this mess. His hand is infected. He can tell. Not only from the smell, but it pulses like it has its own little heart. Thick pus oozes out from under the dirty gauze dressing. It is past time to change it, but he'll have to wait.

Will his mother ever come home?

He hopes so. He's worried that time is running out.

38

The Hospital

Police siren blaring, Newton careened into an ambulance parking space at Ridge Meadows hospital.

"Bear attack!" He jumped out of the car. "Open leg wound. Losing lots of blood."

Two paramedics shot into action. The female, a tiny woman with a calm face, took a quick look in the back seat while the male rolled over the stretcher. "One, two, three." They transferred the blanket with Phyllis in it from car to stretcher. "They said you needed milk?" The woman passed a tiny carton over to Newton.

"Yes, for the bear spray. Make sure you put some on her eyes too." Newton indicated towards Phyllis's prone body.

Don't let her die, thought Barley. He watched in a daze as the broad-shouldered man attached an oxygen mask to Phyllis's face. The woman ripped the plastic cover off a syringe, ripped open Phyllis's shirt and injected something in her arm. It was like watching a telepathic tag team. The man felt for a vein and tied off Phyllis's arm before inserting an IV.

And then they were gone.

Newton told Barley to get out and tilt his head back. He poured the milk directly on to Barley's eyes and in his mouth. The burning dissipated almost immediately.

Barley held up his blood-stained hands and stared. It was all just a bad dream. A nightmare. He followed Newton into Emerg. Someone wearing hospital scrubs said something he didn't catch and led him to the waiting room. Barley looked up and saw a collection of concerned faces staring at him. It was like they were floating. Were they even connected to bodies?

Through enflamed eyes, he made out a bathroom sign and stumbled like a bull, head down, and somehow made it through the door before he threw up in the toilet. The bathroom was small and white and smelled of chemicals. Barley wiped his mouth on his sleeve and noticed blood on the nylon.

Whose blood is this? Mine? No, it's Phyllis's. Syphilis. You shouldn't call her that, Barley.

He swiped at the blood on his jacket, but it was starting to harden. He opened the faucet and let the warm water cascade over his hands. He watched pinkish brown swirl into the sink and down the drain. Was it true that water swirled one way in the northern hemisphere and the opposite way in the southern hemisphere? He'd have to go to Australia to find out.

He left the bathroom, leaning on the door frame for a minute to collect himself. He could see Newton talking to a triage nurse behind an Arborite countertop. She had her head bent over a clipboard taking notes.

"Bleeding mainly from the thigh but superficial wounds to the shoulder," said Newton.

Barley had forgotten about her shoulder. He staggered, sideways like Stanley running down that highway. *That was so long ago. How long ago was it?*

He sat on a blue plastic chair. Newton came over. "Do you have a number for Phyllis's mother?"

Barley tilted his head to one side to ponder the question.

He felt like an ape. But somewhere in the recesses of his mind, he remembered how to open his phone and locate the number.

Newton wrote it on his notepad. Then he put the back of his hand to Barley's forehead. "We might need you to see a doctor too."

Barley looked at the linoleum. "Where did they take Phyllis?"

"She's in surgery now. We'll know more in a while."

"She might not be able to run anymore."

Newton put his arm on Barley's shoulder. "The doctors know what they're doing, but she'll have to stay in hospital until they get her stabilized and stitched up. I'm going to call her mother." Newton paused. "Are you sure you're OK? You're not looking too hot."

Barley had definitely felt better. "They took Stanley," he said.

"I know. I know. I have my people looking into it. How are you so sure it was the kidnapper?"

"The note." Barley dug the beige sheet out of his pocket and smoothed it out. "It's on the same homemade paper. With the tree."

"'The end is near. Miss Henderson should take care,'" Newton read. "Phyllis told me this was in a parking lot near the cruise ship terminal?"

"Yeah, I left Stanley in Phyllis's Mini with the sunroof open. It was so hot." Barley's voice faded. "When we came back, he was gone." The last sentence came out barely more than a whisper.

Newton looked away. "Stay here," he said. "I'm going to call Phyllis's mother and then the office for an update. They'll find your dog, Barley."

While he was gone, Barley started to shiver. He closed his eyes for a minute to regroup. The last thing he saw before he closed his eyes was a man with a tattooed arm. Flames surrounded his elbow, and a demon snake wrapped its way up his arm disappearing into his armpit. Barley thought of the guy with the spider web who had banged into Phyllis's Mini in the tunnel.

Was that just today?

Here is what I know, he thought.

Phyllis is in surgery for a mutilated leg. She may never run again.

Stanley, who I've had all of three days, has been dognapped. The kidnappers have cut off Benjamin's finger.

I am helping my mother's boyfriend track down aforementioned psycho kidnappers.

The US government has scrambled satellite signals making it impossible to find Benjamin.

GeoFind is cancelled.

And my father is still dead.

Overall, it was not a positive recap of the day. Barley was so tired he could hardly lift his head; he decided to leave his eyes closed. He felt himself drifting out of consciousness.

The dream he had the night Phyllis punched him came back in more detail. In it, his father was calling him to follow him through the forest.

"Look at the trees," he said.

Barley looked up. "What about them?"

"They're disappearing." His father was disappearing too. "But don't you worry, Barley-boy. Just think of Boswell and everything will be OK."

Boswell? Why should he think of a praying goat?

Before his father's image faded away, he smiled at Barley. "You can do it, Barley. I have faith in you; you can track him down."

"Track who down?"

Newton touched him on the shoulder.

Barley screamed, silencing the whole room.

"It's OK, Barley. I asked them to get a doctor to see you too."

"No." Barley suddenly felt wide awake. "I know how we can find him."

"Stanley?"

"Yes, and Benjamin too."

"How?"

"We can trace him."

"What are you talking about?"

"The tracking chip, in his shoulder, drives him crazy. We can use it to trace Stanley, and if it was the kidnapper who took him, then we'll find Benjamin too."

39

Paddle Boarder to the Rescue

The Albion Ferry crossed the Fraser River at one of its narrowest points, less than a kilometre between the north bank in Maple Ridge and the south bank in Fort Langley. Two small ferries provided a free fifteen-minute service across the river, taking up to twenty-four cars each run.

En route to the ferry terminal, Newton called Barley's mother. Newton wore a head set plugged into his cell phone, so Barley couldn't hear his mother's responses, but he could hear Newton tell her how they had lost Stanley.

I couldn't even take care of a dog for a couple of days. What kind of loser am I?

Newton didn't mention that Barley was groggy and covered with Phyllis's blood, just said they had been at the hospital with Phyllis, who hurt her leg.

"How is Barley?"

"He's just looking for the name and number of the company that installed the tracking chip in Stanley's shoulder. We're hoping to use it to try and find him."

Barley closed his eyes and put his seat back. He drifted off until they reached the parking lot.

"They're going to call us when they trace the chip,"

said Newton, as he pulled into the ferry line-up. The parking lot was blocked with cars. An attendant sidled over to the driver's window. "Canada Day, you're going to be here a while."

"How long?" asked Newton.

"At least..." she did a rough calculation of the cars in the lot. "A five-ferry wait."

"Five ferries. That's at least an hour and a half," said Newton.

The attendant shrugged.

Newton looked over at Barley. He put his hand under his chin. "You're really not looking well at all. Maybe I should take you back to the hospital."

"No!" Barley tried to sit up straighter. "We have to find Stanley."

"OK. OK. I'll drive around."

"Can't you get a helicopter?" asked Barley.

"No, they're both tied up elsewhere. But I'll go talk to the people in the office. Tell them it's an emergency."

Before Newton left, his phone rang; he held up his index finger to Barley.

"They traced the chip to a house in Morgan Creek," he said. "It appears to be staying in the same location."

"What's the address?"

"2337 133rd Street. I'll be back in a minute."

Barley repeated the address out loud. "2337 133rd Street." He was agitated, but he had no trouble retaining numbers. He got out of the car and ignored a woman who pulled her child in close when he passed. He knew he must look bad, black eye, swollen nose, his clothes matted with blood. He walked down to the shoreline and leaned against a tree. At least twenty paddle boarders were crossing the river just upstream from the ferry. One woman fell off into the Fraser with a splash. She pulled herself up and got back on the board.

Barley looked across the river to Langley. It was so close. Maybe he could swim over. What good would that do him though? He'd still need a vehicle to get to Morgan Creek.

He teetered towards the water, stumbled, and fell forwards. Shoot.

He hadn't hurt anything. Maybe he'd lie in the damp grass for a while. He had made the decision to have a little rest when he heard a familiar voice call his name. He didn't lift his head. He was tired of Newton. It was like he was stuck in an alternate universe with this man trying to take his father's place.

He heard his name again. It was far away, distorted. "Barley. Is that you?"

The voice didn't belong to Newton.

It belonged to Colin.

40

Tracking Chip

Barley looked up at his friend's face through the long grass.

"You're pretty banged up, Barley."

"Yeah well, it's not every day you have a fight with a bear."

As soon as he had heard what had happened, Colin offered to take Barley on the board across the river where he had parked.

Barley looked at the lime-green paddle board. It was about ten feet long and less than three feet wide, with a rainbow painted two thirds the way up.

"We'll both sit, straddling the board, legs in the water," said Colin. "We'll be fine. I've done it lots of times." He took off his life jacket and fed Barley's arms through the holes. "You look like you might sink." He fastened the plastic clasps and looked back to the parking lot. "Maybe we should give Newton a heads up."

Barley stood and scanned the crowd, but Newton was nowhere to be found. He took out his notebook. The pages were stained, as if someone had spilled red wine. He scribbled a message and pointed to the ghost car. Colin ran and left the message on the steering wheel.

Once across the river, they abandoned Colin's board on the banks of the Fraser and began racing to South Surrey in Colin's PT Cruiser; Colin, driving as fast as he could, and Barley riding shotgun.

Colin screamed through holiday traffic until they reached Morgan Creek, a posh neighbourhood with fenced estates and sprawling manicured lawns. He kept glancing over at Barley. As they travelled west on 24th Avenue, they could hear Tom Cochrane singing "Life is a Highway" at the Canada Day concert at the Cloverdale Fairgrounds. The heavy bass reverberated in Barley's head.

Barley used his GPS to give Colin directions. "Turn here on 134th," he said. When the car reached the corner, the arrow on the GPS started turning in circles. "Pull in. We're close."

Colin swerved the PT Cruiser into the curb.

"This is it," Barley said. "2337 133rd Street."

A two-storey detached three-car garage, easily three times as big as any house in Barley's neighbourhood, stared back at them. The main residence was brick and fake stone. A basketball net with a real glass backboard was attached to the side of the garage, and a black Porsche sat idly in front of its middle door.

"You think this is it?" asked Colin. "It doesn't look like a kidnapper's den."

"I guess they could have made a mistake," said Barley. But then a real-life Scooby Doo head appeared over the cedar fence. Did he really just see what he thought he saw? Stanley's huge head appeared for another split second before disappearing behind the fence. Then they could see his nose stick out the big knothole near the gate.

With renewed energy, Barley jumped out of the car.

Stanley let out a deep-throated rumbling woof that Barley felt right down to his toes. He ran to the gate. Locked. Stanley was now jumping up and down like he was on springs, his face appearing and disappearing above the wooden barricade.

"Barley, come back," called Colin.

But it was too late. Barley made a running leap and missed. The fence was too high. He fell and let out an involuntary "ugh."

Colin was out of the car and after him. Barley picked himself up and made a second attempt. This time he was over and in. He landed in a heap. Pain surged through his right side. Stanley looked stunned for a moment, but then ran over and touched his nose off Barley's. He appeared unharmed. A heavy-duty alarm sounded, spooking the dog. He woofed again. Colin stood swearing on the other side of the fence.

Once accustomed to the alarm, Stanley did a victory lap around an in-ground pool, shaped like a horseshoe; it looked as if it had never been used. A ten-person hot tub had been built into the deck alongside. Stanley raced around a monkey-puzzle tree and finally stopped where Barley sat with his back against the fence covered with creeping vines. The Great Dane deposited himself onto his master's lap. Barley winced and pushed 200 pounds of canine over to his left side, which hadn't been damaged in his fall.

Over the alarm's blaring, he could hear something else. A door opened and a woman appeared; she was pointing a handgun at Barley. She cocked it.

"Whoa." Barley stood up, Stanley toppling off.

Colin was outside calling, "Barley, what's happening? Open the gate."

The woman approached Barley; she looked crazed and was motioning wildly for him to move towards the house. "Get away from the dog," she shouted.

Barley pushed Stanley aside and walked up two wooden steps to an upper deck. "Where's Benjamin?"

"Why do you want to know?"

"I'm worried about him."

"Why would you be worried?"

Barley wondered if he could grab her legs and knock the gun from her hand. "He's been away for a few days. We didn't know where he went."

"Are you related?" She motioned for Barley to enter the house ahead of her.

As he passed, he turned and jammed his elbow into the woman's ribs. The gun went off and both of them fell to the ground; Stanley barking loudly.

At that moment a SWAT team in full bullet-proof gear burst through the gate and pulled the woman away from Barley. Newton sprinted in and cuffed her. "Get him to a safe place," he yelled, his eyes lighting on Barley. Two RCMP officers lifted Barley under the arms and brought him through the gate to the driveway, where Colin was freaking.

"Oh my God, Barley. You gave me a heart attack."

Next, a small bald man sprang from the passenger seat of a forest-green Jaguar and fumbled at a keypad near the front door to turn off the alarm. Barley recognized him immediately. Phonse Fagan was surprisingly short—five foot two, tops. Barley had expected a much more imposing figure to be head of BC's best known logging company. Without acknowledging anyone, Mr. Fagan ran up the front steps and opened the ornate door. The K-9 Unit stopped him before he could enter. An argument ensued and Mr. Fagan was thrust back to Newton, who had just handed the cuffed woman to another officer. She was sputtering obscenities, not at them but at Mr. Fagan, who looked at her with an expression of disbelief. A single word came from his mouth.

"Betty."

"Now you know what it's like to lose your family." She spit on the ground at Phonse Fagan's feet and glared at him while the SWAT team dragged her away.

Newton forced Mr. Fagan back to his Jag. The two sat and quietly talked while the K-9 Unit completed their search. Mr. Fagan's arm leaning on the window frame was tanned, but at that moment, his face was as white as a pan of dough.

Two members of the K-9 Unit escorted Barley, Stanley, and Colin back to the PT Cruiser. Barley hesitated for a minute before pushing Stanley's furry mug into the back seat.

Colin began to speak, but his words were cut short by a burst of ambulance siren. The next few minutes were a blur of activity. An ambulance crew entered the house carrying a stretcher. Newton restrained Mr. Fagan from jumping out of the Jag. Another officer came around to hold the man. Within minutes the paramedics reappeared carrying the stretcher, this time with a body on top. Thank God, the face was not covered by a sheet. An oxygen mask disguised the features, but red hair gave away Benjamin's identity.

Once Newton had been replaced in the Jag, he walked over to the PT Cruiser and knocked on the roof. "You must be Colin. I've heard lots about you. If you don't feel it's safe to drive, I can have one of my men bring you home."

"No sir, I'm fine."

"OK then, Colin. Can I trust you to see that Barley gets home safely? He's had quite the day. I'll have one of our cars lead you. You just have to follow."

"Where are you going?" asked Barley.

"I have to go with the SWAT team to the hospital," he said. "I'll check in with you later. Your mother is waiting."

"What about Phyllis?"

"Her mother is with her now. We'll know more in a while." Newton knocked on the roof again and nodded to Colin before heading off.

"You all right, man?" asked Colin. "That was gnarly."

"I'm good." Barley reclined the seat and closed his eyes. Stanley, with front feet firmly on the floor and butt and back feet on the rear seat, cuddled his head next to his master's, lifted his rear end, and let out gas.

41

The Kidnapper

Betty Neilson was sixty-one years old and had been a friend of the Fagan family since long before Benjamin was born. Her electrician husband had worked for Fagan Contracting for decades, until he was killed in 2001 while hooking up power to a new logging site. His wedding band had worn through his work glove. The lawyer for Fagan Contracting offered Betty compensation, and of course, Fagan Contracting sent flowers to the funeral home, but Betty never heard boo from Phonse.

When the company offered her then-eighteen-year-old son some work as tree faller out on remote sites, she was incensed.

"Don't you dare take a job with that company," she said, when he came home with the news. "Stay in school. Wait until you get your business degree."

"Mom, I don't think I'm cut out for a career behind a desk; you know I love working outdoors. Plus, they're offering more money than I'll ever make if I stay in school. I promise, I'll put away half what I make and when the job dries up, I'll use the money to pay for tuition. Even do my Master's."

So, he signed the contract to work as a tree faller; by the time he was twenty, he was making more money than his father ever had. He moved out of the house he shared with his mother and into a flashy apartment on the roof of some posh building downtown. He was helicoptered into sites, where he worked three weeks on and one week off. On his week off, he drank and smoked and popped pills with pill-popping friends. Sometimes he couldn't even get himself up and out the door to work at the end of a week-long bender. He bought a flashy Italian motorcycle. He was never sober enough to ride it. There were no applications to universities. Instead, there were week-long parties in a pent-house suite, a steady string of one-night stands and more than a few nights in the drunk tank. Gerard Neilson's mother never found out that he had advanced to intravenous drugs. No matter, her heart was already broken.

Then, on February 13, the day before Valentine's Day, Betty Neilson opened the door to Phonse Fagan's right-hand man, an RCMP officer, and the pastor from her church. They didn't have to speak for her to know her only son was dead. Her legs crumpled under her.

After they got her to a chair, they explained how the helicopter had dropped him in the woods two days before. He had just started clearing the trees, when one toppled onto him, pinning him across an old log, breaking his back.

"Who was with him?" asked Betty.

Phonse Fagan's man took a deep breath and looked at a spot on the wall over Betty's shoulder. "He was alone."

"Isn't that against company regulations?"

"We're sorry for your loss," said the company rep, touching her arm. "Someone will be in touch to take care of the financial side of things."

"Tell your boss to get in touch," Betty Neilson hissed. "I will not be bought out again."

But Phonse Fagan did not contact her. Betty Neilson left messages with his secretary. She called his home phone. She sent emails. All requests for a meeting were ignored, so Betty Neilson took things into her own hands, marched into Phonse Fagan's office, and demanded that Fagan Contracting admit blame in public.

"We'll take care of you, Betty," said Phonse. "But you know the company would take a huge hit if this became public."

"Phonse Fagan, I will never darken your door again, but mark my words, you will regret what you have just done. Someday, and that may be someday soon, you will suffer a loss as great as mine."

That explained why she took Benjamin and didn't demand a ransom. She didn't need the money. She had reams of money. What she wanted was her family back. So, to exact revenge, she took Phonse Fagan's son on a journey through the backwoods of BC.

Let Phonse Fagan take a tour of his destruction, she thought. Let him see the forest denuded of trees. And at what cost?

Afterwards, she'd leave the boy somewhere he'd be found. Then she'd take the train to Seattle and fly to Mexico.

Or not.

She almost wished she'd get caught. She had nothing left to live for.

42

Home

"That's one special dog, M.J.," said Newton, nodding at Stanley, who was curled up in the old La-Z-Boy chair next to the couch. His four feet hung over the edge, all bunched together like he'd been hogtied. Every now and then, one limb slid off the chair, and he pulled it back and tucked it in.

"Don't we know it, hey, Barley?" Mary Jane Lick rubbed her son's head as she passed by the counter.

"He deserves a medal," said Newton.

Barley glanced up and nodded. "Yup." His mono-syllabic response wasn't because he refused to acknowledge Newton. He couldn't say he was happy to have Newton in his house, but he wasn't repelled by the tartan man-mountain anymore.

It was more that he was worn out. His ankle had lacerations and his ribs still hurt from the fall over the fence. Every time he inhaled, Barley was hit by a tremendous pain in his right side.

He busied himself getting the dog a drink of water. Stanley seemed exhausted too. Barley filled the stainless-steel bowl his mother had bought with tap water and laid it on the step stool. Stanley hobbled over from the chair and lapped it up, getting as much water on the floor as in his mouth. Then he was head and face into his empty food bowl.

Barley's mother pointed at the cupboard where Barley found a tin of dog food. He moved to the can opener and Stanley followed. He turned the tin upside down in the bowl and watched the stuff ooze out. It smelled foul, and when it finally came free of the tin, it sounded like a suction seal breaking. Stanley was so fast getting his head in there that some glopped on his eyebrow.

It was good to be home.

"How could the kidnapper have kept Benjamin in his own house without anyone finding out?" Barley's mother asked Newton.

"Mr. Fagan moved out after the divorce," he explained. "Benjamin's mother continued to live in the family home, but she was vacationing in Portugal. That's why Mr. Fagan sent Benjamin to the camp. He had him for his regular week as well as the week he'd normally be with his mother."

"It still doesn't make sense that they could be in that house. How did the kidnapper get in? In that neighbourhood, they've got surveillance cameras up the yin yang."

"Yes, but Benjamin knew the codes, and his kidnapper shut them down." Newton didn't add that the first time Betty went there after she picked up Benjamin at camp, he didn't want to give up the security code. She had solved that problem quickly with a butcher knife.

He also didn't add that Betty Neilson procured the security code for the house Benjamin's father shared with his new wife, Mrs. Fagan the Second.

What Newton did say was: "We checked the house early on and there was no sign of intrusion. And when she came back from Portugal, his mother was staying in a hotel until we finished the investigation."

"Does she know about the finger?" Barley cringed.

Newton gave Barley a look that told him his own mother didn't know about the finger. He looked at M.J. and smiled. "Benjamin cut his finger."

"Was it bad?" she asked.

"Yup, he got a nasty infection from the cut," answered Newton.

"That's a shame. There's one other thing I don't understand. How did this woman decide where to set up the caches?"

"Betty Neilson sometimes accompanied her husband on trips to set up electricity in new logging camps so she was used to being in the back country, and every clue she hid for Mr. Fagan to find was at a site her son had helped clear-cut for Fagan Contracting. Ms. Neilson used her husband's old Garmin to set up the caches, then wiped the memory and uploaded one set of coordinates for Cathedral Grove. She left the GPS on Benjamin's bed at his father's place for his father to find."

"But he didn't see it right away?" asked Barley.

"No, not until he heard Benjamin was missing."

Someone knocked on the door and Colin appeared with bagels. Barley's mother re-introduced Colin to Newton.

"Ah yes, nice to see you again, Colin, the getaway driver." Newton held out his hand. Colin shook it, something Barley had yet to do.

"I still don't know how you knew Barley was waiting for the Albion Ferry," said Newton.

"I didn't. I was paddling on the river and just saw him tip over into the grass like something out of a horror movie."

"Good thing you were there, and thank you for taking him home."

"No prob," said Colin. He and Barley went upstairs and left the adults to eat their bagels in peace. "Wow, man, you still look like a zombie." Colin shook his head.

"I feel like a zombie," said Barley.

"Word is they found Benjamin in the wine cellar, chained by the ankles to a bed," said Colin. "He had fresh food and water, but the infection in his hand had spread all over his left side. He could hardly breath from asthma. He wouldn't have lasted another day."

"How do you know all this?" Barley held his side as he sat on the bed.

"Larry Lobez called me. He's a distant relation of the Fagans."

"Did he say if Benjamin is going to be OK?"

"They think so; he's on antibiotics to clear up the infection. He'll be in hospital for a while."

"Speaking of hospital, I have to go see Phyllis."

Colin raised his eyebrows. "Last time you mentioned her, you weren't exactly on friendly terms."

"I think we're past that now."

"Ah. So, she forgave you for calling her Syphilis?"

"She told me, in no uncertain terms, that if I ever insulted her, or any woman, like that again, a broken nose would be the least of my worries."

"Good for her. Personally, I think that's letting you off easy."

43

Phyllis and Barley Make Up

Langley Memorial Hospital was on the Fraser Highway not far from the airport. Phyllis had been transferred there after her emergency surgery. She was on the second floor with her leg in traction and her shoulder covered in gauze. Barley crept in the room with a takeout meal.

"You don't have to whisper." Phyllis rearranged herself so she was upright enough to eat. Her left hand had an IV line that ran to a bag suspended from something like a coatrack on wheels. Barley watched as she ripped into the hamburger like a she-wolf. Machines binged and hummed all around her, and an orderly padded past the door wearing scrubs and soft-soled shoes.

"So basically, Fred told me...," she said between bites, "if Stanley hadn't had that tracking chip, Benjamin probably wouldn't be alive."

"Yup." Barley stood next to the bed.

"How is he?" she asked, as she ripped the paper off the straw.

"Who? Stanley?"

"No, not Stanley, Barley. Benjamin."

"Oh, right. I heard he'll be spending a few weeks at BC

Children's Hospital. They're getting his infection under control."

"I think I'm going to be in hospital for a while too." She held up the IV port protruding from her left hand.

A porter wearing white running shoes and a cap covering his hair pushed a stretcher by the doorway.

"I'll come see you whenever I'm not working," said Barley.

Phyllis started to say something, but held back. "Fred said the kidnapper's son and husband were both killed on the job working for Mr. Fagan."

"That's right, remember the police suspected it was a woman. They were right all along. This woman became a prime suspect when the police realized that the GPS that Mr. Fagan had found on Benjamin's bed was actually one registered to his company. It was the one Betty's husband used for work. Remember Newton asked us to look for a serial number inside the battery case?"

"Oh yeah."

"When they went to question the woman, they couldn't find her, so they tracked down the last person to see her."

"Who was it?"

"Her cleaning lady last saw her the day before Benjamin went missing. The woman had told her she wouldn't need her for a while." Barley shifted from one foot to the other. "Anyway, everything was going as planned until she noticed that, instead of Phonse Fagan finding the caches, it was us. That's when she took Stanley."

"Why didn't they pick her up on the surveillance tapes?"

"She wore a different wig or hat at every cache site."

"It's pretty ironic that a tracking chip led you to her." Phyllis laid down the last of her fries. She patted the bed. "Come sit here. It's hard to twist and see you."

Barley sat cautiously on the hospital bed, afraid he'd do her damage or pull out one of the many cords going back and forth between Phyllis and beeping machines.

"What's going to become of geocaching now with the satellite signals scrambled?" she asked.

"Dunno," he said. "Even if the GPS can't get people very close, I suspect the diehards will still do it."

"Like us."

"Yeah, like us."

"Remember that cache we found near Whatcom Falls?" Phyllis took Barley's hand and held it between hers.

"I remember."

It was about two weeks after they had started dating. They were in the early stages of the last GeoFind contest down in Bellingham. The rules weren't the same as this year and they had both showed up to find the same cache at the same time. When Barley's father dropped him in the parking lot, he saw Phyllis and she suggested they find the cache together. Barley was worried about who would get to claim it, but after their earlier forays in the woods, he was thrilled at the thought of doing another cache with Phyllis.

"Remember the mud on the foot bridge?" said Phyllis, stretching and adjusting her position in the hospital bed. "We must have had about a metre of rain that month."

"Yeah, I think they set a record in Washington. Thirty-seven days of consecutive rain or something." Barley paused when a nurse came in the room to check the machines attached to Phyllis that were whirring and broadcasting numbers and graphs on a screen.

"Your sneakers were like moon boots," Phyllis said, laughing and then coughing and finally hiccoughing.

In his mind, Barley could see the thick tree cover as if the hospital room had been transformed to Washington forest. He could see the GPS needle flickering. He could hear Phyllis reading out the clues.

"It was an ammo box, wasn't it?" she said.

Barley could see the ammo box; it was painted red. And the trunk of the fir tree it was under was also painted with a red arrow. "Yes, I said something stupid like: 'Preferred receptacle of geocachers the world over. Sturdy. Watertight.' I must have sounded like a dork."

"You didn't sound like a dork." She paused. "Well, maybe a bit. We argued over who would claim the cache. Remember in the parking lot, we got your father to witness the coin toss."

Barley grunted and took a breath.

"My father is dead." His voice came out a whisper.

"I know." Phyllis smoothed his cheek with the back of her fingers. "I was at the funeral."

"You came to the funeral?" Barley closed his eyes. "I didn't see you."

"The church was packed, and I was afraid to talk to you. You were so mad at me, and I didn't know why. I'm so sorry, Barley."

She hugged him and he found himself hugging back.

Phyllis was at the funeral. Wow. Barley had no idea. Maybe there were a lot of things he was wrong about.

44

A Month Later, an Unexpected Invitation

Barley and Phyllis were officially an item again.

"Can you believe she thought *I* was the one who ditched *her?*" he asked Colin. Mr. Franklyn had finally given them a shift together. "Here I thought she had ditched me, and she didn't know what was on the go." Barley was on cash, but there was lull in the customers.

"I never understood the whole business," said Colin, throwing a round of pizza dough in the air. "Especially once I established that Tyler Kura-whatever was not Phyllis's boyfriend. You wouldn't even listen to me."

"I know. My hormones cancelled out my brain cells. They had been at Phyllis's great aunt's funeral. That's why they were late to the party. They were never going out."

"Ooo, I hope not. They're cousins, aren't they?"

"I know. I'm such an idiot."

The door jingled, and a man came and ordered two large veggie pizzas.

A month had passed since they solved the kidnapping case. Phyllis was out of hospital, and her wounds were healing. She still wore a boot cast and walked with a limp; she wasn't allowed to lift anything heavy, but she could get around. The doctor said she might be able to start some light running after Christmas.

Barley had broken two ribs when he hurdled the fence to get Stanley. It still hurt to inhale. They made quite the pair. He got the Corvette back from the impound yard, and Newton insisted on paying to fix the window. He took care of Phyllis's fender bender too. He was a good guy. Or maybe the RCMP paid. It didn't matter. He was a decent guy regardless.

Barley apologized to his mother for his rudeness. He realized what an ass he'd been. She said she understood how hard his father's death had been for him, for both of them. She knew he didn't really hate Newton; it was just that Fred's presence amplified the absence of Barley's father. "You don't have to tell me that change is hard, Barley. We both loved your father. Letting go and moving on is the most difficult thing I've ever had to do."

As for the police report on the kidnapping case, Barley and Phyllis didn't get any official recognition. Barley did get a lovely new driver's license with no demerit points, however. And his mother finally found the time to set up the insurance and get the car registered. The police had even tracked down the thieves in Hope and found Barley's wallet along with more than fifty others.

There was also no mention of Barley and Phyllis in the news—that would have looked bad for the Surrey RCMP. Imagine announcing that two teenagers had found Benjamin! What they did get was an unexpected invitation from Mr. Fagan. A month and a day after they found Stanley, and the SWAT team rescued Benjamin, Mr. Fagan invited Phyllis, Barley, and Stanley to the house he shared with his second wife in North Vancouver.

Barley didn't know quite what to do with Stanley as they stood on the front step. The butler who opened the door appeared unfazed by 200 pounds of fur, however, and Stanley followed the procession to a massive atrium with a thirty-foot glass cathedral ceiling. Barley felt like a potential buyer on a tour of a real estate property.

The butler led them around a circular oak staircase past a glass-fronted office, then took them past a marble-and-cherry kitchen and through a sunken living room with rough-hewn beams of solid oak holding up the ceiling.

"If you wouldn't mind having a seat, Mr. Fagan will be with you in a moment."

Stanley made himself at home scooching around on his belly on the patterned hardwood. He let go a stink bomb.

"Stanley!" Barley was fanning his arms when Mr. Fagan entered the room. Barley prayed the odour had dissipated somewhat. Mr. Fagan approached Phyllis first. "It is such an honour, Ms. Henderson, to have you as a guest in my home."

"Nice to meet you too."

"How are your wounds healing?"

"They say I might be able to run in the new year. It'll take lots of physio, but I'm up for whatever they give me."

Mr. Fagan pursed his lips and nodded. "I'm happy to hear that."

He turned to Barley and extended his right hand.

"Barley Lick," said Barley. "So happy your son is safe." Barley was surprised to feel his pulse beating in his palm.

"Ah yes, the man with the interesting name. You're the person who found the clues," said Mr. Fagan. "I want to thank you." He still had hold of Barley's hand and squeezed it again. He was like Popeye.

"It wasn't only me," said Barley, feeling hot around the collar. "Phyllis found a bunch too." He smiled in her direction.

"Both of you worked hard," said Mr. Fagan. "And you shall be rewarded." He sounded like he was giving a speech in parliament. "Before we get to that, there's someone I'd like you to meet." Although a small man, he took the stairs two by two, until he realized Phyllis had trouble keeping up. He slowed, and with Stanley in tow, the pair followed him into what was obviously a boy's room.

The walls were painted blue and burgundy—the colours of the Vancouver Canucks—and a large poster of Markus Näslund hung above the dresser. A new white Vancouver Canucks hat was hanging on a bed post.

There, sitting at the desk and working a computer mouse, was Benjamin Fagan. His still-bandaged hand did not appear to slow him down any. He turned away from the screen; his curly red hair had grown so long that the scar on his eyebrow, so visible in the photos, had disappeared under his bangs.

"How's it going, Benjamin?" Barley said. "I'm Barley, and this here is Phyllis."

Benjamin was polite. "Hi," he said quietly, his eyes staying on Stanley. "What's his name?"

"Stanley."

Stanley moseyed over to sniff Benjamin's leg.

"Who owns him?"

"I do," said Barley.

"I heard him, that day at Mom's house." He rubbed his hand along Stanley's spine. "I knew he was big because his bark was so deep." Benjamin imitated Stanley's solitary woof. Stanley's two ears perked up, although one still didn't stand up straight. He brought his nose to Benjamin's cheek.

"That means he likes you," said Barley. He gave Benjamin a dog biscuit to feed Stanley. "You have good taste in hockey players," Barley added.

"I prefer the Sedins," said Phyllis.

"Don't listen to her," said Barley, giving Phyllis a gentle nudge. "Näslund is better than those two combined."

"You're a Näslund fan?"

"Yep, my father too." It was the first time Barley mentioned his father without his throat turning into sandpaper. "In fact, my middle name is Markus."

"That's cool." Benjamin kept rubbing Stanley's head.

They chatted for five or ten minutes, until Mr. Fagan said it was time to go back downstairs. "Can the dog stay here for a few minutes?"

Mr. Fagan looked at Barley.

Barley nodded. "Sure, just don't blame me if he farts."

Mr. Fagan led them to the living room where he presented them each with a cheque for $1,000.

"Ljubljana," said Barley. "You don't have to do that."

"It is a gesture of my thanks," he said. "Without you, I wouldn't have Benjamin. And if you hadn't gotten involved in the whole mess, you wouldn't have got so banged up."

Barley looked at the piece of paper in his hand. He wasn't expecting money. He'd share with Colin. It was enough to know he had helped a boy reunite with his father. And a father reunite with his son.

45

Choo Choos, August 24

"That was amazing," said Barley. He and Phyllis had just come from the Peace Arch border crossing, where they locked on to 49 degrees just north of the border.

"You're easy to please," said Phyllis.

Barley pulled the Corvette into an angled parking spot in front of Choo Choos restaurant in Langley. "Are you sure you want to eat here?"

Phyllis folded her arms. "I suppose you'd rather go somewhere with Colin?"

"No," he protested. "I am happy to be with you. It's your choice of location I have a problem with."

"Langley?"

"No, not Langley. I love Langley. It's just... Choo Choos? I feel like I'm seven years old again. Next year the birthday boy gets to choose the restaurant." Barley held the door for Phyllis and they were led to a table in the back corner. The server took their drink order and passed them small clipboards with menus.

Barley picked up the souvenir pen chained to the clipboard. The steam engine inside travelled from one end of the pen to the other in its liquid channel. He read the list of food on the little piece of paper shaped like a conductor and began ticking off his order. He put an X in the square next to the baked potato. X the rack of lamb. X Coke.

Once Phyllis finished X-ing off her choices, she said: "What do we do now?"

"I can't believe you've never been here before."

"We only moved here when I was in Grade 10."

"Right. You have to wait until the train gets to our table." He indicated the model that ran along the wall behind them. "Then you pull the switch to slow the train. Now."

Phyllis was too slow, and the train continued chugging past them. "Uh oh."

"Don't worry. It'll back again," said Barley.

"What do I do once it slows?" Phyllis's eyes followed the train.

"You put your conductor," Barley detached the little man from his clipboard and waved it at her, "in the train, and it will go to that man over there." Barley gestured to the other side of the restaurant where a male server dressed like a conductor was taking orders from the engine and pinning them to a clothesline for the cooks.

Phyllis slowed the train on its next loop and deposited their orders. "That was fun."

"Barrels," said Barley.

"Don't be such a party pooper, Barley. You said I could choose the restaurant, remember?"

"I'll know better next time."

She picked up the saltshaker and showered him in little white balls.

"Hey," he said brushing off his arms. "I'm happy you didn't choose KFC."

"Oh, I forgot to tell you. I heard that the Colonel Saunders Travel Bug will be on the next supply launch for the International Space Station."

"No way. I wonder if Farmer Bill knows."

"Farmer Bill?"

"The guy with the homemade singing horse I told you about. He's the one who started the Colonel on his journey."

"Oh right, we should set up a Travel Bug to mark this summer, you know, GeoFind and the return of Selective Availability."

"But not the kidnapping."

"No, not the kidnapping."

While they pondered that idea, Phyllis leaned down and picked up the bag she had carried in from the car. "I got you a present," she said. She leaned across the table and gave him a peck on the cheek, just as the waiter arrived with her appetizer of nachos.

Barley reddened. He was still not used to displays of affection in public. "Thanks, Phyllis." He removed tissue paper from the top of the bag and pulled out a tin of SPAM.

"I figured I'd replace it," she said. "I thought about it after. I should have realized by your reaction that it wasn't just any old tin of SPAM."

"No, Dad gave it to me. It was a joke we had about junk emails."

"Sorry, I can be a bit too spontaneous sometimes." She smiled. "There's something else in there too."

It was a rawhide bone for Stanley.

After the meal, Colin arrived just as the server came by with a huge piece of chocolate cake with a dollop of whipped cream. "I'm just in time," Colin said, by way of greeting.

"Ha, ha," said Barley. "You're not getting a bite," he joked, then handed Colin his unused teaspoon to try a taste.

"Mmm," Colin sighed. "Nothing like birthday cake at Choo Choos."

Phyllis laughed. "You all ready for *GeoFind, The Movie?*"

All the GeoFind competitors had been invited to the premiere of Mr. Czanecki's geocaching movie at Colossus. Free of charge.

"Yes," said Colin. "Is it true Mr. C. is going to give away the GeoFind prizes as door prizes?"

"I think so. If you earn free entry into the next GeoFind, want to give it to me as a birthday present?" asked Barley.

"No way, but I do come bearing gifts." Colin passed over a thin package with a tiny troll resting against a mushroom taped to the top.

"What's that?" asked Phyllis.

"That is one of the Kinder Surprise toys from the cache in Hi-Knoll Park," said Barley. "Did you make it to that one?"

"No," said Phyllis. "But Larry and Marcie are trying to do all the caches from the competition."

"How can they?" asked Colin.

"Everyone shared the coordinates they got before the contest shut down."

"Did Mr. C. leave the caches where they were? With the Geocoins?"

"Apparently."

"I'd like to do them all too. Maybe you can come with us, Colin." Barley had finished his cake and was ripping brown paper to expose a Geocaching license plate frame. "How did you know I wanted one of these?"

"You told me about it, remember? The day GeoFind started."

"That seems like a lifetime ago."

"A lot's happened. Do you think they'll ever unscramble the satellite signals so you can geocache again?"

"Hope so. Bush is in the Middle East now trying to sort things out."

"So, maybe you'll get to compete in GeoFind next year?"

"Yeah, I'll finally get to crush Phyllis."

"Barley!"

"Just joking. Come on, we have to go pick up Mom and Newton. I mean Fred."

46

First Edition

When Barley ran in the living room to tell her it was time to go, his mother was sitting on the couch kissing Newton. Déjà vu, thought Barley, but at least he did not feel compelled to pick up a golf club.

Phyllis and Colin followed him in just as Newton passed Barley another flat parcel covered in birthday paper. It was bigger and wider and thicker and heavier than the license plate Colin had given him.

Barley ripped off the wrapping to unveil a first edition of *The Lorax*. He swallowed. A copy like that would be hard to find. He cracked the cover and read the signed inscription aloud: "To Billy, Love, Dad 1972." He was moved; some father had given this to his son. "Wow, where'd you get it?"

"I put in a call into Henderson's Used Bookstore in Bellingham a few weeks ago and asked him to keep an eye out."

"Hey, they're my second cousins," said Phyllis.

"I love that store," said Newton. "They found the book and had it shipped right away from a store in London."

"Ontario."

"No, England."

"Thanks, Fred," Barley said. It still felt strange for Barley to call him Fred. He still called him Newton in his mind. They had been getting along these days. He wasn't a jerk like Barley had thought, although if his mother ever came home with a wad of Newton's chewed gum in her hair—Barley couldn't finish the thought.

Instead, he said, "Did you know this edition has a line that doesn't appear in any of the later editions?"

"No," said Newton. "What is it?"

Barley flipped to the page. "I hear things are just as bad up in Lake Erie."

"What's that all about?"

"Apparently right around the time Dr. Seuss wrote *The Lorax* there was a fire on Cayahoga River on Lake Erie."

"So why did he take the line out?" asked Phyllis.

"I have no idea."

"Another mystery to solve," said Newton, turning to Barley's mother, who seemed to just notice that Phyllis no longer had teeth straighteners.

"Oh, Phyllis, you got your braces off," she said. "Flash us a big smile."

Phyllis showed off her teeth.

"You know Barley had braces when he was younger."

"He didn't tell me that."

"Yeah, the braces were fine, because he couldn't take them off to lose them, but his retainer was a nightmare."

"Do tell." Phyllis looked delighted to hear an incriminating story.

"One day Barley and his father and I went to the PNE. We had finished all the rides. I was tired and wanted to go home, but Barley insisted we get something to eat at the fairgrounds."

"You're not going to believe her version, are you?" Barley said, but Phyllis nodded for his mother to continue.

"After he finished, he dumped his food tray and came back to the table. He had this funny look on his face. I asked him what was wrong. He said he must have thrown away his retainer in the garbage with the rest of the stuff.

"I told him to go look through the garbage. He said no way. So, his dad went and got the guys to unlock the bin and walked through the whole exhibition grounds with a clear plastic garbage bag with everyone's pizza crusts and fries in them.

"I thought Barley was going to die of embarrassment. But of course, I had no sympathy for him. He was always losing his retainer. It had already been replaced twice, and there was no way we were going to fork out money for another one. Barley had his hoodie pulled up over his head even though it was about thirty degrees, and every time he saw someone he knew, he put his face down and pretended he didn't know us."

"Let me tell the rest," Barley interrupted. "When we got to the car, I reached in my hoodie pocket and pulled out my retainer. Dad almost killed me."

"I never figured you for a retainer kind of guy." Phyllis flashed her now brace-less pearly whites.

"The cat's out of the bag," said Barley.

"Everyone ready to go to Colossus?" Newton asked. "We all here?"

"The only person missing is Stanley," said Barley.

"Stanley is not a person," said Fred. He could still be an idiot on times.

"He is to me," said Barley.

"He's over having a hot date with Fifi. They're going to share Stanley's doggy bed," said Phyllis. "Isn't that adorable?"

That was not adorable. If Barley were Stanley, he'd eat Fifi. Barley still thought Phyllis's dog was a mutant.

The old Barley would have voiced this opinion; the new Barley kept it to himself.

The End

Barley Lick Discussion Questions

1. Two themes in this novel are acceptance and healing. Moving through the five stages of grief is rarely a linear process. Do you feel the novel offers a realistic portrayal of how Barley moves through denial, anger, bargaining, depression, and acceptance?

2. Healing takes many forms. Give some examples of how Barley finds a way to stay connected to his father. What ways have you stayed connected to someone who was very important to you and is no longer with you?

3. *The Degrees of Barley Lick* deals with serious issues like kidnapping, the dissolution of a happy family after an unexpected death of a parent, and the misunderstandings between youth that can lead to alienation. Another theme is loss and the different forms it can take: the loss of a child, of a parent, of a friendship. How do we cope, recover, and move on from these losses? What roles do others play in easing loss? For example, the shop owner who gives Barley a job, and Colin and his family who try to make life normal for Barley after the death of his father.

4. Saving old-growth forests is a theme in *The Degrees of Barley Lick*. In the novel, activists feel so strongly they camp out in the branches of ancient trees. What do you think can be done about deforestation? Who do you think is responsible for changing the situation? How in our daily lives can we make a difference?

5. Although the novel deals with serious matters, a great deal of comic relief is provided by Stanley, Barley's dog. How does the character of Stanley develop, and how does his presence help Barley resolve many of the dilemmas he faces?

6. It is rare that someone who's lost a parent, no matter their age, reacts favourably when the remaining parent takes on a new love interest. Did you find Barley's reaction believable? Does Newton deserve Barley's hostility or is he an innocent bystander?

7. Barley's treatment of Phyllis is unacceptable and she lets him know. Do you feel she was justified in punching him in the nose? Were you surprised that they hadn't been able to clear up the misunderstanding of Hallowe'en sooner?

8. By the end of the novel, Barley's relationship has changed not only with Phyllis, but also with his mother. Are there any parallels between the arc of Barley's relationship with Phyllis and the arc of his relationship with his mother?

9. Geocaching remains a popular international sport with more than three million geocaches worldwide, and some of the geocaches mentioned in the book are real. Have you ever tried geocaching, and if not, would you like to after reading about it here? What part of geocaching sounds the most interesting? Or difficult? Or challenging?

Acknowledgements

Thanks to Marnie Parsons and the team at Running the Goat, Books & Broadsides (Rachel Dragland, Michelle Porter, and Emma Allain); to WANL for their Manuscript Evaluation Service and their inaugural Pitch the Publisher event where I met Marnie; to Marie Wadden for her encouragement; to Ryan and Liam Flanagan and Madison Bailey, my video team; to Michael Levine, Glenn Deir, and Maria Clift for their contract expertise; to Marie Snippa for my author photo; and to Brian Marshall for patiently answering many automotive questions.

Thanks to Alastair Allan for introducing the Flanagans to geocaching; to Rocky Snippa for gifting me my first GPS; to Chris Flanagan and our children, Conor, Liam, Ryan, Marie, and Declan, for coming along on all those geocaching adventures; and to geocaching.com for keeping the treasure hunt going all these years. TFTC

Special thanks to all my beta readers and editors: Ben Cowburn; Marie and Joshua Snippa; Paul Butler; Claire Wilkshire; Jessica Grant; Cathy Smallwood; Kelly, Don, William and Patrick Anthony; Kim Shipp; Margot Kennedy; Hannah Browne; Liam French; Benjamin Avery; Gerry Marshall; John Marshall; Liam Flanagan; Marie Flanagan; and the Ram's Head Writers' Group (especially Lisa Hatton, Michael Hebert, and Bob Jacoby in Langley, B.C. without whom, this novel would still have an unlikeable protagonist).

A final thanks to Cyril Blake for providing the inspiration for Barley Lick's name, and to all you readers who chose my book out of all those other amazing reads on the shelf.

Note: I have adjusted the timing of the 2006 Stanley Cup Play-offs to fit the narrative.

Susan Flanagan has worked as a freelance journalist (BJ, King's College, NS, 1991) for thirty years. A lover of nature, she joined geocaching.com in September 2002, and under her username 48degrees, hid her first cache in Kelligrews, NL that December.

Susan's first novel, *Supermarket Baby*, won the 2019 Percy Janes First Novel Award. Her non-fiction works have appeared in *Canadian Geographic*, *National Geographic* (maps), *Canadian Running*, *Newfoundland Quarterly*, *Queen's Quarterly* and the *Hockey News*, among many others.

She is married mother of five and lives in St. John's, NL. She continues to get out in nature whenever she can. For more information, visit susanflanagan.ca

This book was designed by Emma Allain
and printed in Canada.

978-1-927917404

Running the Goat, Books & Broadsides is grateful to Newfoundland and
Labrador's Department of Tourism, Culture, Industry and Innovation for
support of its publishing activities through the province's Publishers Assistance
Program, to the Canada Council for the Arts for support through its Literary
Publishing Projects fund, and to the Canadian Department of Heritage and
Multiculturalism for support through the Canada Book Fund.

Running the Goat
Books & Broadsides Inc.
General Delivery/54 Cove Road
Tors Cove, Newfoundland and Labrador A0A 4A0
www.runningthegoat.com